DATE DUE

8/1	
Quinn	
N.C.B.	
B.Webb	
D.Jenkins	
Fischer	

GAYLORD   PRINTED IN U.S.A.

Summer Snow

**Center Point
Large Print**

**This Large Print Book carries the
Seal of Approval of N.A.V.H.**

Summer Snow

STAN LYNDE

CENTER POINT PUBLISHING
THORNDIKE, MAINE

This Center Point Large Print edition
is published in the year 2008 by arrangement with
iUniverse Star, an imprint of iUniverse, Inc.

The text of this Large Print edition is unabridged. In other
aspects, this book may vary from the original edition.
Printed in the United States of America.
Set in 16-point Times New Roman type.

ISBN: 978-1-60285-215-0

Library of Congress Cataloging-in-Publication Data

Lynde, Stan, 1931-
    Summer snow / Stan Lynde.--Center Point large print ed.
    p. cm.
    ISBN-13: 978-1-60285-215-0 (lib. bdg. : alk. paper)
    1. Montana--Fiction. 2. Large type books. I. Title.

PS3562.Y439S86 2008
813'.54--dc22

2008004859

To Michael H. Price—

Merlin's godfather

CHAPTER 1
Breakout at Dry Creek

As a deputy U.S. marshal, I had entered the Dry Creek jailhouse many times, but that Sunday night in the fall of 1886 was the first time I'd been taken there as a prisoner. Deputy Sheriff Glenn Murdoch shoved me across the threshold and followed me inside. "Damn, Merlin," he said. "It ain't that a lawman's never gone bad before. I just never thought *you* would."

Glenn carried my belted six-shooter looped over his shoulder. His eyes were slits, his mouth a bitter line pulled down at the corners. He looked like a man who'd swallowed a double shot of vinegar. He poked me with the sawed-off shotgun he carried, and I stumbled and nearly fell. "Quit *pushin'* me!" I said. "It's hard enough, tryin' to walk in these durned leg irons."

"You'd be better off if you'd been wearin' 'em last week," Glenn said. "If you'd had your ankles chained together, you couldn't have rode off on another man's horse."

"Hell I couldn't," I said. "For a horse like that grulla, I'd have rode him side-saddle."

I had acquired the horse from Thane McAllister's remuda two weeks before. The animal was clear-footed and tough, and there was no quit to him. Trouble was, the brand on him was Thane's, not mine. When Glenn questioned my ownership, I couldn't pro-

7

duce a bill of sale because, well . . . because I didn't *have* one.

Across the office, the door leading to the jail cells stood open. Beyond, in the gloom, the other prisoner, Rufus Two Hats, watched from his cage. I'm sure he figured I would soon be his next-door neighbor there in the crowbar hotel. Outside, at the hitch rack, the horse in question stood saddled and loose-tied next to Glenn Murdoch's blue roan.

Glenn had a stiff leg from his cowpuncher days, and he never liked to take a chance that a prisoner might rabbit on him. He stood the sawed-off in the gun rack and crowded in close. "Why'd you do it, Merlin?" he asked. "Why did you turn outlaw?"

I shrugged. "Why's anybody? The money, I guess. Peace officers are underpaid and overworked."

Glenn shook his head. "Stand hitched," he said, "and I'll take those irons off."

When he bent to unlock the shackles, I looked down, and there were the ivory grips of my .44 showing above the holster at his shoulder. I saw my chance, and I took it. My manacled hands flashed out and jerked the gun from its leather, and Glenn's eyes went wide. He looked into mine, measuring me. I took a step back, holding my Peacemaker out in front of me—aimed at his belly.

"Back off, Glenn," I said. "I'll shoot you if I have to."

"You're bluffin', son," he said, and he made a grab for my gun.

The sound of the shot rang out in that closed room,

rattled the windowpane, and rocked the hanging lamp above the desk. White smoke billowed in the lamplight, acrid and bitter. Glenn looked stunned, disbelief stamped on his face. For a moment, the fingers of his right hand gripped my arm and then loosened, and Glenn toppled to the floor at my feet and lay still.

I dropped to one knee, fished the keys to the cuffs and leg-irons from his vest pocket, and a moment later, I was free. As I picked up my gun belt and buckled it on, bright blood stained Glenn's shirt and pooled on the office floor. I turned and looked through the open door to the cell where Rufus Two Hats stood watching. He was a big man, over six feet, with long, straight hair and a face like an axe blade. Expressionless, he asked, "You kill him?"

"What do you think? You want outta here?"

Rufus gripped the bars and his eyes glittered.

Hurrying, I turned the key in the cell's lock, swung the door wide, and Rufus Two Hats stepped out. "Merlin Fanshaw," I told him, "also known as The Bodacious Kid."

Two Hats studied me. "You used to be a lawman?"

"Once," I said. "I've done a lot of things."

I grabbed a rifle off the rack and scooped cartridges from the cabinet. "Help yourself," I said, "but let's make tracks. If somebody heard that shot—" Two Hats was already buckling on a gun belt. "I got no horse," he said.

"Take Murdoch's roan. Glenn sure won't need him."

Outside, silence ruled the darkened street. Up

beyond the bank, lamplight glowed in the windows of the Oasis Saloon. Somewhere in the darkness beyond, a dog began to bark. I swung up onto the grulla and turned the animal away into the night. Behind me came the hoof beats of Glenn's roan, and Two Hats's voice. "Where we goin'?" he said.

I spurred the grulla, and the animal struck out on the road at a lope. "Anywhere," I said, "as long as it's away from here."

That's how Rufus Two Hats and me departed Dry Creek on a quiet Sunday night in September. But before I tell you what happened next, I need to step back a week or so and tell you what happened before.

Dry Creek, Montana lies east of the Cayuse Hills on the sometime stream that gave the town its name. Wasn't much of a town, I guess, but it was *my* town, and two weeks ago, I had been glad to come back to it. As a deputy under U.S. Marshal Chance Ridgeway, I had just closed out an assignment down on the Crow Indian Reservation, and it was good to be back among the folks I grew up with.

I checked my horses into Walt's Livery, treated myself to a meal down at Ignacio's Café, and lifted a few cold ones with the boys down at the Oasis Saloon. The first couple of days, I played cribbage and swapped stories with my friend Glenn Murdoch, and spent some pleasant hours a-courting my long-time lady friend, Pandora Pretty Hawk.

During the warm afternoons, after she got off work at Blair's boarding house where I was back in my old room, Pandora and me used to stroll together among the cottonwoods down by the creek. We held hands and talked foolishness, the way lovers do. Those were special times. Pandora always gave me the feeling that she understood me, but that she loved me anyway—which struck me as a rare thing.

Pandora and me must have seemed quite a contrast, not just because she was a female and I wasn't. I stand five foot ten in my boots, while and Pandora is a good five inches shorter. My hair's unruly and dark brown; hers is sleek and black as a raven's wing. My eyes are blue; hers are brown. I tend to be clumsy sometimes—except when I'm a-horseback—but Pandora moves with easy grace, confident and poised.

I recall one Sunday afternoon that September, a warm day, full of that special golden autumn light, Pandora and me walking down among the cotton-woods. She had on her green-checked gingham dress, and I could tell from the look on her face that she was especially happy. She was looking up to where the leaves in the tops of the bigger cottonwoods had already turned bright yellow. "They seem to know summer's over," Pandora said. "They're putting on their autumn finery."

"Yes," I said, feeling poetic. "They know the seasons are changin'. Soon, they'll shed their leaves entirely and bed down for the winter." I looked down at her pretty face and smiled.

11

Pandora smiled back and gripped my hand a little tighter and leaned her head against my shoulder. "But they'll wake again when spring comes," she said. "They'll yawn and stretch and dress again in tender green."

By that time I was caught up in it, like we were writing a story together. "Then along about the first of June, they'll cast their seeds to the winds, and cotton-wood fluff will burst out and drift down on the air."

"Like summer snow," Pandora said.

I had turned twenty-two in June, and I was making good money—two dollars a day—as deputy under U.S. Marshal Chance Ridgeway. Most federal deputies were paid on a fee basis. However, Uncle Sam tended to be less than prompt in settling his accounts, so Ridgeway paid his deputies a straight salary against fees, and for the first time in my life, I had a steady income. But then the money had begun to give me ideas.

Walking among the cottonwoods with Pandora that day, my financial status suddenly took on new importance. It may be true, as Tennyson wrote, that in the spring a young man's fancy turns to thoughts of love. All I know is that on that sunny afternoon my own fancy took a turn toward matrimony.

Once I allowed the notion into my mind, it commenced to grow on me. I had five hundred dollars in the Cattleman's Bank of Dry Creek. A place of my own—maybe a small horse outfit somewhere, with Pandora at my side—seemed like a real possibility.

I didn't say anything to Pandora about my notion, and that turned out to be a good thing, but early the next morning, I rode out to the M Cross to see about buying a horse I had admired. It was just my bad luck that while I was away, outlaws held up the Dry Creek bank, shot Bob Dingle, the teller, and made off with all the cash on hand—including my five hundred dollars.

It was Deputy Sheriff Glenn Murdoch himself who broke the news. I rode into town leading my new gelding, to find Glenn waiting for me at Walt's Livery. I grinned as I drew rein and was about to brag about my horse trade when I noticed Glenn's expression; his face was serious as a miser's funeral.

"About time you got back," Glenn said. "Outlaws robbed the bank yesterday. They killed young Bobby Dingle and made off with the cash."

My right foot had just touched the ground, my left foot was in the stirrup, and I still had the reins and saddle horn in my hands. When he said that, I just stopped and stared at him. "Robbed the bank? They killed *Bobby?*"

Glenn scowled. "Is there an echo in this barn? I believe I just told you that." He paused. "Ridgeway's in town, over at the hotel. He wants to see you."

As I followed Glenn through the front door of the Grand Hotel, I was still trying to get my mind around Bobby's being dead. I was full of questions ready to be asked, but Glenn just pointed me toward the staircase and said, "Your boss'll fill you in. He's upstairs. Number ten."

The stairs creaked underfoot as we climbed, and the hallway seemed unusually dark as we moved toward room number ten. Glenn stopped and rapped sharply on the door. "It's Glenn Murdoch, Marshal," he said. "I've got Merlin with me."

There was a muffled "Come in," and I followed Glenn inside.

U.S. Marshal Chance Ridgeway sat by the window at a small table littered with papers. He glanced up as we entered the room, and nodded. "Good of you to join us, Deputy," he drawled. "I understand you missed the robbery yesterday."

"I was out at the M Cross," I said, "buyin' a horse from Thane McAllister." I felt guilty, but how was I supposed to know outlaws would pick yesterday to rob the bank? "I should've been here," I said. "What happened?"

Ridgeway nodded at the empty chairs. "Set down, boys," he said. "It hurts my neck talkin' up to you."

Glenn eased himself into one of the chairs. I sat down in the other.

Ridgeway leaned back and laced his fingers across his vest. "The long and short of it is that Original George Starkweather is back in business. Mostly, he's been busy rustlin' cattle, but I guess he ran short of operatin' capital. Yesterday, George and five known members of his gang cleaned out the Dry Creek bank and murdered Bobby Dingle."

Scattered among the papers on the table were a number of wanted posters. Ridgeway gathered up a handful and dealt them out like playing cards. As each poster fell, the marshal called its name: "George Starkweather. Shorty Benson. Crazy Ike Mullins. Pronto Southwell. Tom Blackburn. Chickasaw Wilson. Rufus Two Hats." His brows narrowed. "As depraved a pack of human hellhounds as a man could ask for."

Ridgeway turned in his chair and looked down at the street through the open window. "They hit the bank at ten forty-two yesterday morning. Tom Blackburn held the horses while the others went inside. They made the customers lay down on the floor and dragged banker Sheets out of his office. When Dingle didn't come up with the money fast enough to suit them, they shot him and helped themselves.

"They cleaned out the cash drawers and the vault and headed for their horses. Apparently, Rufus Two Hats was a mite slow gettin' mounted. A farmer from over on the Big Porcupine pulled a Winchester out of his wagon and went to shootin'. He missed Rufus, but dropped his horse—I suppose because the horse was a slightly bigger target."

The marshal nodded at Glenn. "Deputy Murdoch heard the shootin' and showed up just as the boys were leavin' town. He found Rufus Two Hats pinned beneath his dead horse and took him into custody. The rest got away."

"How much did they get?" I asked.

"Banker Sheets says forty thousand. That means it was probably twenty-five or thirty."

I picked up the posters from the table. "How do you know it was George and his boys?"

"Good question, Deputy," Ridgeway said. "One of the customers in the bank yesterday was Jackrabbit Annie, proprietress of the local joy parlor and a long-time acquaintance of George Starkweather. Ordinarily, she wouldn't have identified the thieves—professional courtesy, you understand—but some of the money they stole was hers."

Glenn shook his head. "One robber even took her jewelry. I never saw Annie so mad. She called those boys names even *I* never heard before!"

I was numb. "I know how she feels," I said in a half whisper. "I had money in that bank, too."

Ridgeway seemed not to notice what I'd said. His eyes narrowed. "George Starkweather is a murderer, a thief, and a whoremaster," he said. "Decency does not abide in him."

"That sounds personal, Marshal," Glenn said.

"I take all evildoers personal," Ridgeway replied. "But yes, George Starkweather and I are longtime acquaintances. You might say I have a history with the man."

The marshal looked at me. "So does young Merlin there," he said. "Merlin helped bring George to justice back in eighty-two. Helped us send him off to the penitentiary at Deer Lodge for life."

I nodded, thinking how Starkweather had paroled himself a couple of months back, how he'd gone over the wall one night with two other prisoners and disappeared into the tall and uncut. But all I said was, "The marshal's right—Original George Starkweather's bad to the bone."

"So what do we do now?" Glenn asked. "How do we get our hands on this world champion bad man?"

"We're not the only ones askin' that question," Ridgeway said. "Lawmen all over the territory are lookin' for Starkweather, even the Pinks." By which he meant the Pinkertons, the biggest detective agency in the country, the outfit that helped break up the James-Younger gang. Ridgeway carefully straightened the wanted posters into a neat, square stack on the table before him.

"Well," I said, "they haven't caught *George*."

"No, "Ridgeway agreed. "They haven't caught George."

I turned to Glenn. "Speakin' of lawmen who haven't caught George," I said, "how come *you* didn't raise a posse and go after those boys?"

Glenn snorted. "Oh, I did! I rounded up a store-keeper, a bartender, two farmers, and a drunk. We rode out until it seemed we might actually catch up to 'em. About then, my fearless posse decided it was gettin' on toward suppertime, and they'd better go home and do their chores."

"Back to your question, Glenn," Ridgeway said. "I have an idea about that."

Glenn fell silent, his eyes on Ridgeway, and waited.

Ridgeway looked thoughtful. "That desperado you arrested," he said, "Rufus Two Hats. You still have him locked up?"

"You know I do," Glenn said. "My deputy, Bucky Shavers, is watchin' him."

I had seen that gleam in Ridgeway's eye before, and I waited for the marshal to make his play. "What do you suppose would happen," Ridgeway said, "if we turned him loose?"

Glenn's gaze turned into a surprised stare. "You *know* what'd happen! He'd run like a turpentined cat!"

"And where," the marshal said, "do you suppose he'd run?"

"Hell, I don't know!" Glenn said. "I guess he'd—I suppose he—why, he'd run straight back to George!"

"Not if he thought we'd follow him, he wouldn't," I said. "Two Hats may be dumb, but he's not that dumb."

Ridgeway smiled, looking straight at me. "That's right," he said. "That's why you're goin' with him."

So that's what brought Glenn and me riding up to the jail a couple of nights later.

It was a dark night, no moon, the only light being the pitiful glare of the flames in the little glass coffins atop the lampposts that lined either side of the street. The street was empty—not a soul in sight. My ankles and wrists were already raw under the iron shackles, and I was thinking of Pandora, all unsuspecting and in her bed asleep. We dismounted, made sure the reins would slip easy on the hitching rail, and about the time I had one foot on the jailhouse step, I turned around and glared at Murdoch.

"Get the muzzle of that Greener outta my kidney!" I whispered.

"Rest easy; it ain't loaded," Glenn said, "no more than your .44 is!"

"That's not the point! The durned thing *hurts!*" He pulled the scattergun back, and I glanced down at it. Loaded or not, those were the two biggest, darkest holes I'd ever seen. "Is it really necessary to have those hammers cocked back?"

"Bellyache! Bellyache!" he said. "I'm the man about to ruin his own perfectly good shirt with a pig's bladder full of blood."

CHAPTER 2
Across the Yellowstone

Rufus Two Hats led the way on Glenn's roan, whipping the animal, putting distance between us and any possible pursuers. I followed on the grulla a length or two behind, matching the big man's pace and wondering just what in the green-eyed Nellie I had got myself into.

Where was Two Flats taking us? I'd thought he'd go north to Rampage, the abandoned ranch George and his boys sometimes used as a hideout. But we were riding south.

Moonlight broke through the clouds and lit the broad sagebrush-studded plain, all white and still. Beyond, at the edge of the plain, low hills dotted with juniper and jack pine rose up. Off to the right, the peaks of the

Crazy Mountains loomed ghostly and pale, and directly ahead, the dark mass of the Absarokas stood tall against a starry sky.

The grulla was double tough and willing, but the pace was taking its toll. The little horse gasped for breath, faltering, and nearly stumbled. I spurred the animal up alongside Two Hats and saw that the roan was faring no better.

"Let's rest these mounts!" I said.

Two Hats made no reply, but he eased Glenn's roan back to a trot, then to a walk, and finally to a stop. Lather flecked the roan, and the animal struggled to catch its breath.

The big man pointed toward the broken hills before us. "There," he said, and rode on at a trot. I touched the grulla with my spurs and followed. Moments later, we broke out into a sort of hollow atop the hill and stepped down. The big man looked back at the moon-shadowed plain, his eyes narrowed. "Maybe somebody follows," he said.

I watched for movement below, but I saw nothing. I remember wondering why a man holds his breath when he's trying to see better, but I couldn't come up with an answer. Maybe, I thought, he does it so he can hear better, but that didn't make much sense. We wouldn't hear someone back yonder on the plain unless they had a brass band, and that seemed unlikely.

"See anything?" I whispered.

Two Hats shook his head. "Nobody comes. No damn lawmen, like you."

"I'm not a lawman," I said. "I've stole a horse and killed Glenn Murdoch. A lawman tends to lose his standin' when he guns down one of his own."

Two Hats looked at me for a long moment, then back at the plain. He said nothing; his face was blank. "We wait," he said. "By and by, sun comes up."

Well, so far it always has, I thought. "How much farther?"

Two Hats studied me with cold, suspicious eyes. Seconds passed. Finally, he looked away. "Two days," he said. "Maybe three."

Both Two Hats and me had brought Winchester carbines from the marshal's office. I watched as the big man jerked his from the saddle scabbard and then pulled mine as well, and I wondered what he was up to. But he tossed my rifle to me. "Here," he said. "I'm gonna sleep some. You watch."

Two Hats leaned back against the base of a tree, his rifle cradled in his arms. From the sound of his breathing, it was obvious he fell asleep almost at once.

The moon seemed to race across the night sky, hiding its face behind the clouds, and then flooding the land with light every time it broke through. Grass was sparse there on the hilltop, but I loosened the cinches and took off the bridles so the horses could graze on what forage there was.

As I kept watch, I thought of how sparse grass was all over Montana. The range was overcrowded, new herds coming up the trail from Texas every year joining the thousands of cattle already here. The grass was free to all, and everybody wanted a piece of the pie. Trouble was, now the pie was nearly gone.

Cattle were just about everywhere—worth maybe fifty dollars a head. So it wasn't hard to see why George and his gang were back in the cow-thieving business.

It hadn't rained in a long time, and now the land was dry as a lizard's breath. All but the biggest streams and waterholes had dried up. Thirsty cattle bawled and bellowed in the coulees. But Two Hats and me still had a long ride ahead of us, and I hoped our horses were up to it.

I looked around to see the grulla and the roan standing quietly asleep on their feet. The roan was a big animal, but then Rufus Two Hats was a big man. And he was hard on a horse. That worried me some. If, as Two Hats had said, our destination was still two to three days distant, we'd need to go easy with our mounts.

I liked the way the little grulla carried himself. He was colored and marked like most of the breed— which, some say, goes back to the stock the Spaniards brought over. He was a sort of mouse gray with black mane, tail, and socks, and a black line down his back. I'd begun to call him "Mouse."

My pa taught me a good horse will give a man everything it has, up to and including its life, so he had no use for a man who'd mistreat a horse. I don't believe he would have cared much for Rufus Two Hats. I didn't care for him much myself.

The way Two Hats looked at me sometimes made me think he would just as soon gun me down, take both horses, and ride on alone.

I turned my eyes back to the valley. The clouds had thinned out, and moonlight dusted the plain. Scrub cedar and pines dotted the foothills, dark smudges that took on the shape of buffalo or cattle or stealthy Indian warriors sneaking up the slope. Sometimes one of those smudges would seem to move, and I'd catch my breath and stare until I realized my imagination was working overtime.

Seated alone there in the rocks, I considered what I'd agreed to do. Original George Starkweather had escaped from the territorial prison at Deer Lodge and returned to his old pursuits with a vengeance. Marshal Ridgeway had sent me out to find him and to convince him that I was a lawman gone bad who wanted to join his gang. If by some chance I made him believe me—and if he didn't shoot me on sight for my part in his capture back in eighty-two—I was to send word to Ridgeway and stand by to assist in George's arrest.

Ridgeway was a good boss, and he knew me about as well as one man can know another. He'd sent me off on other assignments, and I'd always delivered. Because he believed in me, I believed in myself—mostly—but this time was different. This time I knew something Ridgeway didn't know.

One month earlier, at an abandoned cabin in the Bighorn Mountains, I had faced down and killed Ed Hutchins—a murderer who had escaped along with

Starkweather. Hutchins had come at me with a gun, and I had shot him twice in the chest, putting him down. Then I'd learned his revolver had not been loaded; he had chosen to die rather than return to prison.

Since that day, I hadn't been able to get Ed Hutchins out of my mind. The shooting even invaded my dreams.

I had used deadly force before in the line of duty when threatened by armed and dangerous men, but this had been different; I'd killed an unarmed man. Now I wasn't sure that I could shoot another human being, even in self defense.

The lids of my eyes took on a will of their own. One minute I'd be watching the plain below, and the next, I'd come suddenly awake, realizing I had fallen asleep. I'd chide myself and determine to stay alert. Then a moment later, I'd drift off, only to wake up again with a start.

I was still sitting there three hours later, somewhere between drowsy and dead to the world, when I felt a hand on my shoulder. I came wide awake then, I can tell you! Eyes wide open, I twisted my head around like a burrowing owl and saw Rufus Two Hats standing looking down at me.

"Scared you, huh?" he said. "Get some sleep. I watch now."

"Hell, I wasn't scared," I lied. "I heard you come up. I was just thinkin' of somethin' else is all."

Two Hats didn't believe a word of it. "You was scared," he said.

So I lay down, and wouldn't you just know? Now that it was all right for me to fall asleep, I found I couldn't. I lay there with my eyes closed, but I kept worrying that Two Hats might murder me in my sleep. *If I drop off now,* I thought, *I might never wake up again.*

Two Hats hadn't done anything to make me think he wanted to kill me. Still, I figured I'd rather be awake and safe than asleep and sorry—especially if my sleep turned out to be permanent. However, I finally dropped off into a deep and peaceful slumber. I have oft-times been a marvel to myself.

I woke up hungry. I was stiff from sleeping on the ground and cold as a carp, but I was alive. Overhead, darkness was fading fast, pale stars winking out one by one. Above the skyline the eastern sky blushed red as paint. I sat up, stretched, and looked around. Ten feet away, the grulla grazed on the short grass beneath the trees. The little horse raised its head, chewing, and looked at me as if to say, "Where's breakfast? This grass is pretty thin."

I offered him my sympathy. "I know how you feel, Mouse," I said. "I could eat a bite myself."

Down the slope, Two Hats stood looking out across the valley. Glenn's roan stood near him, bridled and ready for the trail. The big man turned, saw me watching him, and led the roan uphill toward me. "About time you woke up," Two Hats said. "We're burnin' daylight."

"We need to find some feed for these ponies," I said, "and for ourselves. My belly thinks my throat's been cut."

Two Hats looked south. Gentle hills and coulees sloped to a tree-lined river maybe six miles away. Railroad tracks stretched out along the valley floor, steel rails shining in the early light. "Pretty good grass over there," Two Hats said. "Water for the horses. That's the Yellowstone."

Beyond the river, sandstone cliffs rose sharply, and mountains stood tall in the distance. "We cross over," Two Hats said. "Have plenty grub, coffee, soon."

Mounting our horses, we turned downhill. With the coming of daylight the land began to take on a familiar look, and I realized I'd been there two years before. Across the water, at a bend in the river, the great sandstone cliff called Young's Point stood, barren and stark except for a scatter of thirsty pines at its top.

On the opposite shore lay the new settlement of Park City. Seventeen miles upstream was the town of Columbus, which in its short and active life had known a variety of names. At different times, the place had been called Eagle's Nest, Sheep Dip, and Stillwater— among other things—and was finally christened Columbus because the Northern Pacific wanted it that way. I didn't know where Two Hats was leading us, but I couldn't believe he would take us to either of those towns.

We crossed the tracks and descended to the river. A

deep, fast-flowing stream in spring and early summer, the Yellowstone was low that fall, and the horses crossed it easily. We watered them both and rode up a ravine to the top of the bluffs. Broken hills and timbered draws lay before us. Rufus Two Hats took the lead, headed south. Minutes later, we topped out on a low hill above a grove of cottonwoods and drew rein. In a clearing below, nearly hidden by thick brush and trees, stood a low, sod-roofed cabin. A corral containing maybe fifty saddle horses lay west of the cabin.

In a round corral near the bigger one, two men had a bay gelding tied down and were heating irons at a branding fire. The men looked up as we rode down from the bluffs. They watched for a moment and then turned their attentions back to the gelding. I heard the horse squeal as a hot iron burned its hide.

Fifty yards from the cabin, Rufus Two Hats drew rein. I did the same. Raising his cupped hands to his mouth, he sounded the call of the killdeer—*kill dee dee dee*—so perfect I found myself looking for the bird. Moments later, the same call came back from the cabin. Two Hats nodded. We turned our horses out of the timber and into the clearing.

The cabin door opened, and a pinch-faced man of about fifty stepped outside. He was short, maybe five foot two or three, and lean as a whippet. He held a rifle in his hands and looked up at Rufus through narrowed eyes.

"I thought you was dead," he said. "Thought that sodbuster back in Dry Creek blew out your lamp."

Rufus grunted and stepped down from the roan. "You think too damn much," he said. "Get the skillet on. We're hungry."

"Who's *we?*" the man asked.

"Me an' him," Two Hats said, pointing to me. "Calls himself the Bodacious Kid. He broke me out of the Dry Creek jail."

"Hell you say. Never heard of no Bodacious Kid."

"Well, now you have, you skinny old bastard. You gonna feed us or not?"

"You don't watch your mouth, I'll feed you rat poison, by god."

The man lowered his rifle and grinned a gap-toothed smile. He looked at me. "I'm Shorty Benson. Get down, Kid," he said. "Don't pay the big breed any mind. He's ignorant, and he don't respect his elders."

I dismounted and tied the grulla to a sapling.

"Come on in," Shorty said. "Got beans and fry bread on the stove. Won't take but a minute to hot 'em up."

I stepped inside. A rough table and a rusted cook stove took up most of the room. "I sure am obliged," I said, "but don't trouble any on my account. I'm so hungry, hot or cold makes no never-mind, long as there's plenty of it."

Shorty was already adding wood to the stove's firebox. He replaced the lid, opened the damper, and turned to me. "You are an affable young feller," he said, "an' polite, too. Most of the boys who ride through here are surly sons o' bitches—and about as friendly as rattlesnakes."

"What is this place exactly?" I asked. "Some kind of line shack?"

"Some kind. More like a way station for long rope artists. The boys bring horses and cattle in from up north, rework their brands, and move 'em on south to the headquarters ranch."

Behind us, Two Hats bulked up the cabin's doorway. "Except for the poor bastards who starve to death waitin' for this old fool to feed 'em." He rummaged through the shelves beside the stove. "You got any whiskey?"

"Hell, no," Shorty said. "Have you?"

"Damn," Two Hats said. "I could sure use me a drink of whiskey."

"Whiskey ain't good for Injuns. Makes 'em crazy."

"Makes white men crazy, too," Two Hats said. "I don't see no difference."

The pot on the stove had begun to steam. Shorty dished up two heaping plates of beans, added a man-sized piece of fry bread to each one, and set them before us. Then he poured us both a cup of coffee.

"Eat hearty," Shorty said. He didn't have to tell me twice.

I felt a sight better when I finished eating. I stacked my plate, cup, and eating tools and placed them in the dishpan on the counter as I stepped outside. Rufus Two Hats borrowed the makings from Shorty and rolled himself a smoke. Then he stepped out behind me, and Shorty followed.

All through the meal Shorty had talked pretty much

nonstop even though he hadn't said anything. But as we stepped outside, his palaver began to get interesting.

"You boys headin' down to Arrowhead?" Shorty asked.

Two Hats shrugged.

Shorty looked off toward the big corral where the horses were penned. "Reason I ask," Shorty said, "is the chief wants them ponies brought down to the home ranch. Can you and Bodacious take 'em when you go?"

The two men we'd seen when we rode in were walking toward us from the direction of the corrals. One was a man about my size and weight, with long hair and high-topped boots. The other was a tall, raw-boned ranny in a checkered shirt and black hat. As the men approached, I could see they were arguing, although I couldn't hear their words.

Two Hats nodded at the men. "How about them two?" he asked. "Why can't they take them horses?"

"I need 'em here," Shorty said. "I've got some more ponies comin' in, and those boys are real artists at changin' brands."

The grulla and the roan stood where we'd tied them, switching flies in the sunshine. Twenty yards away, the two men stopped and turned to face each other. The argument seemed to be heating up. The big man's face was red, and his eyes flashed as he cussed the other man. "I've had a belly full of you," he snapped. "You're a goddamn sneak thief? No man steals from me!"

"Go to hell," the smaller man said. "I told you before—I never touched your watch."

"Oh, shit," said Shorty. "They're arguin' about that damned watch again."

"What about the watch?" I asked.

"Luke Fedders, that tall drink o' water, lost his pocket watch while he was trailin' horses with Stub Hartley, the smaller man. Accused Stub of stealin' it from him. Stub says Luke's crazy. Says he never took the timepiece, but Luke won't let it go."

Shorty stepped away from us and toward the argument. "I'd better take a hand, before those two—"

Suddenly, Stub Hartley pulled a short-barreled Colt revolver and, just as fast as he could pull the trigger, fired three slugs into Luke Fedders! The three shots slapped the silence, running together in a blur of sound. The big man jerked like a puppet on a string as each bullet struck him. He swayed, dropped to his knees, and toppled forward into the dirt.

"Guess you won't need your damned watch now," Stub said. "Your time just ran out."

I reached for my .44, but my hand stopped just short of drawing and would go no farther. My mouth went dry as dust, and my belly felt like I'd swallowed a cold rock.

For a moment I'm back in the Bighorns facing Ed Hutchins again. I see him step out of the cabin, hatred twisting his face, coming toward me, raising his stolen gun. He points the revolver, and I fire—once, twice. Then he's down in the tall grass, dying. I've killed a man who met my challenge with an empty gun. I shook my head to clear the memory and looked again at Stub Hartley.

Stub took hold of the grulla's reins and swung into the saddle. "Tell George Starkweather I quit!" he said. Jerking the little horse around, the small man sank spur and rode off through the brush and into the breaks beyond.

For a moment, Shorty, Two Hats, and me just stood there frozen in midstride like actors in a tableau. It had all happened fast. Stub Hartley had killed the big man, stepped up onto my Mouse horse, and quit the country before I could get my mind around what was happening.

Surprise turned to outrage. The shooting didn't bother me; one horse thief had gunned down another, and that was that. But the killer had stolen Mouse, and that made it personal.

"Hey!" I shouted. "That's my horse!"

I reached Two Hats's roan in three strides and was a-straddle of him in a bound. The big gelding was already turning to follow the grulla; my spurs just made him do it faster.

The roan took me through the brush at a go-to-meeting trot. Branches slashed at my face. Thorns tore my shirt and scratched my hands. I ducked my head and pulled in my neck like a turtle, taking the buffeting on my shoulders and arms. Ahead, Mouse carried Stub Hartley toward the broken country that led back to the river, but I wasn't far behind.

We broke out of the undergrowth and plunged into a

dry coulee. Scrub cedar and low pines studded the slopes ahead. Dust raised by Mouse's hooves hung in the air. I couldn't see the little horse, but I knew I was close—right on his heels. The roan dropped into a steep gully, hitting stiff-legged, rattling my teeth. I heard him grunt, then felt him spring up, climbing the bank. We reached the crest of the hill and plunged down again. I took a short hold on the reins and pulled my .44 out of the leather.

And then, suddenly, the roan decided he'd had enough. He reared, front legs pawing the air, his head thrown back. Off balance, I flew forward, my face colliding with his head. Pain blinded me. Stars exploded behind my closed eyes. I wondered if I had broken my nose.

The big horse fell to pitching in earnest. He reached the top of a steep hill and bucked down over its crest. Loose rock and clumps of dirt sailed past me. I lost a stirrup, and then my balance. Flying free, I saw the ground rush up. I tried to get my feet under me, intending to touch and roll with the fall, but I hit the ground like a dropped boulder, and bounced and tumbled until I came to rest upside down on the hillside.

I tried to breathe but could not; the fall had knocked the wind out of me. I lay there gasping for air like a carp on a riverbank. I wanted to breathe even more than I wanted to stop hurting. After what seemed like a week, I caught my breath, sat up, and took stock of the damage.

To my surprise, there wasn't all that much. I had a

few cuts and welts from the branches, a nosebleed, and a headache, but nothing appeared to be broken, and I hadn't lost my hat. And I still had my .44; it jammed into the loose dirt when I fell, but I hadn't lost it. All I had lost was my horse, the man I was chasing, and my dignity.

It occurred to me that I wasn't doing all that well at playing outlaw. A real outlaw wouldn't have gone loco just because someone stole his horse, would he? As an outlaw, you'd think he would expect it.

Is that so? I thought. *You just saw a real outlaw kill another one over what he claimed was a stolen pocket watch. I reckon an outlaw is just as touchy as an honest man about being robbed. Maybe more.*

So I gave up my philosophizing and returned to the business at hand. Outlaw ethics or no, Stub Hartley had made off with my horse and my saddle, and I aimed to get 'em back.

I scrubbed the dirt from inside my gun barrel with a pine twig and slid the weapon back into its holster. I got to my feet and brushed myself off some. Then I turned my thoughts to hunting for the roan.

I scrambled through loose dirt and rock to the top of the slope, hoping to catch sight of the big gelding. Had he made his way back to the cabin? Or headed for the cottonwood trees along the river? Or had he quit the country altogether? I had no idea. All I knew for sure was that I was on foot and hunting my horse. I found his tracks in the soft, loose dirt and set out to follow them.

The roan's trail led downhill toward the Yellowstone.

The pine-studded bluffs descended into brushy bottoms, thick with willows, and I kept my eyes on the tracks before me. Before long, I could hear the river. Cottonwood trees stood tall along the banks, and the ground was littered with leaves and fallen branches. And then, in the dappled shade at the water's edge, I found the roan.

There he stood, head high and watchful as I stepped out of the willows. His nostrils flared as he caught my scent; nervously, he scratched the gravel with a forefoot. By some miracle, the Winchester was still in its saddle scabbard.

I began with an apology. "Sorry I pushed you that way, Roanie," I said. "Rufus Two Hats treated you bad, and so did I."

The roan cast a wary eye in my direction, but he was listening—his ears pointed my way as I spoke to him.

"I don't blame you for buckin' me off back there either," I said. "I sure had it comin'." I walked slowly toward the big horse, my voice low and easy, and held my hand out toward him. "Thing is, that Hartley feller stole Mouse, your little pardner. I have to get him back, and I need your help."

Again, the gelding pawed the ground and tossed his head, his eyes fixed on me. I stood still, watching him. After a time he calmed some; I walked slowly toward him again, my voice low and easy. "Now if you'll just let bygones be bygones, I promise to treat you better," I said. "I won't handle you rough, and I'll try not to spook you. What do you say, Roanie?"

The big horse trembled, but he didn't move away. My hand touched his neck and lingered. I grasped his trailing bridle rein with my other hand, then stroked his neck awhile, talking soft until he grew calm again. "Much obliged, big horse," I said, easing into the saddle. "Now let's go find Mouse."

CHAPTER 3

My Death and Resurrection

By the time I picked up Stub Hartley's trail again, I figured the outlaw was maybe twenty minutes ahead of me. The signs were clear; hoofprints in the soft mud and sand plain as day. Torn leaves and bent branches marked where Hartley had spurred the gray through the brush. From time to time I'd come to a place where they broke out of the willows and followed the riverbank, and I'd slow down and read sign to make sure he hadn't crossed over.

Then, a half-mile farther on, I came to a place where he'd done just that—crossed to the other side. Beyond, on a raised grade, rails of the Northern Pacific cut through the valley. I knew the town of Columbus lay maybe two miles upstream, so that's where I figured I'd find Hartley.

I turned the roan into the river, watching the opposite bank in case Hartley lay in ambush. Roanie waded out, feeling his way along the bottom, and then, all of a sudden, we plunged into deep water. Head high, he swam for the shore while I gave him free rein. The current carried us downstream a ways, but in just a little bit, we reached the other side, and Roanie clattered up the rocky bank. I reined him away from the river into the sunlight, and following the riverbank, we struck out for Columbus.

I had last seen the town back in eighty-four when it went by the name of Stillwater. Since then, the Northern Pacific had brought it a new name—Columbus—and a new prosperity. The place still had its share of saloons, dance halls, and such, but new businesses had sprung up, and it had a more settled and permanent look.

The town's main drag fronted on the railroad tracks, and I turned Roanie up the street, keeping an eye out for a mouse-colored grulla wearing my old Texas saddle. Horses aplenty stood hitched in front of the saloons and beer joints, but none of them was Mouse. I checked the side streets and was about to inquire at the livery barn, when I heard a commotion from the other side of the tracks.

Crossing over, I saw a little crowd standing in front of a low stone building. Other townsfolk were rushing that direction. I rode over and dismounted. Making my way to the front of the crowd, I discovered what the excitement was all about. There he lay—on his back in the street—Stub Hartley, riddled with buckshot and dead as a beaver hat!

Beyond the dead man stood a slope-shouldered gent I'd met two years before—Horace Wisdom, city marshal of Columbus. The marshal hadn't changed much.

He still wore the big Stetson hat and the black frock coat he seemed to favor, and his nickel-plated badge reflected splinters of sunlight. He held a long-barreled shotgun and posed before Hartley's corpse like a dude hunter with a dead rabbit.

For a moment, I feared Horace might recognize me. Then I remembered that without his eyeglasses, the man was nearly blind. As he stood there playing to the crowd, he had taken them off out of vanity. He wouldn't know me unless I announced myself, and I sure didn't intend to do that.

Seeing Stub Hartley dead was interesting enough, but what really caught my attention was the young man behind the city marshal. A youth of about eighteen stood in front of the stone building, a badge pinned to his shirt, and he was holding the bridle reins of my horse, Mouse!

"What happened, Marshal?" asked a townsman.

"I had a telegram from Dry Creek last evenin'," said Horace. "Two days ago, a peace officer gone bad, one Merlin Fanshaw, killed deputy sheriff Glenn Murdoch in that town and helped a prisoner escape. Telegram said Fanshaw was ridin' a grulla horse and an old-style Texas rig." He pointed to Mouse with a flourish. "Like *that* one."

Horace puffed out his chest; this was his moment in the sun. "I saw this feller come ridin' up the street on that animal," he continued. "He kept lookin' back over his shoulder like somebody was chasm' him. I recalled the telegram and recognized the horse—and Fanshaw—from the description. When I ordered him to rein up, he went for his gun. My shotgun was cocked and ready. I beat his draw and shot him out of the saddle."

"You beat his draw?" the townsman asked. "You just said you had your shotgun cocked and ready."

Horace frowned and cleared his throat. "Yes. Well, the man was a killer. A peace officer can't be too careful."

I eased my way to the edge of the crowd and then back down the street to where I'd left Roanie. Clearly, there was no way I could claim Mouse and my saddle—not under these circumstances. Then it occurred to me that that telegram might have described the roan too. I figured the sooner Roanie and me left Columbus, the better—even if I *was* officially dead.

I rode north out of town, watching my back trail. No one followed or even seemed to notice me. After twenty minutes or so, I turned around and followed the Yellowstone south to where I'd forded it earlier. Minutes later, I re-crossed the river and rode Roanie back to the cabin.

The sun had set by the time the cabin came into view. Overhead, the sky was ablaze with color, but down in the trees the light was fading fast. Beyond the cottonwoods, at the edge of the clearing, Rufus Two Hats and Shorty Benson stood together beside an open grave. At their feet lay the body of Luke Fedders.

Both Shorty and Rufus looked up as I topped the hill.

I tried to imitate the call of the killdeer as Rufus had done, but I was less than successful. I sounded like a man trying to sound like a killdeer. Rufus returned my call, and then, with his foot, rolled the corpse into the grave.

By the time I rode down to where the burying was in progress, Rufus was already shoveling in dirt. Shorty watched me dismount. "I don't see no mouse-colored horse," he said. "Did you forget what you went after?"

"No," I said, "but I decided to let him spend a little time in town. Even a horse needs a day off now and then."

Shorty watched me, waiting for the rest of the story. "Stub rode him into Columbus," I said. "That turned out to be a mistake. City Marshal Wisdom had a telegram from the marshal's office in Dry Creek. Telegram described Two Hats and me—described the horses we rode, too. Wisdom saw Stub ride in on the grulla and braced him. Stub pulled his gun, and Wisdom blew him out of the saddle with a ten-gauge."

"Stub's dead?" Shorty asked.

"Dead as a horse thief ever gets. Wisdom's deputy has my horse in custody. The marshal was still making a speech to the citizens when I left. He thinks Stub was me."

Shorty spat. "Stub was a damn fool," he said. "Killed Luke. Stole your horse. Caused us all this grave-diggin' trouble."

Two Hats snorted. "Caused *us* trouble? *I* done all the damn work."

Shorty shrugged. "I ain't the manual labor type," he said. "My specialty is bank robbin' and cookin'. I leave the heavy liftin' to the riffraff."

"Your specialty is runnin' your mouth," Rufus said. "You better watch out, old man. I ain't too tired to dig another grave."

We ate supper together that evening by lantern light. Shorty had made a venison stew and a batch of biscuits. Again, he brought up the subject of the horses in the corral. "What about them horses I asked you about? Will you boys drive 'em down to Arrowhead?"

Rufus ignored the question. I said, "I wouldn't mind. What is this 'Arrowhead' you keep talkin' about?"

Shorty glanced at Rufus before he answered. "It's the home ranch," he said. "I thought you knew. It's down in the foothills of the East Pryors—on Layout Creek this side of the Bighorn River."

"How do we get there?" I asked.

"Ride east until you pick up the Meeteetse Trail," Shorty said. "Then south to Red Lodge and across the Clark's Fork."

I knew about the Meeteetse Trail. Located by the army back in eighty-one, it began at Billings and ran the full length of Carbon County and into Wyoming before it finally terminated at the town of Meeteetse. Freighters used the trail to haul supplies to the ranches and army posts in the area. Stagecoaches made the trip in fair weather and foul, covering sixty to eighty miles a day.

"Is George at Arrowhead?" I asked.

"That's right. Rufus knows the way."

"How long a drive is it?"

"Two days. If you boys leave before first light, you can be there day after tomorrow."

I stood up. "Then I reckon I'll get some shut-eye," I said. "You got a spare blanket?"

Shorty's laugh was a dry cackle. "Hell, boys—I've got two complete bedrolls you can use. Neither Luke nor Stub'll be needin' theirs tonight."

That's how I came to spend the night on the cold ground in a dead man's bedroll. Stub's blankets were filthy and ragged. They smelled of sour sweat and cheap whiskey, but the night was cold and I was glad to have 'em. Overhead, the pale moon shed its light on clearing and cabin. Beyond the treetops, the sky was scattershot with stars, and a chill wind rattled the branches of the cottonwoods.

I lay there on my back looking up into the night sky, thinking about the twists and turns a man's journey takes. I had left the safe and steady life in Dry Creek to partner up with a hard-eyed breed. Now I was wanted by the law for murder, and a horse thief named Hartley had stolen my horse and saddle—only to get himself killed by a small-town lawman who thought Stub was me.

I figured Ridgeway would come to Columbus when he heard about my untimely demise. Likely, he'd ask to see the dead man and find it wasn't me. I hoped he would be relieved to learn I was alive. I know *I* was.

And now, come morning, I'd be driving stolen horses to a place called Arrowhead, to an outlaw chief who might or might not shoot me on sight. My life was safe and steady no more.

I said a prayer for the two dead men, and asked the Lord to shuffle the deck and give them a square deal. Then I burrowed deep in the blankets and fell asleep like a January bear.

"Roll out, boys," Shorty Benson called from the door. "There's coffee on the stove and horses in the corral."

I sat up rubbing the sleep from my eyes. The lantern in Shorty's hand cast a pale circle of light on the grass. Ten feet away, Two Hats threw back the tarp that covered the late Luke Fedder's bedroll, then sat up and reached for his boots.

"It sure don't take long to stay all night around here," I groused. "What time is it?"

"Time you got up," Shorty said. "It's a little past three in the mornin'."

"That late, huh? Good thing you woke me—I might have lazed around till three-thirty or four."

Shorty turned back to the cabin and took the light with him. "Fetch some stove wood when you come in," he said.

I didn't linger. The morning's chill was biting. I knew the day would warm with the dawn, but sunrise was still a good three hours away. I shivered, shrugged into my brush jacket, and pulled my boots on. After I'd rolled and tied up Stub's bed, I gathered an armload from the woodpile beside the cabin and stepped inside.

Shorty stood at the stove cooking hotcakes and bacon. He nodded curtly as I tumbled my burden into the wood box. "Coffee's hot," he said, "Help yourself." I poured myself a cup and stood—well out of Shorty's way—warming myself at the stove. I was still half asleep, but the good smells of coffee and bacon drew me to wakefulness.

Minutes later, Rufus filled the doorway. He wore only a thin cotton shirt and seemed unaffected by the cold. "You can ride Stub's horse," he said. "He's fiddleheaded, but he'll get you there."

I nodded. "I'll ride Stub's saddle, too. Seems only fair, seein' as he took mine."

Rufus grunted. "Didn't do the dumb bastard much good, did it? Stealin' your outfit got him killed."

"And now the law has your horse and saddle," said Shorty, setting the cakes and bacon on the table. "Hell of a thing."

"Luck of the draw," I said, "but I am gonna miss that Mouse."

After breakfast, Rufus and me wrapped the leftover hotcakes and bacon in the pages of an old newspaper and put the bundles in our saddle pockets. I was glad to find that Stub's saddle was of the Texas iron-horn type, a lot like my own. The stirrup length was perfect; I wouldn't have to replace the leathers. I tied a blanket roll behind the cantle and hefted the rig up onto my shoulder.

Shorty was waiting for us at the round corral. He'd

run Stub's gelding and Roanie in the night before and had grained them for the ride. Shorty held the lantern high where Stub's horse was tied short and high to a corral post. "That's one of the best horses in the string," he said. "I hope you like buckskins."

"Best horses I ever had were buckskins," I said. "Ones I've owned were tough and willin'."

"I had a woman like that, once," Shorty said, grinning, "but she was a strawberry roan."

I brushed the buckskin's back and swung the Texas hull into place. The gelding stood, calm and steady, as I tied off the latigos. "Well," I said, "let's see what he's got."

I stepped up into the saddle and reined the little horse about. He was cat-quick, I found, and he answered well to both rein and knee. He made no move to pitch, and I took that as a bonus. I never minded a horse that would buck some when first saddled—I figured better early in the day than later, when he might take me by surprise—but the buckskin's good behavior on that particular morning meant we could start earlier. We had a long way to go.

The fifty horses stirred inside the corral as Rufus and me rode up to the gate. Moonlight shone on their necks and backs, dappled by the shadows of the cottonwoods. The wind had fallen off during the night, but the morning was still and cold. I shivered, anxious to get moving.

Rufus stepped down and swung the gate open. "I'll ride point," he said. "You eat dust."

Riding point was the hard part of the job. Rufus would have to ride swing, point, and flank all at the same time to keep the ponies headed in the right direction. It was a job I knew well, but Rufus was familiar with the trail and I wasn't. "Lead off," I told him.

I turned the little buckskin inside and began a slow circle of the corral. Restless, the horses began to mill and found the open gate. Outside, Rufus kicked Roanie into a lope, flanking the leaders as the ponies poured through the opening. I touched the buckskin with my spurs and felt him bolt and carry me into the darkness. Glancing back, I had a last quick look at Shorty; he was still holding the lantern as he watched us ride away. Then I turned my attention to following running horses by moonlight.

The ponies thundered away, flying free. Ahead, Rufus flanked the leaders, holding the bunch together. I followed behind, tasting the dust of the horses' passing, my eyes watering from the cold wind we made. Scrub cedar and pine loomed up and flew past, dark shapes in the gloom. We clattered up hillsides and dropped into moon-shadowed gullies. I trusted the buckskin to make his way through the rough and broken country over obstacles I couldn't see.

At length, the horses slowed. Rufus had held them together during their breakaway from the corral; now they seemed satisfied just to move along at a dogtrot. In the east, stars faded and winked out. Mountains reared up, dark against the sky. High overhead, the moon grew pale. Ahead, Rufus waited astride Roanie, watching the bunch jog past. I reined up as I approached him and stopped.

"Big coulee up ahead," he said. "Good grass. We'll ease the ponies down there."

It was the longest speech I'd heard Rufus make. I nodded, and we rode up the bench, pushing the horses down into the bottom. Light was hitting the hilltops by then, but the low-lying gullies remained shaded and dark. A cold breeze arose with the coming daylight, and I shivered. Always darkest before the dawn, goes the old saw. Always coldest just after the dawn, I've found.

The ponies fanned out and grazed on the dew-wet grass. At the head of the coulee, a spring trickled out of the rocks and formed a stream. We watered our mounts, and then we drank. Shadows gave way as sunlight came on, and I turned my face to the sun and welcomed its warmth.

Rufus and me took the bridles off and turned our saddle horses out to graze in their hobbles. For the better part of the next hour, we just sat beside the stream thinking our own thoughts. Rufus rolled himself a smoke and lit up. I figured some friendly conversation might help pass the time.

"Where you from?" I asked.

"Around," he said.

"How long have you rode with George?"

"Awhile," he said.

"You're not real talkative, are you?"

"No," he said.

So much for friendly conversation.

Rufus looked out across the valley; his eyes narrowed, his face expressionless. So far, I had found talking with Rufus to be pretty much like conversing with a granite boulder. But I tried again.

"Some good ponies in that bunch," I said. "Shorty said the long-rope boys brought them in from up north. From where, exactly?"

Rufus shrugged.

I looked again at the horses. They were saddle stock of many colors: buckskins, bays and sorrels, roans and blacks, grays, and pintos. I saw a zebra dun, two whites, and a glass-eyed appaloosa. Backlit by the morning sun, browsing on the green grass of the bottoms, the bunch was mighty easy on the eyes. At a rough estimate, I figured the animals were worth between three and four thousand dollars.

"How far do we take 'em tonight?" I asked.

Again, the shrug. "Clark's Fork, maybe. Other side of Red Lodge."

I had heard of Red Lodge. The town lay in a fertile valley at the foot of the Beartooth Mountains just fifteen miles from the Wyoming line. Twenty years earlier, a prospector name of "Yankee Jim" George had come to the valley looking for gold. What he found instead were rich deposits of coal. Last I heard, the Northern Pacific was building a branch line to the area from the main line at Laurel. The town had a post office, a handful of tent-and-log saloons, a short order house, and not much else.

Rufus looked out beyond the grazing horses and nodded. "Meeteetse Trail is just over that ridge," he said. "Red Lodge ain't far."

"I expect we'd best ride clear of towns," I said. "We're wanted men movin' fifty head of stolen horses. Last thing we need is to attract attention."

Rufus was quiet for so long I thought he hadn't heard me. Finally he said, "One of us better go in and bring back some grub. We're gonna be damned hungry by tonight."

"I don't know. Towns mean peace officers. Peace officers mean trouble."

"I ain't gonna make it on a few cold hotcakes and some stale bacon. I'm goin' in.

"I like to eat better than most anything," I said, "but our job is to get those horses delivered. I don't like takin' chances."

Rufus set his jaw and frowned. "I ain't askin' you," he said. "When we get there, I'm goin' in, goddammit! You can do what you want."

A man has to choose his battles—and his time. "We'll talk about it later," I said. "Right now, let's gather those ponies and get 'em lined out again."

We proceeded on, pushing the horses ahead of us along a broad, open bench. At noon, we moved the herd down into a valley marked by a wide road, and crossed over onto the grassland beyond, allowing the horses to graze. Since our discussion that morning, Rufus had clammed up entirely. The stubborn set of his jaw made it clear that he hadn't liked my objection to his going into Red Lodge. He was mad as hell and in no mood for palaver.

That was all right with me. More talk would likely have led to a fight, and butting heads wouldn't get the horses delivered. I ate the leftover breakfast I'd brought and sat beneath a tree reading the newspaper page I'd wrapped it in.

I thought again of George Starkweather. It had been him that got me started reading again. That year I rode with him and his gang, George told me he had taken up reading while doing time for rustling. George was a bad man, no question about that, but he'd been quick to lend me his books, and they'd opened my mind to new worlds.

Since then, I always tried to keep a book or a newspaper close at hand. In fact, Mr. Twain's book *Tom Sawyer* had been in my saddlebag when Stub Hartley stole my horse. Now, both Mouse and my book were in the hands of the Columbus city marshal. I missed Mouse, but I think I missed having a book to read even more.

The newspaper page was from the Helena *Independent,* and it had a story on the drought in Montana and the problems facing the territory's cowmen. Prices were too low to sell their animals, but the range was too overstocked, overgrazed, and dry to hold them. "Much," the article said, "depends on the coming winter."

Well, that's always true in Montana, I thought. The

weather seldom suits the cowman. Either too much rain and snow, or too little. When the moisture does come, it comes at the wrong time. Cattle die of Texas fever. Calves die in spring snowstorms. The cowman loses stock to wolves, Indians, and rustlers—like George and his boys. Being a cattle king, I decided, wasn't all it was cracked up to be.

It was time to get the horses back on the trail. Carefully, I folded the newspaper page and put it in my shirt pocket. It was crumpled and torn, greasy from the bacon, and I had read every word. Even so, I kept it. It was the only reading material I had.

It was late afternoon when Rufus spoke to me again. We had moved the horses steadily south since midday, coming at last to a wide valley below the rising peaks of the Beartooths. A lively creek flowed out of the mountains and made its way northward down the valley. Ahead, Rufus drove the herd across the creek and up to the valley's east bench. At the top, he drew rein and waited, watching my approach.

I smiled when I neared him, but my hand was near my .44. Rufus Two Hats was a wild card. If it was his intention to do me harm, I figured I'd go down shooting. At least, I hoped I would. I reined up and looked him in the eye. Mule stubborn, Rufus scowled and lowered his gaze.

"Red Lodge is just ahead," he muttered. "I'm goin' in."

I kept my eyes on him, but I said nothing.

"We need some grub," he muttered.

I looked beyond the big man. The horses had fanned out across a grassy hollow and were grazing again. "All right," I said, "but if you're not back in an hour, I'm goin' on without you."

"You don't know where Arrowhead is."

"On Layout Creek, Shorty said, this side of the Bighorn River. I'll find it."

Rufus flashed a quick smile. It startled me some; I didn't know the big half-breed *could* smile.

"Hell, Kid," he said. "I'll be back before you know it."

"Watch yourself," I advised, but he had already turned Roanie down off the bench. I watched as he splashed across the creek and disappeared, riding south.

Rufus was not back before I knew it—not hardly. One hour passed, and then another. The sun dropped low, and the shadows grew long. The ponies showed no inclination to wander, but seemed content to graze on the short grass that lined the hollow. Twice, I rode a slow circle around the bunch, pushing back the few animals that had drifted away from the others.

I remembered the way Rufus had looked the day before as he rummaged through the shelves back at the cabin, a kind of naked hunger in his eyes when he asked Shorty if he had any whiskey, and a quiet desperation when Shorty told him no. Growing up back at Dry Creek with my pa, I knew those signs all too well. Pa had been, and Rufus Two Hats was, a man controlled by drink. As I waited, I knew why he wasn't back yet.

I commenced to reproach myself. I had been a durned fool to let Rufus go into the settlement alone. I should have roped and hog-tied him, kept him from riding off—at gunpoint, if necessary. I had said I'd take the horses and go on alone if he wasn't back in an hour, but we both knew that was a bluff.

The truth was, I didn't know how to find the home ranch. I knew it was on Layout Creek this side of the Bighorn River, but that was all. I wasn't familiar with the country. I didn't know the way.

Maybe, I thought, Rufus getting drunk wasn't the worst of it. Maybe he'd been arrested—or shot. Maybe he was wounded and trying to get back to me. Maybe Roanie had bucked him off, the way he'd unloaded me while I was chasing the horse thief. Rufus might be hurt and on foot someplace this side of Red Lodge.

As much as I hated to leave the horses, there was only one thing to do. I turned the buckskin back past the aspen grove and down into the valley. As twilight settled among the foothills, I struck out for Red Lodge.

The "town" turned out to be a handful of cabins, shacks, and tents scattered across a sagebrush flat. The fast-flowing stream we'd crossed earlier cascaded along its rocky bed, bordered by willows and cottonwoods. There were no people in sight, but two saddle horses stood hitched outside one of the bigger cabins. A hand-painted sign above the door read "Cowpunchers' Retreat." I stepped down and tied the buckskin next to the other horses. Then I opened the door and went inside.

The cabin was spacious and warm. Tables and chairs filled most of the room. At one table, two riders who sat across from each other eating, looked up as I came in, decided they didn't know me, and returned to their food. Across the room a big caboose stove blazed away, cracking and pinging as it warmed the building. The rich smell of a savory stew drifted my way from a kitchen range in the rear, and that woke my hunger.

An older man in shirtsleeves and an apron walked toward me from the kitchen. "Welcome, cowboy," he said. "I'm John Webber, and I own this hash house. What can I do for you?"

The smell of the stew made me light-headed, so I pulled out a chair at an empty table and sat down. "Bring me a double order of whatever I'm smellin'," I said, "with all the trimmin's. I'm so hungry I could eat a skunk."

The man smiled. "Sorry, cowboy," he said. "We only serve skunk on Tuesdays. Today's special is venison stew and biscuits. Will that do?"

"As long as it's fast," I said. "It doesn't even have to be good."

Webber brought me a big bowl of stew and a mug of coffee with a plate of biscuits on the side. It took no time at all for me to go through that serving and another. When I'd finally had my fill, I slumped back in my chair. Webber came out of the kitchen to clear up the debris.

"They must not eat very often where you come from," he said. "You ride for one of the cow outfits over east?"

"No," I said. "I'm a deputy sheriff out of Billings. I'm lookin' for a man."

"That right? He wouldn't be a big half-breed, would he? Man of that description raised Billy Hell over at the saloon this afternoon!"

"Sounds like my man," I said. "What'd he do?"

"Drank up half the whiskey in the place and then refused to pay for it," Webber said. "Bartender called him on it, and the big breed broke the man's nose and a couple of ribs. Two other customers tried to stop him, and he beat hell out of them, too.

"After that, he stepped up onto a big roan horse and pulled foot, bold as brass and full of stolen whiskey."

"Nobody went after him?"

"Nope. The breed said if anybody followed him, he'd kill 'em slow and painful. That tended to discourage the local heroes. Broken bones and bruises heal, and a man can always distill more whiskey."

I paid Webber for the grub. "Much obliged," I said. "I'd better get on his trail before it goes cold."

"With a lawbreaker like that big sum'bitch," Webber said, "a cold trail might be just the thing."

Dusk had settled across the valley by the time I started back. I followed the road to where I'd crossed the stream, watching for Rufus and the roan, but found no trace. Shadows were deep there along the creek, and I gave the buckskin his head, trusting him to find his way. He splashed across, hooves clattering against the rocks, and carried me up the slope beyond. At the top, the aspen grove I'd passed earlier was still, the trunks of its trees ghostly white in the gloom.

In the darkening sky, the first stars of evening began to appear. Looking below, toward the hollow, I found I could just make out some of the horses. They were grazing where I'd left them. I reined in the buckskin, listening. Born with the setting sun, a gentle breeze sighed through the grass and stirred the aspen leaves. I turned in the saddle, straining my eyes, still hoping for some sign of Rufus, but saw only shadows. *Where was he?*

I turned the buckskin down toward the grazing horses and, standing in the stirrups, took one last look back. It was then I heard a horse whinny, high pitched and clear, loud in the stillness. The buckskin turned his head toward the aspen grove, ears pointed toward the sound. I followed his gaze and saw it—Roanie stood just beyond the tree line, outlined against the sky! The big horse pawed nervously at the ground and whinnied again. I steadied the buckskin and peered into the darkness—there! Just there, on its side in the grass, lay the figure of a man—Rufus!

I was glad but angry as well—I had been worried about him! Now I had found him, too drunk to ride, fallen from his horse, passed out! I rode up and dismounted. I wasn't gentle with the toe of my boot. "Hey!" I said. "Get up, durn you!" I bent to shake him awake and quickly drew back. He was cold—cold as stone.

Impressions flashed through my mind like summer lightning. Rufus lay still, eyes wide open and staring. His shirt was wet along his back, shiny and black in the gloom. *Blood,* I remember thinking, *Rufus Two Hats is dead!*

It was then that a sudden movement caught the edge of my vision—a tall, bearded man, rifle at the ready, moving out of the trees and coming fast. I took a step back, reaching for my gun, but my hand froze in mid-draw. The man swung the rifle up sharply, and I felt the shock of the blow as the gun butt struck my jaw. Lights exploded inside my brain. A red haze flared behind my eyes. The earth seemed to drop away beneath my feet, and I fell with it into darkness.

CHAPTER 4
Old Acquaintance

When I came to my senses, I lay on the ground with my face in the dirt. The pain in my jaw throbbed in time with my heartbeat, and my teeth felt loose. My tongue felt swollen big as a cow's. I smelled smoke and wondered if I was a newcomer in Hell.

My arms were stiff and cramped. When I tried to bring my hands up to roll over on my side, I couldn't do it; they were bound behind my back. I didn't groan, but I guess I must have grunted some, because a high-pitched voice, nasal and mean, called my name.

"Good mornin' to you, Merlin Fanshaw," said the voice. "You are not dead, young sir, at least not yet."

I lifted my head in the direction of the voice and opened my eyes. Twelve feet away, an old man with a gray beard sat beside a campfire. Dressed all in dusty black, the stranger peered at me through thick spectacles and smiled a gap-toothed grin.

"I usually ain't inclined to make a man suffer," he said, "but you was fixin' to pull your pistol on me. That's when I had to put you under."

I rolled on my side, and pain stabbed through my head and left me feeling queasy, but somehow I managed to sit up. I tried to focus. The man was thin as wire, all elbows and knees. Beneath a battered hat, his hair hung dirty and lank to his shoulders. Tobacco juice stained his beard and spotted his shirtfront. My .44 Colt revolver was stuck in the waistband of his pants.

Behind him, at the edge of the grove, a saddle horse and a pack mule grazed. The stranger leaned closer to the fire and stirred the contents of a cast-iron skillet with a Bowie knife. Laying the knife aside, he picked up a battered Bible and leafed quickly through its pages.

"Here it is," he said. "First Kings nineteen, verse five: 'And as he lay and slept under a juniper tree, behold, then an angel touched him and said unto him, Arise and eat.' "

He closed the Bible. His laugh was a dry cackle. "You lay and slept nigh unto an aspen tree, not a juniper, and I ain't any angel unless I be Asrael, the angel of death."

Thirty yards away in the short grass behind the man, the body of Rufus Two Hats lay where I'd seen it the night before. The hard brown face had gone to ashen gray. The mouth gaped, and the eyes stared at the sky, unseeing. The flies had already found him.

"You could at least close his eyes," I said. "Did you kill him?"

"I surely did. Waited till he passed the grove yonder. Shot him in the back with my .45–70. Kilt him clean, though the light was fadin'."

"Couldn't have been all that hard. I understand he was dead drunk."

The old man shrugged. "He be drunk no more, but merely dead," he said. "I blowed him clean out of his saddle. Bled like a stuck hog. I reckon the bullet took him through the lungs."

I stared at him. "Who are you, mister? Some kind of lawman?"

Again, the man laughed his dry cackle. "Not hardly," he said. "I'm a hunter. Bounty man. Name is Ezekiel Graves. You and me have met, young sir, but I don't expect you'd recollect."

"We have?"

"Last winter in Dry Creek. I stopped by the marshal's office to see Glenn Murdoch. Was talkin' to him one mornin' when you come in."

"You're right," I said. "I don't recall."

"I passed through Dry Creek again the day after you

murdered Glenn and broke Rufus Two Flats out of jail. Didn't take the U.S. marshal long to put a bounty on you both. Five hunnert dollars reward for the late Rufus yonder, and seven hunnert an' fifty for you. Dead or alive."

"How'd you find us?"

"Picked up your tracks goin' away from Dry Creek. Appeared you was headed south. I took the train as far as Columbus."

"I'd call that a lucky guess."

The man called Graves nodded. "Turned out that way. But ain't it queer how the lucky hunters are always the best hunters?"

"So how'd you come to follow us here?"

Graves took the skillet off the fire and scooped the contents onto a tin plate. "Had the good fortune to be in Columbus when Horace Comfort killed that feller," he said, "the one he thought was you."

"But you knew it wasn't."

"That's right. I didn't tell Horace, of course. I could see how he made his mistake, though. That mouse-colored horse of yours matched the description right enough."

Graves waved a hand at the plate and began to eat. "I'd offer you some of this," he said, "but there'd be no point to it. I don't expect you're hungry just now, anyway."

"Let's get back to the shootin' at Columbus. You knew the man Comfort shot wasn't me, but you recognized my horse. What then?"

The bounty hunter chuckled. "I saw you slip away from the crowd. Recognized you right off. Saw you get up on that big roan and sneak out of town."

"Why didn't you stop me?"

Graves finished the food on his plate and picked up the Bible again. "Didn't like the odds," he said, leafing through the pages. "Besides, I figured you'd lead me to Rufus—if I was patient."

"So you killed him."

"Indeed, young sir. I am the avenger, and huntin' evildoers is my trade. You slew Glenn Murdoch. You and Rufus was runnin' from justice." Graves pointed a bony finger at a passage in the book. "You ran, as it says here in Deuteronomy nineteen, 'Lest the avenger of the blood pursue the slayer, while his heart is hot, and overtake him, because the way is long, and slay him.'"

Graves closed the Bible and assumed a smug expression. "I have already slain one of you evildoers."

I didn't try to keep the anger out of my voice. "From behind, in the dark, while he was drunk. All right, what about me?"

Graves stroked his beard. "Been thinkin' 'bout that, Deputy. The reward for you is the same whether you're warm or cold. I just might fetch you back alive."

"Why so generous?"

"I need a little help. It'll take two of us just to load Rufus's body on a horse. Besides, I could use somebody to talk to. Bounty huntin' is lonesome work."

"Well," I said, "I can't help much with my hands tied behind me. How about cuttin' me loose?"

Graves took off his eyeglasses, breathed on their lenses, and polished them with a dirty bandana. He seemed to be thinking my question over. After a pause, he fitted the wires of the spectacles over his ears and nodded. He picked up the Bowie knife from the skillet and wiped the blade on his pants leg. "Seems like a reasonable request," he said, getting up from the fire. "Get up and turn around."

I struggled to my feet and turned my back. As I did, I noticed again the corpse of Rufus Two Hats. It had not improved since I saw it last. The thought passed through my mind that turning my back on Obadiah Graves and his big knife took a large measure of stupidity. I stuck my bound hands out, felt the man cut the ropes, and turned around.

Graves must have seen something in my face. He took a step back, the Bowie still in his hand. "Don't even think about tryin' to jump me, Deputy," he said. "I'd gut you like a fish."

My arms were cramped and my hands were numb; I couldn't have jumped him if I'd wanted to. I shook my hands to get the circulation back, felt the painful tingle as the blood resumed its flow, and I smiled, buying time.

"Jumpin' you is the last thing on my mind, mister," I said. The campfire had died to ashes and coals. I nodded toward a blackened coffeepot that stood on a flat rock off to one side. "The first thing on my mind is a cup of that coffee."

Graves glanced down at the coffeepot, and I bet the

farm. I kicked out hard and felt my boot collide with the man's crotch. My left hand caught his wrist, keeping the knife at bay, but the strength still hadn't come back to my fingers, and I felt my grip weaken. Graves pulled free. I grabbed for my gun, still tucked in Graves's waistband, jerked it free—and dropped it!

I dived for the revolver just as Graves's Bowie knife whistled like a scythe through the space I had just vacated. I struck the ground scrambling for the six-gun. Graves was coming at me, the blade slashing the air, when I picked up the weapon and turned it on him. "Hold it!" I said. "Drop the durned knife!"

Graves hesitated. In spite of the pain on his face from that kick between his legs, with his gapped teeth bared and his eyes burning hate, he weighed his chances. I eared the Colt's hammer back to full cock and told him again. "Drop it, you psalm-singin' butcher, or I'll drop *you!*"

I was running a bluff; I still had no idea whether I could shoot the man, but I hoped *he* believed I could.

Slowly, Graves lowered the knife, then let it fall. He straightened his hands shoulder high and open. Then I noticed his eyes; he seemed to be looking at something in the distance behind me. "There's riders comin' this way, Deputy—two men."

"I didn't just fall off the turnip wagon, you durned ghoul," I said.

Graves shrugged and put his hands down. "They'll be here d'rectly," he said, still staring into space. "Then we'll see."

I hesitated. I had no intention of taking my eyes off the bounty hunter even for an instant, but . . . did I hear horses approaching? I wanted to turn and look, but I didn't dare.

Then I heard a man's deep voice calling out behind me, "Hello, the camp! All right if we come in?"

Before I could act, Graves called back. "Come ahead! You men are just in time!"

Still holding the gun on Graves, I turned. Two men were riding up the slope toward us, one a tall man on a blood-bay stud, the other a slim-built ranny about my age riding a sorrel gelding.

The tall man wore a heavy buffalo coat and a black hat. He drew rein as he neared the campfire. Behind him, his companion did the same.

Graves was all smiles. "I surely am glad to see you fellers," he said. "I'm a federal marshal out of Billings." He nodded at me. "This young man is my prisoner. He jumped me just before you showed up— got the drop on me!"

The tall man looked down at me from the saddle. "Put up your gun," he said. Behind him, the morning sun was a blazing ball in the sky. I lowered my .44 and slid it back in the leather. Shading my eyes, I looked up at the man against the brightness.

The stranger turned his attention again to the bounty hunter. "What's he wanted for, Marshal?" he asked.

Graves looked nervous. He kept glancing sideways at Rufus's body over by the aspen grove. "Uh . . . horse stealin' and murder," he said. "I had to kill his pardner yesterday night. The man attacked me."

The tall man rode over to Rufus's corpse and looked down at it. "Attacked you with his back, did he? I see that's where you shot him."

I spoke up. "Don't listen to him," I said. "He's no marshal! He's—"

"I know who he is," interrupted the tall man, "and I know who he ain't. He's a back-shootin' bounty hunter name of Zeke Graves, and he ain't worth a gob of warm spit."

The tall man rode back toward the campfire. Again, I squinted into the sun, trying to make out his face. The morning was cold, and the turned-up collar of his buffalo coat helped hide his features. Still, there was something familiar about him, about his voice, but I couldn't put a name to it.

Graves was sweating now, and trembling. Behind the lenses of his spectacles, his eyes were wide and fearful. He wasn't wearing a short gun, but he kept glancing nervously at the carbine he'd propped beside the campfire. "D-do I know you, sir?" he asked.

"You ought to, by god," said the tall man. "That feller you killed worked for me.

Everything seemed to happen at once. Graves's nerve broke; he made a desperate lunge for the carbine, and a long-barreled Colt revolver suddenly appeared in the tall man's hand. I saw flame belch from the gun's muzzle, heard and felt the blast. The bullet took Grimes in the back and threw him sprawling. He lay kicking in the grass, still trying to reach his rifle, but the tall man rode over to him and casually shot him in the head. Graves twitched and lay still.

"Damn!" complained the tall man. "I never used to have to shoot 'em twice."

I saw his face then, and I knew his name. "Cap'n?" I asked. "Is that you?"

"Who the hell did you think I was?" he replied. "Hello, Bodacious."

Original George Starkweather hadn't changed all that much. His hair and beard were whiter, but his face bore no trace of prison pallor; George was still brown as an old saddle. His smile showed the strong white teeth I remembered, and the jagged scar that marked the left side of his face still reminded me of a lightning bolt. His cold, yellow eyes fixed on me and held.

Then he said, "Nobody ever called me 'cap'n' except you. It's been four long years since I heard it."

He stepped down off the bay and spoke to the ranny on the sorrel. "This here's the Bodacious Kid, Pronto—leastways he used to be. Kid, meet Pronto Southwell."

The man called Pronto was guarded and cool. Beneath a flat-brimmed hat, a shock of wheat-yellow hair spilled down over his brow. His gray eyes were close set, his cheekbones high and wide. He sported a thin moustache, and he wore high-topped boots and Mexican spurs. He also wore two belted Colt revolvers. I had the feeling he knew how to use them.

I reached up and shook his hand. "Howdy," I said. Pronto nodded, but said nothing. George bent over and rifled the pockets of the dead bounty hunter. His efforts produced a thick roll of bills and a money belt.

"I don't reckon a decent person would touch this here blood money," George said, "so I'll just have to keep it."

He raised his head and spoke to Pronto. "Put a rope on this mankiller," he said. "Drag his carcass up next to Rufus while I fix us some breakfast. No use lettin' this grub go to waste."

Pronto dismounted, drew a noose about the dead man's feet, then swung back into the saddle and spurred the sorrel up toward the trees with the corpse bouncing along behind.

George dug through the bounty hunter's panniers and came up with a slab of bacon, an onion, three potatoes, and half a loaf of bread. "Fetch some firewood," he said, "and we'll get that cook-fire goin' again. We left Arrowhead before breakfast, and I'm hungry as a wolf pup."

If I hadn't known George as well as I did, I might have wondered how he could eat after murdering a man in cold blood. My own appetite had disappeared entirely.

If George Starkweather had a conscience, I'd never seen any evidence of it. His own wants were all that mattered to him, and he put upon them no limits whatever.

In spite of my helping to put him in prison, George's attitude this morning was matter-of-fact, almost friendly. I took a deep breath and waited for the other shoe to drop.

George crisped the bacon, sliced the potatoes, and chopped up the onion, then fried it up in Graves's fire-blackened skillet. He brewed a second pot of coffee and got plates and cups from the pannier. "Come and get it, boys," he said.

Odd—two corpses lay just downwind, and I was hungry again. *So much for death ruining my appetite. I've been around George Starkweather thirty minutes, and already I've grown calluses on my heart.* I forked the grub in with gusto, thinking only how glad I was to be alive.

We finished breakfast and divided what coffee was left in the pot. Pronto drank his and went to see to the horses. George lit up a stogie and offered me one.

"Much obliged, Cap'n," I said, "but I don't use tobacco. Never did."

George exhaled blue smoke. "You didn't four years ago," he said. "I thought maybe you'd took it up since then. People change."

He sipped his coffee. Above the rim of the cup, his yellow eyes were intense. "Take you, for example," he said. "I heard you became a lawman—deputy marshal under Chance Ridgeway. Is that a fact?"

I forced myself to meet his gaze. "That's a fact, Cap'n," I said, "but like you say, people change. I'm runnin' from the law these days."

"Why is that?"

"Stole a horse from Thane McAllister out of Dry Creek. Glenn Murdoch was fixin' to lock me up. I got hold of a gun. We struggled, and I shot him."

George nodded. "And then you broke Rufus out of jail and the two of you lit out. Was that the way of it?"

My mouth was dry. George was testing me, asking questions he already knew the answers to. "Yes," I said. "That's how it was."

"How did killin' Glenn make you feel?"

"Bad. I never meant to shoot him."

"Why did you break Rufus out?"

"To tell the truth, Cap'n—I figured he might lead me to you."

"So you could maybe bring me in? Chance Ridgeway would like that."

"You're forgettin' about Glenn. There's no goin' back from a killing."

George was silent for what seemed like minutes. Sweat crawled down from beneath my hat brim. I felt like a mouse being studied by a snake.

This time it was George who looked away. He seemed to accept my answers. "No, there ain't," he said, "especially from the killin' of a lawman. All right, why did you want to find me?"

"I wanted to ride with you again, Cap'n."

Again, George fell silent, like he was weighing my words. At last he said, "I reckon you ain't the first man to walk on both sides of the law."

"Can I ask you a question?" I said.

"Go ahead."

"You already knew I killed Glenn and broke Rufus out. How?"

"I had a man in Dry Creek that day. He was fixin' to

break Rufus out himself, but you beat him to it. When he heard about you killin' Murdoch, he came to tell me.

George looked off toward the hollow. The horses Rufus and me brought over from the Yellowstone had scattered somewhat, but they seemed content to graze in the sunshine and hadn't drifted far.

"I've been expectin' those ponies. Pronto and me rode out this mornin' to see what was keepin' them."

"There's forty-nine head in the bunch," I said. There was fifty, but I cut out the buckskin to ride. All their brands have been reworked."

"What about the big roan?"

"Used to be Glenn's horse. Rufus was ridin' him."

"Which one do you want—the buckskin or the roan?"

"I'll take the roan. We can throw the buckskin in with the others."

Pronto came leading the bounty hunter's horse and pack mule. "What about these two?" he asked.

"Bring 'em along," George said.

Pronto's cold eyes glinted. "I put Graves's rifle in his hands," he said, "and Rufus's short gun in his. Whoever finds them two will think they shot it out and died together."

George chuckled. "It'll be coyotes and magpies that find them," he said, "They won't think a damned thing. They'll just be grateful for the meat."

We rode down the slope together, moving slow so as not to spook the grazing horses. Pronto pushed

Graves's saddle horse and pack mule ahead of him, riding a little apart from George and me. Some of the ponies raised their heads, watching our approach. As we drew near they moved out together and became a herd again.

"Take the point," George told Pronto. "When we hit Clark's Fork, we'll let 'em drink." Pronto nodded and moved ahead at a trot. George and me fell in behind.

I was nervous; Lord knows I had reason to be. Over the past few days, four men had been killed, two of 'em right in front of me, and I was riding with a bandit chief who thought no more of murdering men than he did of swatting flies. Now I was on my way to his hideout where I would doubtless meet other cold-blooded killers. An empty, lonesome feeling grew in the pit of my stomach. I was a long way from home and a long way from help.

George seemed to accept my story—at least he hadn't killed me on first sight—but that didn't mean he wouldn't do it later on. George Starkweather could sniff out treachery and danger the way an old loafer wolf could smell a trap. Else he couldn't have survived so long. Anyway, I knew he could take my life at any moment, and that surely did cast a cloud over my sunny disposition.

For a time, I tried to engage George in talk. I told him how Stub Hartley had killed Luke Fedders back at the cabin and how he'd stolen my Mouse horse. I told of following Stub into Columbus, and how Stub had got himself gunned down by Constable Horace Comfort, and how Horace believed Stub was me. George made no answer to my palaver; he was distant and seemed preoccupied. My pa used to say a man should never miss a good chance to shut up. I did just that.

When we reached the Clark's Fork we let the horses drink before driving them on into the Pryor Mountains. The day continued sunny and clear, but a cold wind out of the north offered a chilly reminder of coming winter. As we rode, we saw grazing cattle everywhere, but the grass was sparse and the country dry. Twisted junipers and mountain mahogany lined the trail, but the top of the mountain was crowned with fir.

Late in the afternoon, we turned the horses up a shadowed ravine and out onto bench land. Just ahead lay a wide gate. As we approached it, two men, heavily armed, stepped out of the shadows, swung the gate open, and stood watching as we drove the horses through. Ahead sat a spacious looking log house and out buildings and corrals. George rode up beside me and pointed. "Welcome to Arrowhead," he said. "This is the home ranch."

Those were George's exact words. Why was it then that what I heard was "Come into my parlor, said the spider to the fly?"

CHAPTER 5
Welcome to Arrowhead

We drove the horses past the house and outbuildings to a fenced pasture and turned 'em inside. George reined up, and I stepped down to close the gate. "I'm gettin' too old for these long rides," he said. "That bullet wound in my hip . . ." He sat up straight, arched his back, and rubbed the spot with the heel of his hand.

I put my shoulder to the gate and slipped the wire over the upright. "I remember. Kiowa John, four years ago. Shot you with a Spencer."

George nodded. "That's right. Just before Jigger St. Clare gunned him to doll rags. You remember of Jigger, don't you, Bodacious?"

"Yes, Cap'n. He was quite the Jigger."

"Top hand with a short gun and loyal as a hound. Went down shootin' it out with Chance Ridgeway's posse."

Yes, I thought. *And you know it was me who told Ridgeway where to find you.*

George looked away, toward the mountains, but he wasn't seeing the mountains. "Wild times," he said. "All them boys are gone now . . . except you and me.

He shifted in the saddle and gazed toward the house. "Arrowhead's way more than just a ranch," he said. "We've got a store, a saloon, a blacksmith shop. Even got a little whorehouse back yonder in the trees. If your tastes don't run to debauchery, you can move into the bunkhouse with the boys. Supper's at six up at the cook shack. Chinee cook's a world beater."

The mention of food got my full attention. To keep the talk light, I asked him, "So where'd you find a Chinee cook?"

"Met him in the pen. Name's Wang Lee. He just finished a four-year stretch for tryin' to poison his employer."

I grinned. "I sure hope he's changed his ways."

"Oh, he has," George said. "He hasn't poisoned anybody in weeks. Ain't it wonderful how prison can rehabilitate a man?" George swung down from the saddle, favoring his hip.

About that time, Pronto rode up and took George's stud and his own sorrel to a log barn beyond the bunkhouse. I led Roanie and followed. Once inside, we stripped the saddles off, put the animals in stalls, and fed them each a ration of grain. As we stepped outside, Pronto turned toward the cluster of outbuildings. "Come on up to the bunkhouse," he said. "Meet the boys."

The bunkhouse, built of logs, had a sod roof and a raised veranda, all nestled back in the trees at the far end of the outbuildings. Inside, double-decker bunks occupied each corner, and a rusted Sunshine stove crouched on sturdy legs at the room's center. A bucket and washbasin occupied a stand inside the door beneath a roller towel that had seen better—and cleaner—days.

Three men sat at a rude table by the window, playing pitch. They looked up as Pronto and me came in, but said nothing. Pronto said, "New man, boys—the Boda-cious Kid. He'll be takin' the halfbreed's place. Big Rufus got hisself dry-gulched over Red Lodge way."

One of the card players, a heavyset man with a bull neck and a cast eye, laid his cards down. "Hell you say!" He sat a minute like he was thinking, his good eye staring at the stove while his other looked up into the rafters. Then he picked up his cards again.

Pronto turned to me. "That's Crazy Ike Mullins, Kid. The dark-eyed scarecrow next to him is Tom Black-burn—and the fat man with all the face hair is Chick-asaw Wilson."

I matched each name with a face. With Pronto South-well, Shorty Benson, and the late Rufus Two Hats, these were the men who had helped George rob the Dry Creek bank.

I met their eyes. "Howdy," I said. Nobody stood or offered to shake hands.

The fat man looked me over. "Where's your bedroll, Kid?"

"Don't have one."

The man nodded at a lower bunk against the back wall. "Might as well take Big Rufus's roll. Seems like he's done with it."

Another dead man's bed, I thought. "Obliged," I replied.

The supper bell rang at six and found me ready. Ike, Tom, and Chickasaw quit their card game and headed for the door with Pronto and me following. Outside, the sky clung to the light, resisting the coming darkness. Across the way, lamplight glowed in the windows of the cook shack while a cold wind sighed down the western slopes and hastened our steps. We crossed the threshold and went inside.

The cook shack was an open room with a stove and cabinets at one end and a long table and benches at the other. At the stove, the "Chinee cook" held sway, watching us with neither word nor expression. The table was set with cups, plates, eating tools, and big blue speckleware bowls and platters of grub. Three hard-looking hombres already at the table looked up as we walked in, then went back to talking among themselves. We took our places and set to filling our plates.

The two who came in behind us, I recognized as the men who'd opened the gate for George and me. As they sat down at the table, they didn't take their guns off . . . and neither did I.

Wang Lee came around the table and filled our cups from a four-quart coffee boiler. A short man, stocky and solid, his skin reminded me of yellowed parchment. His hair, gray at the temples, was in a long braid that fell down his back like an oiled rope. As he filled my cup, he looked me over just a bit longer than he did the others—but that may have been my imagination.

Supper was boiled potatoes, roast beef and gravy, and green beans. I figured the meat had likely come from rustled beef, but that didn't keep me from going back for seconds.

Nobody did much talking, except to say "pass the beef" or "send them spuds up here." Wang Lee kept the serving dishes filled and made sure nobody's cup ran dry.

As each man finished, he stacked his dishes on the counter and went outside. I followed Pronto out, feeling better for the grub but dog-tired from the day's adventures. Above the canyon rim, the sky still held some color, but night was settling in and stars were breaking through the darkness like pinholes in a wagon sheet. Some of the boys drifted off toward the log saloon, and one or two headed off toward the little bawdy house back in the trees.

Back at the bunkhouse, Ike, Tom, and Chickasaw took up their card game again. Pronto Southwell sat down on his bunk to clean and oil his guns. The tender way he handled his weapons put me in mind of a mama cat grooming her kittens. I pulled off my boots, crawled into Rufus's bedroll, and fell asleep before my head hit the blankets.

I spent the week that followed catching up on my sleep and getting acquainted with my new surroundings. The weather turned bitter cold with chill mountain mornings and a stiff wind out of the north that promised winter. At the store, I bought a heavy wool shirt, two pairs of wool socks, a pair of knee-high Dutch socks, two pairs of chopper's mitts with liners, two suits of underwear, and a Scotch cap.

My buying spree pretty well wiped out my ready cash, but I had something to show for it; I had been cold a time or two in my life, and I was not fixing to be so again if I could help it. The boys who spent their money at the saloon and among the whores mostly wound up with empty pockets and memories. Not that there's anything wrong with memories, understand—but they won't keep a man warm at forty below.

Some of the boys began to bellyache about their poverty, said George hadn't split the money from the Dry Creek raid yet and owed them for horses and cattle they'd stolen, said the storekeeper overcharged, and the card games were crooked. They muttered and whined and grumbled, all in low voices around the bunkhouse and corrals. I couldn't help but smile; for some reason, I never heard 'em complain where George could hear.

I spent some time down at the horse barn taking care of Roanie, combing the burrs out of his mane, trimming his tail back even with his hocks. Working with the big gelding, I noticed a sign of a cold, hard winter coming—the horses had haired out early and were already wearing heavy winter coats. There were other signs too: wild game and birds had left the plains and headed south and west, and the Arctic owls had been seen heading south to warmer country. Even the range cattle, some said, were wearing thicker coats of hair.

I learned that George always posted full-time guards above the roads that led in and out of Arrowhead Canyon. Three days after I got there, it was my turn to stand guard. So late on a cold Sunday afternoon, I was huddled beneath a wind-twisted pine, watching the trail that led up from Wyoming.

Roanie was tied short and high to a green branch out of the wind behind me. He was rested and fit, and so was I. Sitting there, I considered my options. Till now, I'd had no chance to break away, but at last, I was alone. I could ride back to Red Lodge or north to the Yellowstone and get word to Ridgeway that I'd found George Starkweather. I could do my job.

I'd have to circle back in the timber below the canyon's rim and keep out of sight of the other sentry. Once past him, I'd have a clear track all the way north. With any kind of head start, no rider in the camp could catch me. Yes, I thought, that's what I'll do. But right then, I heard George's voice behind me, and I knew my chance was lost.

"Evenin', Bodacious. How's guard duty goin'?"

I turned, startled. George and Pronto Southwell stood in the lee of a big pine tree, watching me. I'd been so lost in my thoughts I hadn't seen or heard them. Down the slope, in a patch of cedar, I saw where they'd left their horses. "Fine, Cap'n," I said. "Nothin' movin' on the road tonight."

George smiled his big go-to-hell grin. "Didn't mean to spook you," he said, "comin' up on your blind side like we done."

"Oh, I saw you fellers," I lied. "What's up?"

George pointed to the road below. In the fading light of evening, a fat man in a buckboard was driving a struggling team up the slope. "I've been expectin' that feller," he said. "Just let him pass. I'll wait for him back at the house."

I stood watching George and Pronto pick their way downhill in the twilight. *George must think I'm the poorest sentry there ever was; I didn't see him come up, and I didn't spot the buckboard.*

Then a second thought answered that one. *What do you care what George Starkweather thinks?*

That was even harder to answer.

Chickasaw Wilson came to relieve me just after supper. He was still picking his teeth and patting his belly when he rode out onto the canyon's rim. "Wang Lee outdone hisself this evenin'," he said. "He served a cider pie that was sweet as a baby's breath!"

"I suppose there won't be any left when I get down there," I observed.

"Hell there won't!" said Chickasaw. "When I reached out for seconds, the old Chink threatened to take my hand off with a cleaver. 'You takee *one* piece,' he said. 'Save piece pie for men on guard.' So I backed down. Only a crazy man argues with a mule or a cook."

I grinned and untied Roanie from his branch. "I knew there was somethin' about Wang Lee I liked," I said.

Huge and swollen above the canyon's rim, an orange moon rose into the night sky. Somewhere in the distance a coyote choir sang a lament that made me shiver in spite of my sheepskin coat. I rode down through slide rock and cedar to the ranch, passed through the gate, and started past the house.

The buckboard was parked nearby. I was curious about George's visitor. I had only seen the man briefly in the waning light, but he'd seemed somehow familiar. I recalled his girth—he was fat as a boar hog, well-nigh overflowing the buckboard's seat— and he was dressed in a dark suit, overcoat, and bowler hat. I'd thought it was strange how he'd urged the team up the road without glancing left or right. Who was he?

I was still thinking about that when Pronto stepped out onto the porch and motioned me to stop.

"Hold up," he said. "George wants to talk to you."

"Durn!" I said, "I was on my way to meet with a piece of cider pie."

You had to look quick if you hoped to see Pronto's smile. It flashed, briefly, and then his face returned to stone. "You want me to tell George you're too busy?"

I reined up and stepped down. "Oh," I said. "I guess not."

"The pie will keep," Pronto said. "George won't."

I dismounted and loose-tied Roanie to the hitch rail. Then I stepped up on the porch, moved past Pronto, and knocked on the door.

Through the window, I saw George cross the room carrying a lighted lamp. The door swung open. George smiled. "Evenin,' Bodacious," he said. "Come on in.

I took my hat off and stepped inside. George closed and barred the door. "Let's go into the keepin' room," he said, "and set by the fire. There's somebody here you ain't seen in a while."

George led the way, the lamp casting moving shadows as we passed. We entered a spacious room that contained a massive stone fireplace. Behind the andirons, four-foot logs blazed. Leather covered easy chairs faced the fire. In one of them sat the fat man I'd seen in the buckboard, his face serious with a kind of overstuffed dignity. George took me by the arm and spoke to him. "Say howdy to Merlin Fanshaw, the Bodacious Kid," George said.

Turning to me, George said, "You remember Slippery Mayfair, don't you? Ran that rustler's roost over at Rampage back in eighty-two?"

"I remember," I said. I offered the fat man my hand, and we shook. "You were in the stolen cattle business back then. How are you, Mr. Mayfair?"

"I still am, Bodacious," he said. "And business is good, as am I. Good of you to ask."

He glanced at George. "You could take a lesson from this young man," he said. "He has impeccable manners. After four years he still remembers how much I dislike the appellation 'Slippery.'"

George placed the lamp on a table beside the chairs. "Set down, Kid," he said. "We've got some catchin' up to do."

I settled into one of the easy chairs. George picked up a whiskey bottle from beside the lamp and pointed to three glasses. "Figured we might have us a taste of this sheepherder's delight while we talk," he said. "It came all the way from Tennessee just to smooth out life's rough spots."

I seldom drink whiskey. Didn't care for it. I had watched whiskey take over my pa's life until it wasn't my pa who took strength from the bottle, but the bottle that took strength from him. Still, it was an insult to turn down a man's offer of a drink, and I couldn't very well say no to George. "Sounds good," I said.

George filled the glasses and raised his. "Here's how," he said.

"How," I replied, and we drank. It wasn't rotgut, but it burned like it was, all the way down.

"Now that you're ridin' for this outfit, there's a few things you need to know," George began. "First off, I don't go by the name Starkweather no more. My name hereabouts is Shannon, George Shannon. Folks in these parts know me as a legitimate cowman and a good neighbor. I own this spread free and clear, and I run maybe five hundred steers on my range, spring through fall.

"It's a small outfit compared to some, but that's the way I like it. No point in callin' attention to myself."

George took a sip from his glass and studied me with his cold, yellow eyes. "Slippery has a spread of his own outside Wolf City, Wyoming. Owns most of the town, including the bank. He still fences stolen stock for me. Riders pick up cattle and horses in small bunches all over Montana and drive them here with stops along the way. Sometimes, like those horses you and Rufus brought, the brands are changed at one of the stopovers, but not always."

Slippery Mayfair cleared his throat. "Once the live-stock arrives," he said, "George gets word to me. I send riders up here; they take delivery and move the stock down across the border."

George nodded. "That's right," he said. "Slippery peddles the critters to small operators and home-steaders down in Wyoming. Them raggedy-ass dirt farmers are so glad to get a cheap horse or a steer they don't ask many questions."

I took another sip of whiskey. I was wondering when he set all this up, being out of prison no longer than he had. George read my mind.

"Slippery put most of it together for me after I went up in eighty-two. Far as my neighbors know, 'George Shannon' is just one more absentee owner. This damned country's full of 'em—cattle kings and bovine queens livin' back east, over in Europe, and whatnot."

George stood up, walked over to the mantelpiece, took down a book, and then came back to his chair. "You kept up on your readin', Bodacious?" he asked.

I smiled. "Yes, sir, I have. Been readin' Mr. Twain's *Tom Sawyer* lately."

George nodded. "Yes," he said. "I admire Twain's writin'."

He leaned near the lamp and opened the book. "This author don't write as well as Twain, but he's had a powerful influence on the cattle business."

The book's cover was green with black accents, and there was a shorthorn steer head in gilt above the title:

Beef Bonanza; or, How to Get Rich on the Plains.

"Written by a feller name of Brisbin," George said. "For years people believed the West to be parched, no-account country, mostly desert. Brisbin had a different idea. Listen to what he says. 'These arid plains, so long considered worthless, are the natural meat producin' lands of the nation.' A whole lot of folks believed him. Too many, as it turns out.

"Now the range is overstocked and overgrazed. We've had prairie fires and drought. Water holes and streams've gone dry. Bad news for the beef barons. I figure a reckonin' is on its way."

George closed his eyes and the book. Firelight and shadows played upon his face. He opened his eyes again and stared into the darkness beyond the lamp-light and said, "If this country gets one really hard winter . . ."

Then, looking at me. "Anyway, all them cattle on the range gave me the chance to make a new start—to become a whole different person."

You're not all that different if you're still stealing cows and robbing banks, I thought.

"All right," I said, "But what's all that have to do with me?"

"I need a good man, someone I can depend on," he said. "I've got outlaws ridin' for me, and cowpunchers. The outlaws rustle cattle, steal horses, and help me hold up a bank now and then, but most of 'em ain't all that bright. They're in the life for the money. Except for Pronto maybe, loyalty does not abide in them.

85

"Cowpunchers, on the other hand, are mostly honest. Some of 'em are even halfway loyal. But they're drifters, hired hands for a season. When the work's done, they ride on to other ranges.

"You know me, Kid. All my life I've been a rake and a rounder. I've robbed and I've killed. I've cheated at cards, and I've betrayed my friends. I've drunk whiskey, smoked opium in the pipe, and I've run with the whores. Now I'm lookin' to make a change—I figure it's time to quit ridin' the owl hoot trail."

I was so surprised, I nearly fell off my chair. George Starkweather giving up the outlaw life? I could hardly believe my ears.

"Peace officers are thicker than prairie dogs these days. There's town law, county law, Indian police, federal law, bounty hunters, range detectives, even the damned Pinkertons—all of 'em bound and determined to catch themselves an outlaw.

"They use the railroads and the telegraph to get ahead of a man, and they flood the country with spies, informers, and wanted notices. Now, in some of the bigger towns, they're even usin' *telephones,* by god! The bastards sure have took the fun out of lawbreakin'."

George sipped his whiskey, but it didn't pacify him much. He turned back to me. "This brings me to the reason I wanted to see you. Now that I'm 'respectable,' I need someone to help me run this outfit. Maybe you. Job pays two hundred a month and board. What do you say?"

If I had been surprised before, I was downright astonished then. I took a minute to recover and get my wits back in line. "Why . . . I appreciate the offer, Cap'n, but I'm just a wrangler and a sometime cowhand. I don't know if I could be anybody's cow boss."

"Nothin' to it," George said. "Just be slightly smarter than the cows, and work your ass off."

It was time for frank talk, at least as frank as I was prepared to go. "Are you forgettin' I helped get you sent to prison back in eighty-two? I'm surprised you'd even let me on the place."

George shrugged. "I never blamed you for that," he said. "You were workin' for Ridgeway, and you done your job."

"I call that mighty generous, considerin'."

"You did what you figured you had to. If you hadn't told Ridgeway where to find me, I'd likely have got myself to the pen another way. I'd been there before. The outlaw life is a high stakes game, son. I've shot the moon and bucked the tiger since I was younger than you.

"One thing I know. The only way to beat the house is to quit while you're ahead. I figure to do that before a bullet or a rope does it for me."

George smiled his broad smile then, and his yellow eyes took on a sly look. "Leastways I figure to," he said, "after you help me rob just one more bank."

CHAPTER 6
A Visit to Blue Rock

In the fireplace, a smoldering log burned through and broke in half. The broken piece fell from the andirons with a thump, loud in the stillness. George stood, took a poker from its stand and pushed the piece back onto the coals. Behind the screen, bright flame blossomed. George replaced the poker, turned, and sat down facing me. "Well?" he asked.

"You want me to help you rob a bank?"

"That's right. What do you say?"

"Well, Cap'n, you know me. I'm game for anything. I'm just a little surprised, is all. If you're planning to go straight—"

George leaned over and refilled my whiskey glass. "Even a law-abidin' rancher like me needs a little operatin' capital."

Slippery Mayfair held out his glass, and George filled it with the good Tennessee. "Actually," the fat man said. "George intends to rob the same bank *twice*.

"About twenty miles south of here is a small town called Blue Rock," Mayfair continued. "It's not much of a town, but it's the supply center for two major Wyoming ranches. Four days from now, J. T. Hightower, the owner of one of those ranches, is making a major purchase of livestock from the owner of the other—fifty thousand dollars worth, in cash. That money is already in the bank's vault."

"That's right," George said. "The fruit is ripe for the pickin'. Trouble is, Hightower's hired a small army of gunmen to see that nobody steals the cash."

"Which is why," Slippery said, "George means to rob the bank twice."

I raised my eyebrows in question.

"Hightower's equipped his gun hands with the best horses money can buy," George said. "Anyone who tries to rob the bank will have to deal with a well-armed and well-mounted posse.

"I figure two can play at that game, so I aim to send in two riders, each mounted on a fast horse. They'll go into the bank, fire a couple of shots into the ceiling, and ride out like their shirttails are on fire. The cowman's gunnies will follow, ridin' hell for leather!

"Soon as the posse leaves town, the real robbery takes place. The time to take honey from a hive is after the bees are gone."

"What about the decoys?" I asked. "How are they goin' to outride the posse?"

"They'll have fresh horses waitin' a few miles from town."

"And if the posse catches them anyway?"

George shrugged. "Well, Bodacious," he said, "into each life a little rain must fall."

What could I say? In the end I told him I'd go. Oh, I had my misgivings, of course, but a man didn't say no to George Starkweather in his own house.

He smiled his reckless smile and grasped my hand and told me how glad he was that I'd agreed. He offered me more whiskey (I did manage to say no to that), shook my hand again, and fixed me with his proud, mad eagle stare. He looked at me as if I'd hung the moon.

It was all an act. Still, George had a way of making a man feel special. Call it charm; call it leadership— whatever; George had long since mastered the skill. He could fool you with a card trick, then show you how he'd done it and fool you again. George could sell whiskey to a Mormon elder.

He smiled. "I reckon I've given you enough to think about for one evenin'. Why don't you go on now and get some sleep? We'll talk more later." I got to my feet. "Maybe I'll do that, Cap'n," I said.

Outside under the stars, I breathed in the cold, clean air and tried to clear my head. The full moon was high in the sky and smaller than at moonrise, but its glow lit up the land. A man could have read a newspaper by its light.

The cook shack was silent and dark as I passed. I figured Wang Lee had long since cleaned up the supper dishes and gone to bed. My piece of the cider pie, if it still existed, was likely shut away in the pie safe. Across the way, the bunkhouse, too, was dark. Even the card players had turned in.

I made my way across the moonlit field, opened the bunkhouse door, and went inside. I found my bunk by feel, shucked my boots and britches, and slid between the soogans. The room smelled of leather, tobacco, and old sweat. Someone turned over in his sleep. One of the boys was snoring softly.

I lay there thinking about the men who slept in that room. Wanted men and fugitives and me, an officer of the law, had spread my blankets among them. I wondered what thoughts disturbed their sleep. What fears attended their dreams?

I closed my eyes and looked ahead to a bank and a town I'd never seen. I looked ahead to a place called Blue Rock and a rancher's private army. I knew without a doubt what troubled my rest.

Pronto and me were just leaving the cook shack after breakfast the next morning, when George took us aside. "I'm sendin' you two down to Blue Rock," he said. "I want you to take a good look at that bank and report back."

"Sure, Cap'n. What should we be lookin' for?" I asked.

"Anything and everything. Time the bank opens. Location of the vault. Slippery says the banker'll be in his office and two tellers out front in their cages."

I glanced up toward the house; Slippery's team and buckboard were gone. George caught my glance. "Slippery left early this mornin'," he said. "Figures a storm is blowin' in and wanted to be home before it hits."

George reached inside his coat, took out a hundred dollar bill and handed to me. "Talk with the tellers. Ask them to change this bill for you. Watch for guards inside the building or barricades on the street. Before we take that bank, we're goin' to want all the information we can get."

I felt my spirits lift. This could be my chance! Surely, Blue Rock had a telegraph office. I'd telegraph Ridgeway, and I'd warn the town. Losing Pronto Southwell long enough to do it wouldn't be easy, but I'd find a way.

"I understand, Cap'n," I said. "The middle of a holdup is no time for surprises."

"That's a fact," George said. "There's always somethin' a man didn't figure on. I believe in bein' ready as I can for whatever comes up."

Pronto and me dressed for the weather and saddled our horses. The morning was cold and windy with a hint of snow in the air. I wore my sheepskin coat, mittens, and shotgun chaps, and Pronto was in a heavy wool overcoat, California pants, and batwings. Folks in Blue Rock might see we were strangers, but there'd be nothing about our appearance to stir up their suspicions. We looked for all the world like two drifting cowpunchers, nothing more.

We rode out through the ranch gate and dropped into the narrow canyon that led down into Wyoming. Steep cliffs marked our passage, with pine and scrub cedar clinging to the upper slopes. As we traveled, Pronto and me spoke but seldom; it was hard to hear each other over the wind. Mostly, we gave our attention to covering the distance and to our own thoughts.

George Starkweather was no fool. He knew I had been a lawman, maybe he thought I still was. Sending me to scout out the bank at Blue Rock was his way of testing my loyalty, and he was sending Pronto Southwell to keep an eye on me. If ever I seemed a threat to his plans, George would kill me without so much as a second thought. If I made a suspicious move while we were in Blue Rock, Pronto Southwell himself might do it. Either way, I'd be dead, and being dead was not a condition I aspired to.

It was bitter cold and snowing in earnest by the time we hit town. The road circled the base of a low, timbered hill before dropping down to become Blue Rock's main and only street. As Slippery Mayfair had said, the town wasn't much: two dozen or so weathered buildings facing each other across a wide and rutted street. Horses lined the hitch rail in front of the saloon, heads down and eyes closed. A top buggy and a farm wagon were parked in front of the mercantile. At the end of the street, a cavernous livery barn humped up beneath the blowing snow like an old range bull.

It wasn't hard to find the bank. Built of quarried blue stone, the building stood two stories tall, looking down on its neighbors from the very center of town. We drew rein before the raised boardwalk in front and stepped down. At the doorway, we stomped the snow off our boots and brushed off our clothes before going in. Painted in gilt letters on the front window was, *First Bank of Blue Rock. Hours 10-3.*

"Banker's hours," said Pronto.

It was good just to be in out of the wind. A coal stove radiated heat from its place at the lobby's center. Behind the grillwork, a bank teller sat at a desk, writing in a ledger. A second teller in a green eyeshade looked up from his work and smiled. "Howdy," he said. "Snow still comin' down?"

I gave him back his smile. "It sure don't seem to be goin' up," I said.

The teller laughed. "No," he said, "I guess not. I have seen it go sideways many a time, but never up. What can I do for you fellers?"

"We just rode up from the Big Horn," I said. "Lookin' for a ridin' job. Wouldn't know anybody who's hirin', would you?"

The teller shook his head. "Afraid not," he said. "The big outfits around here are layin' off all but their permanent hands for the winter. You might ask over at the saloon. The barkeep may know of somethin'."

"Obliged," I said. "This town have a hotel?"

"The Shoshone. Two doors down from the saloon, but you might be out of luck there, too. Bunch of special deputies has pretty well filled the place up."

"Special deputies?"

The teller looked down at the floor and frowned. He seemed to realize he'd said too much. "Well, not deputies exactly," he said. "More like posse men. I don't really know what they're doin' in town."

He turned back to straightening out his cash drawer. "If there's nothin' more I can do for you—"

"There is one thing," I said, taking out the hundred George had given me.

"Would you change this bill for me? I owe my pardner twenty dollars."

The teller took the bill and looked it over. "You want that in paper, or gold?"

"Gold," I said.

The teller put the bill in his cash drawer and handed me five double eagles. Pronto had wandered over toward the offices at the far end of the bank, but I could feel his eyes on me. In a room behind the latticework, the heavy steel door of the vault stood open.

"We'd best be movin' on," I said. "Much obliged."

Turning to Pronto, I handed him one of the gold pieces. "Here's that twenty I owe you. Let's go down to the saloon, and I'll buy you a beer."

The teller looked up and smiled. "Good talkin' to you," he said. "Maybe I'll see you fellers again."

I opened the door. "You never can tell," I said.

Outside, we stepped down and untied our horses. The snow had stopped, but the wind was blowing stronger than before. Pronto looked up, squinting at the clouds. "I hope the weather holds off a day or two," he said. "Fresh snow would make trackin' too easy for them 'special deputies.'"

He lowered his eyes, studying me with that cold gaze of his. "What do you think?" he asked.

"We gathered some information. Two tellers at the bank, like Slippery said. The vault was open. Bank's hours are ten to three. Did you see anything of the banker?"

Pronto nodded. "His office door was open, too. Fat man at a desk. He was wearin' a stiff collar and a sour expression. Back door opens onto the alley next to a coal shed."

We walked up the street toward the saloon, leading the horses. The street was frozen mud, its ruts dusted with white. Gusts whipped the snow against the buildings and slashed at our faces. The day had gone dark, though it was only early afternoon. Then, just beyond the coal shed, I saw a small building that bore the sign, "Telegraph Office." Poles and wire faded into the fog. A light shone dull orange in the window.

"Go on ahead down to the saloon," I said. "I want to take a closer look at that shed."

Pronto's eyes narrowed. "I'll go with you," he said. "What are you lookin' for?"

My heart was racing, but I kept my voice calm and easy. "I just want to see the place. Like you said, it's just off the bank's back door."

"And next door to the telegraph office," he said. "You aimin' to send a message somewhere?"

The odds had been too long, only a slim chance I could have wired Ridgeway anyway, and now that was gone. "Hell, no," I said, "but we might want to cut those wires on the day we hold up the bank. Keep those posse men from gettin' help."

Again, Pronto studied my face, respect taking the place of suspicion. "Yeah," he said. "We might. You think of things—like George does."

"Let's look the shed over and go get that beer," I said.

There was nothing remarkable about the coal shed except that its door was locked with a hasp and a pad-lock. Through a gap between the boards I could see maybe a half-ton of coal inside. A sign on the wall next to the door read: "Bank property—KEEP OUT."

I can't say I ever saw a locked coal shed before, but I wasn't all that surprised. Banks, in my experience, like to lock up pretty much everything that belongs to them.

Pronto noticed the padlock, too. "Why in hell would anybody put a lock on a coal shed?" he asked.

I shrugged. "Because they can, I guess."

Pronto scowled. "Tight bastards," he muttered. "They're prob'ly scared some poor widow will steal their damn coal to keep her kids warm. Heartless sons o' bitches deserve what's comin' to them."

I walked around the corner. Maybe six feet from the ground, there was an opening covered by a hinged door, and it was unlocked. "Guess they're not worried about people putting coal in," I said. "They just don't want anybody takin' it out."

Pronto had lost interest in the subject. "Hell with 'em," he said. "You gonna buy me that beer or not?"

It was truly a small town in those days that had only one saloon. Most settlements in the west had at least two or three. We tied our horses with the others at the rail, opened the door, and went inside.

Coming out of the cold into the noise, smells, and heat of the saloon was a shock to the system. Voices of the patrons were a constant babble; men were two deep at the bar; gamblers and drinkers sat at green-topped tables playing poker and faro. The blended smells of beer, whiskey, and unwashed men made a potent mix. Cigar smoke eddied in layers above the din.

A coal stove, nearly seven feet tall, stood at the room's center, radiating dry heat like a furnace. I elbowed my way through the crowd at the bar until the saloonist in charge paid me heed. I bought two beers and bulled my way back to where Pronto waited just inside the door.

We stood there drinking our beers and watching the room. I suppose neither Pronto nor me were in the mood for talking even if we could have made ourselves heard. We drank, we watched the patrons, and we warmed up. Then we went back outside, mounted our horses, and set out for Arrowhead.

What we had seen in the saloon struck me as curious. Blue Rock was a small town in the middle of nowhere, but its saloon had been crowded. Some of its customers were cowhands from the big ranches George had told us about, but surely not all. Among them were a number of well-armed gents who could only be J. T. Hightower's special deputies and posse men. A cold chill passed along my backbone, but it had nothing to do with the weather.

The trip back to Arrowhead seemed even colder than our ride down to Blue Rock had been. The storm had passed, but gray clouds hung low and ragged above the canyon walls, and fresh snow lay in drifts along the way. A bitter wind gusted out of the north, moaning through the trees and taking my breath away.

From time to time, I checked our back trail, but I saw no one. In all that windswept canyon, nothing seemed to move but the grass beside the trail and the swaying pines on the slopes above.

A mile from the ranch, I spotted Crazy Ike Mullins serving his stint at guard duty. He sat huddled in a buffalo coat beneath an outcropping above the trail. Recognizing us, he stood and waved his rifle overhead before hunkering down again out of the wind. I smiled. Ike was a Texan, and like other riders I'd known from the Lone Star State, he disliked cold weather above all things. I heard him opine one night at the bunkhouse that dying and going to hell might not be so bad. "At least," he said, "a man would be warm."

When we rode in, George was waiting for us outside the cook shack. He stood in the lee of the building, watching as we drew near. "Good to see you boys," he said. "Any trouble?"

"No trouble, Cap'n," I said.

"Put up your horses and come inside. There's fresh coffee, and there's stew on the stove."

"Sounds good," I said. "We'll be along d'rectly."

We dismounted at the barn and led the horses inside. I was so stiff from the ride I could hardly walk, and my fingers felt cold and awkward. We stripped off the saddles and wiped the horses down in their stalls and gave them each a forkful of hay and a ration of oats. Then we closed the barn door and made our way across the lot to the cook shack.

George was waiting for us inside. The other boys had long since eaten and gone, so except for George and the cook, we had the place to ourselves. We sat down across from George while Wang Lee poured us each a cup of coffee and set out the stew and biscuits. While we ate, we told George what we'd seen and heard in Blue Rock. We described the low hill outside of town. We told him about the bank, the open vault, and the two tellers. We related what the teller had said about the "special deputies" who were gathered in town. We even described the coal shed behind the bank.

George puffed on his cigar. Finally, he nodded and stood up. "You boys did good," he said. "Slippery says the money transfer will take place three days from now. What them cowmen and special deputies don't know is that we'll be transferrin' the money to *us*.

"Tomorrow mornin' after breakfast, I'll tell the boys what we're fixin' to do and how we're goin' to do it. See you then." Then he opened the door and walked outside.

Neither Pronto nor me said anything to the others, but somehow they seemed to know something was in the wind. They knew we had ridden down through the canyon that morning. Crazy Ike had seen us return. Pronto spent that evening cleaning and oiling his guns. And George himself told the boys to be at the cook shack the next morning.

A man could see the difference in their attitudes. Following Pronto's lead, Tom, Ike, and Chickasaw cleaned and loaded their weapons. They laid out their warm clothes and riding gear and joked with each other. They even abandoned their nonstop card game.

The two well-armed riders I'd seen when first I came to Arrowhead showed up at the bunkhouse that evening. Neither of them said anything to the rest of us, but merely nodded in greeting as they entered. They spread their bedrolls in the empty bunks and lay there in the half light of early evening, obviously thinking their own thoughts.

As for me, I was awake late into the night. I'd set out to find George and his men, my assignment being to convince him I was a renegade lawman, and here I was about to become a member of his gang. Not only had George accepted me, now he expected me to help lead a raid on the Blue Rock bank! I hadn't succeeded too well.

I remembered the tellers. Suppose the robbery went bad? What if somebody in the bank or an innocent bystander on the street got killed? How could I live with that? And what if I had to use my gun to defend myself? Could I? Or would the ghost of Ed Hutchins come back and stop my hand? George was testing me. I'd told him I wanted to ride with him, and now I would have to prove my words.

I had never been much of a praying man. Mostly, I turned to the Almighty only when I was in deep trouble and couldn't find my way out. This occasion sure seemed to qualify. I closed my eyes and asked for help, not only for me but for the people of Blue Rock. I don't know if the Lord heard my prayer or not, but somehow I felt easier in my mind. The next thing I knew, it was morning.

The ranch triangle jangled at five. By twenty after, all seven of us had washed up and were dressed for the day. We stepped out into a cold and cloudy morning with a fresh wind blowing out of the north. I was pleased to see that no new snow had fallen during the night; as Pronto had pointed out, fresh snow would have made it easier for the special deputies to track us. We crossed the frozen ground and went into the cook shack where Wang Lee was serving up platters of hotcakes and bacon, and we fell to eating.

The boys were quieter than usual; none of the joshing and rough humor that usually marked the morning meal. The men ate quickly, their eyes alert as they passed the platters and the coffeepot without being asked. They finished their breakfasts. They waited.

Promptly at six we heard the stamping of feet outside. The door swung open, and George walked in. He glanced about, surveying his men with that intense stare of his, then went to the head of the table and smiled at us all. Wang Lee brought George a cup of coffee and placed it in his hand. George looked fit, eager, and confident.

"Mornin', boys," he said. "It's cold as charity out

there, with a wind that could blow the nuts off a bull. Fact is, it's downright miserable. But it's a fine day to rob a bank."

Tension lifted like fog from a sunlit lake. One or two of the boys chuckled. Some smiled. All eyes looked to George. Once again, I had to admire his skill as a leader. Every man at that table looked to him, waiting for his direction.

"We're hittin' the bank at Blue Rock today," he said. "There's cash on hand, and it's ours for the takin'." He caught my eye and held it for just a moment. "I've got reason to believe there may be as much as twenty thousand dollars there—say, four thousand for each of you boys."

Twenty thousand? I'd heard Slippery Mayfair say there was *fifty* thousand! George looked at me again. His glance seemed to say, "A leader doesn't always tell his men everything he knows."

The men were with him now, each mentally counting his share of the loot. George took a sip of his coffee and said, "Bodacious and Pronto rode down to Blue Rock yesterday to case the bank. They say there's a couple of tellers and the boss banker inside. No guard.

"Now there ain't much real law in Blue Rock as a rule, but that twenty thousand belongs to a rich cowman name of Hightower, and he didn't get rich by being careless. He's hired a passel of gun hands and outfitted them with good horses. If anybody should try to rob the bank, he intends for his boys to pounce on

103

'em like a barn cat on a chickadee. That's why we're doin' this job a little different.

"Just this side of town, there's a low hill topped by scrub pine. Bodacious, Pronto, Ike, Tom, and Chickasaw will ride up there and wait."

George looked at the two men who had joined us the night before. He nodded. "Haynes and Morris there are horsemen," George said. "They'll be ridin' hot-blooded horses bred for speed. They'll go into the bank, fire a couple of shots, and ride out of town fast. Hightower's boys will be hot on their trail, but there's no way they can catch 'em. There'll be fresh horses waitin' three miles out of Blue Rock, and another change of mounts three miles beyond that.

"As soon as the posse leaves town, the rest of you boys will hit the bank. I won't be goin' with you on this one. Bodacious and Pronto will be in charge. Follow them like you would me."

George opened a cabinet drawer and removed four seamless feed sacks, each one secured by a drawstring. He gave two of the sacks to Pronto and two to me. Then he said, "Get the money, put it in these bags, and leave town fast. Split up and ride out in different directions. Make sure you ain't followed. Circle around, and come back here to Arrowhead."

He looked at each man in turn, meeting his eyes. Then he said, "Luck to you boys," and walked out of the cook shack.

The dice were cast, as they say. Every gambler knows those ivory cubes can fall a thousand different ways, and I knew no man could predict the events that day would hold. Except George, maybe. They were his dice, after all.

CHAPTER 7

A Banking Transaction

Pronto stood beside me watching the men file out of the cook shack. One by one, they stepped down off the porch and headed for the bunkhouse. As we turned to follow them, I was surprised to find George waiting. He stood, dressed for the trail, his blood-bay thoroughbred saddled and ready.

"Hold old up, boys," he said. "I've got more to say, for your ears only."

I stopped and waited. Pronto leaned against the wall of the building, a frown on his face. "Two things," George said. "First, I want you to keep the boys here for an hour or so. I need time to ride down to Blue Rock ahead of you.

"By the time you hit town, I'll be over at the hotel, havin' dinner with J. T. Hightower himself. Told the man I wanted to talk about buyin' some steers from him. Figured that'd give me a fine alibi—I couldn't very well be eatin' dinner with him and robbin' the bank at the same time.

"Second, I want only you two to handle the money. Take the bags around to that coal shed behind the bank and toss them in through that narrow door you saw. Then get out of town, fast."

"But, if we leave the money in the coal shed—"

"—them posse men can't catch you with it and take it back. They'll never think to look for the money in a locked coal shed. Happens I've got a key to that padlock. On my way home, I'll stop by and pick up the bags."

"I notice you told the boys there was twenty thousand in that bank. Slippery said there'd be fifty."

George grinned. "Caught that, did you? Yeah, that's a fact. I'll split the twenty with the boys, but the other thirty is mine. You have a problem with that?"

"No, Cap'n. You're the boss. I was just wonderin'."

George turned the thoroughbred out away from the cook shack and faced it into the wind. "Remember," he said, "give me an hour before you start out. I'll see you back here." Then he swung into the saddle, turned his horse away, and rode out at a trot.

An hour and thirteen minutes later, Pronto and me led the rest of George's men out on the road to Blue Rock. The thoroughbreds that Haynes and Morris rode danced and fought their bits, eager to be moving out, but I told their riders to hold the horses back. We'd need their strength—and their speed—when we hit town.

Snow began to fall as we entered the canyon, growing heavier and thicker with each mile. Pronto, riding beside me, squinted at the sky and spat. "There's that snow I hoped we wouldn't get," he muttered. "The damn posse won't have any trouble trackin' us now."

"That's true only if it stops snowin' before the holdup," I said. "If it keeps comin' down, it'll cover our tracks."

I turned in my saddle and looked at the men behind us. Most were dressed for the weather in heavy coats and sheepskins. Crazy Ike wore his buffalo coat, its collar turned up about his face. Chickasaw Wilson was dressed in a blanket capote with a hood like the old-time mountain men and Indians wore. Toni Blackburn was the only man in our party who seemed ill-dressed. The oldest of the men, he huddled wet and shivering inside a shabby frock coat of black wool. His hands were covered with thin cowhide gloves, no protection at all from the cold. I noticed he kept changing the hand that held the reins, warming his free hand by placing it beneath the saddle skirts, next to the warm body of his horse.

I dropped back and drew up alongside him. "Those all the clothes you've got?" I asked. "You're not goin' to make it, dressed like that."

The old man's face was drawn and pale. Beneath a battered hat, a woolen scarf covered his ears. Bright spots of red marked his cheekbones and nose. His lips trembled as he spoke. "I f-figured on gettin' warm clothes before winter set in," he said. "I spent my money on them damn whores, and I've b-been too b-broke."

"I've got an extra pair of mittens I can lend you," I said, "but I've got my doubts you can make it. You know I can't let you slow us up."

He bared a mouth full of rotten teeth in what was meant to be a smile. "Let me come, Kid," he said. "I-I'll keep up. I n-need the money."

I did what I had to do. "No," I said. "You can't pull your weight. I'm sendin' you back, Tom."

He lowered his eyes, accepting my decision. The old outlaw looked like a whipped dog. I felt sorry for him, but I couldn't let one man put us all in danger. I watched him rein his horse around and turn back toward the ranch. He faded away into the storm until he disappeared from view.

I rode back to the head of our column and pulled in beside Pronto. Passing the men, I felt their eyes on me. There was something very like respect in their expressions. Pronto was not impressed. "You're soft, Kid," he said. "George would have shot the old fool and left him beside the trail."

I sounded tougher than I felt. "I've got better things to do than shoot burned-out old outlaws," I said.

The snow was still falling when we reached Blue Rock. We circled the base of the low hill and drew rein. I took Haynes and Morris aside. "The bank is the two-story stone buildin' in the center of town," I said. "You know the plan. One man goes inside, the other stays with the horses.

"Raise a little ruckus, maybe fire a shot or two, and then ride out as fast as those hot-blooded horses'll carry you. Hightower's posse will be hot on your trail."

"Three miles east of town you'll find a pole corral, an abandoned cabin, and two fresh horses waitin' for you. Make the switch and ride another three miles. You'll come to a cabin on the creek and a log barn.

Two more fresh horses are in the barn. Take 'em, circle on around, and head back to the ranch."

"Anybody live in the cabin?" Haynes asked.

"Homesteaders. They're expectin' you."

"What happens if that posse catches us?"

"Not much chance of that. You'll be better mounted than the posse men. But if they do, you haven't stolen anything, just made a little noise."

Haynes nodded. He and Morris turned their thoroughbreds toward town, and we watched through the blowing snow as they rode away.

Crazy Ike and Chickasaw waited at the bottom of the hill while Pronto and me led our horses up to its crest. Once there, we lay beneath the spreading branches of a pine while I surveyed the town through field glasses. The street was deserted. A half dozen horses lined the hitch rail at the saloon, and four more stood tied outside the hotel. One of them was George's blood bay stud. George would be inside talking cattle with J. T. Hightower.

Smoke billowed from the chimneys and stovepipes along the street and faded away in the wind. At the general store, a man shoveled snow off the boardwalk and hurried back inside. I handed the glasses to Pronto.

"Looks clear," he said. "Posse men are likely at the hotel, maybe some at the saloon. I count ten horses."

"More inside the livery barn, I expect. Do you see Haynes and Morris?"

"Yeah," Pronto said. "They're movin' up the street toward the bank."

I took the field glasses back. "All right," I said, backing away from beneath the tree. "Let's get mounted."

Back in the saddle, I leaned forward, watching the bank through the glasses. I saw the men dismount. Morris held the horses while Haynes went inside.

Two gunshots sounded, muffled but surprisingly clear even at this distance. Outside, Morris pulled his pistol and fired three times into the air. The door flew open and Haynes dashed out and vaulted into the saddle. Then the boys sank spur, and the thoroughbreds bolted, running east out of town.

Men poured out of the saloon, staring and pointing in the direction of the bank. I heard shouting, saw the men move toward the horses. Down at the hotel, other men appeared. They untied horses at the hitch rail and swung into their saddles. In minutes a dozen riders were thundering through town in hot pursuit of Haynes and Morris.

Pronto and me came down the hill, our horses stiff-legged and sliding on the snowy slope. We pulled our bandanas up over our faces as we rode. Chickasaw and Ike saw us coming and did the same. "Let's go, boys," I said.

We rode into town at a lope and slid to a stop at the bank's front door. I was out of the saddle and running before Roanie stopped moving. Pronto was right behind me, both guns drawn. "Hold the horses, Chick-asaw!" I shouted. "Ike, watch the door—we're goin' in!"

The door had been closed again after Haynes had fled the bank, but I didn't let that slow me down. My boot caught the door just above the latch and kicked it open. Then we were in the bank's lobby and moving toward the counter. Behind the grillwork the two tellers were on their feet, eyes wide and staring. To our right, near the stove, a man I took to be a merchant threw his hands up and took a step back.

"On your belly!" Pronto said, his pistol leveled at the man's face. The townsman dropped like a rock and spread-eagled on the floor.

The young teller I'd talked to earlier had lost his surprised look. His face took on a determined expression, and I knew what that meant. "Don't try it!" I said, but he bent beneath the counter and came up with a shotgun! I pointed my .44 at him and shouted, "Drop it, kid! Don't try to be a hero!"

He didn't hesitate. He brought the scattergun up, cocking the hammers as he straightened. *I can't shoot the boy,* I thought, *but I can't let him shoot me, either!* I hesitated. "Drop it, kid!" I yelled. "I don't want to kill you!"

Behind me, I heard Pronto say, "Hell, I don't mind." I turned my head in time to see him fire his revolver directly at the teller, and the shot slammed the boy back against the wall. The shotgun clattered to the floor and the boy followed it, falling forward and lying sprawled and still on the dark, oiled wood.

Gunsmoke drifted above the counter, its smell as bitter as my feelings. "Watch the storekeeper!" Pronto yelled. "I'm goin' after the boss banker!" He walked past me in two long strides, moving back toward the vault.

I felt sick. I had hoped we could pull the robbery off without gunplay, but now a young teller had been shot, and the stakes had been raised sky high. I stepped back, watching both the merchant and the second teller. I called out, "On the floor! One dead fool is enough!"

The second teller dropped to the floor, his face raised toward me. He stared as I kicked open the pass-through and stepped behind the counter. The first teller lay face down in a spreading pool of blood, the shotgun mere inches away from his outstretched hand. Covering the second teller with my pistol, I tossed the shotgun out into the lobby.

Pronto and me carried the feed sacks inside our coats. I pulled one of mine out and tossed it to the second teller. "All right," I said, trying to sound as scary as possible, "Put the money from the cash drawers in this sack. Do it now!" The teller scrambled to his feet. Trembling, spilling coins onto the floor, he quickly filled the sack.

When the contents of the cash drawers had been dumped into the bag, I closed the drawstrings and moved out toward the banker's office. Pronto was kneeling inside the open vault like a man at worship, filling his bags with bundles of bank notes. A fat man in a black broadcloth suit lay unconscious beside the heavy vault door, bleeding from a scalp wound.

"Damn banker tried to lock the vault before I could get to it," Pronto said. "I had to pistol-whip him some."

I bent, scooping some of the bundled bills into my bag. "Hurry up," I said. "That shot might bring some local heroes. I doubt they all left town."

"Don't rush me, goddammit!" Pronto snapped. "Why the hell didn't *you* shoot that kid?"

"I was about to. You beat me to it."

"Hell you say. I still think you're soft."

We finished filling the bags and were cinching up the drawstrings when gunfire exploded outside the front door. The shots came in a ragged volley, like fire-crackers popping. I heard bullets strike the stone wall and scream away. A window shattered, sending a shower of glass glittering into the lobby. Then, loud and close at hand, shots answered the volley, and I knew Chickasaw and Ike were in a fight for their lives.

Pronto drew both his revolvers, moving swiftly toward the door. "Seein' as you ain't much inclined to shoot people," he said, "I'll go help the boys while you take the cash out the back way. Think you can handle that?"

There wasn't time to argue, and I didn't. I holstered my .44, grabbed all four bags, and dashed out the back door. Snow was falling heavily as I ran across the alley to the coal shed. My hand found the fastener that secured the high door. I opened it, threw the bags inside, and fastened it again. That done, I ran through the drifted snow around to the front of the bank.

The scene that met my eyes as I turned the corner was a jumble of sound and confusion. Six men advanced on foot toward the bank, firing as they came. Ike and Pronto were mounted and firing back. Chickasaw had been hit—more than once, from the look of things—but he held the reins of his horse and mine in a death grip, struggling to stay on his feet.

As Pronto and Ike broke away, one of the advancing men found an opening between the rearing horses and shot Chickasaw point blank with a shotgun. The shot drove the bearded outlaw back against the stone wall of the building and left him dying on the boardwalk. Released from Chickasaw's hold, the horses dashed away. I had nearly reached Roanie, but saw my chance for escape vanish as the big roan and Chickasaw's horse raced on up the street.

I pulled my .44 and turned to face our attackers, but lost my footing and fell in the deep snow beside the bank. It was well that I did, because at that moment the man who shot Chickasaw fired the other barrel of his shotgun at me. The scattergun belched flame and hurled lead pellets into the space I had only just vacated.

Somehow I dropped my six-gun into the snow. Desperately, I scrabbled for it and found it. My fingers had just closed over its grips when the man with the shotgun pinned my wrist to the ground with his boot. "No, you don't, by god!" he said. The pain shot up my arm as the man put his weight down. I looked up just in time to see him lift his other foot and lash out with a hard kick. Pain exploded like a bomb inside my head. I felt the shock, saw the world shatter into splinters of light, and fell away into darkness.

I awoke to the sound of a man groaning, and then realized it was me. My head throbbed with a grievous ache. The salty taste of blood was in my mouth and my teeth felt loose. My tongue felt swollen, too big for my mouth. I lay still, my eyes closed, and surrendered to the pain. Where was I? I seemed to be lying on a cold, hard surface of some kind, but where?

Piece by piece, memory returned. I recalled the robbery and Pronto shooting the teller. I remembered my dash out the back door and throwing the moneybags into the shed. I remembered the noise and confusion of the gun battle in the street, and seeing Pronto and Ike ride out through a hail of bullets. I recalled the men advancing through the smoke and falling snow like ghosts and the way Chickasaw's horse and Roanie had raced away in their fright.

I heard again in my mind the shotgun blast that ended Chickasaw's life and the second blast meant for me. I remembered losing my revolver and finding it again. And the big man and the pain and that was all.

I turned my head and opened my eyes. I lay on the cold, stone floor of a jail cell, a cage set off from the rest of the room by iron bars. Beyond the bars, a big man poured coal into a box stove. A smoky oil lamp hung on a wire nearby, its glow casting dark shadows across the room. I guess I must have groaned again, because the big man put the coal scuttle down and turned to look at me.

"I was hopin' you wouldn't wake up," he said. "Damned if you ain't a disappointment all around."

As he walked toward the cell, I recognized him as the man who had killed Chickasaw and fired at me, the one who had knocked me cold with a kick. "Now I'm gonna have to feed you and keep you alive till your hangin'."

When I sat up, pain exploded inside my head. I was afraid I'd have to air my paunch right there in the cell. "Hangin'?" I mumbled. My tongue still felt too big for my mouth.

"That's what we do with killers in Wyoming. We're peculiar thataway."

There was a painted iron bunk, and I pulled myself up and sat on it. "Never killed anyone," I said.

"You were in the bank," said the big man. "Bank teller's dead. I figure there's a connection. So does the other teller. He saw you do it."

"Not me."

The big man stretched, and the badge inside his coat caught the lamplight. "Law says you have the right to a speedy trial by a jury of your peers. That's what you'll get. Twelve good men and true, all bank depositors and friends of the deceased. Circuit judge will be here in a day or two. We don't have a gallows, but we've got plenty of telegraph poles. When the time comes, I'll let you take your pick."

I closed my eyes against the throbbing in my head and the churning in my belly.

The big man pulled up the sturdy wooden chair opposite the cell door and sat down.

"My name is Shackleford," he said. "Bud Shackleford. I'm town marshal here when I'm not shoein' horses. I'm also the town blacksmith. You want to tell me your name?"

"All right. I'm Merlin—"

"—Fanshaw," Shackleford interrupted. "Also known as the Bodacious Kid. You killed a deputy sheriff up in Dry Creek, Montana. Broke a bank robber out of jail and rode away on a stolen horse.

"I found your name on a receipt in the inside pocket of your sheepskin. Seems you bought a sack of oats from Walt's Livery in Dry Creek a week before you killed Glenn Murdoch. I telegraphed the marshal's office there. Young deputy name of Shavers told me all about you."

Damned secrecy, I thought. *Even Bucky Shavers believes I'm guilty.*

Things were out of hand. I took a deep breath and showed my hole card.

"All right," I said. "I am Merlin Fanshaw, all right. I'm a deputy marshal on special assignment for U.S. Marshal Chance Ridgeway. You can telegraph him at his office in Helena."

Marshal Shackleford chuckled. "Deputy marshal, you say. This gets better and better. You always go around robbin' banks and killin' tellers, Deputy?"

"Another man killed the teller. Telegraph Ridgeway. He'll back my story."

"I'll do that," said Shackleford, "soon as we can repair the line. It went dead just after I wired Dry Creek."

"The line went dead?"

"I suppose the storm took it down."

"When do you reckon it'll be workin' again?"

Shackleford shrugged. "Hard to say. Hopefully, sometime before your hangin'."

He stood up. "Like I said, I'm obliged to feed you until then. You reckon you could eat some stew?"

What the hell. My head still throbbed, my teeth ached, and my nose had started to run. I was dog-tired, half froze, and fresh out of hope. Even so, I told the man yes, you bet I could eat. I didn't know how many more chances I'd have.

CHAPTER 8
A Guest of the City

When Shackleford left the jail, two other gents stepped inside. They were hard-looking men, well-armed and serious. They said nothing, but seated themselves in chairs near the stove, watching me. I gave then a rueful smile, but they just stared at me the way a man might look at a skunk. After that I gave up all attempts to be sociable, lay back on the bunk, and closed my eyes.

I must have dozed off because when I opened my eyes again, the two men were gone and Shackeford had returned. The big man walked toward my cell carrying a tray holding a bowl of stew, a small pot of coffee, and a tin cup. He unlocked the cell door, placed the tray on the floor, and raised his eyes to me. They were cold, blue, and steady.

"Try and jump me if you've a mind to," he said. "We can save the county the cost of a trial and execution, take care of the whole thing right here."

I waited until he backed out and then picked up the tray. The smell of the stew reminded me how hungry I was. "Thanks, but no thanks," I said. "You don't like me much, do you?"

"Let me put it this way. No."

"Can't say as I blame you," I said. "I'm obliged for the supper."

Shackleford closed and locked the cell door, pulled a chair up, and sat down. "I aim to do what's right," he said.

I set the tray on my lap and sampled the stew. "You must think I'm pretty dangerous," I said, "sendin' those two fellers in to make sure I didn't break out while you were gone."

"Those boys are my deputies. They weren't here to keep you from breakin' out. They were here to keep the citizens from breakin' in. There are more than a few folks in this town who'd like to get their hands on you. They take it personal when a pack of thieves robs their bank."

Shackleford shifted in his chair. "Like I said, I'm only a part-time peace officer. Mostly, I run the blacksmith shop over by the livery. I like this town. My wife died a few years back, but I've got me a son name of

Elwood. Elwood's a good boy. Only nine years old, but he already helps me out at the forge."

Shackleford paused, and I thought the color of his face deepened.

"Elwood has a problem, though. He was born with a clubfoot. Hampers him some. I took him down to Denver a few years back to see a doctor I'd heard about. The doc said he could fix Elwood's foot, but it wouldn't come cheap. Said the operation would cost me three thousand dollars."

Shackleford was silent for a time. When he spoke again, his voice sounded weary and sad. "Do you have any idea how long it might take a small-town black-smith to save that much money?"

I finished the stew and set the tray on the floor inside the cell door. I was about to say no, I didn't know how long it would take, when he told me.

"Long time," he said. "That was four years ago. Since then, workin' nights and days, I managed to put away nearly twelve hundred dollars."

Shackleford unlocked the cell door and picked up the tray. "Every last cent of it was in the bank you boys robbed," he said. "So—no, I don't like you very much."

If the bank robbery had made Shackleford sad, it had put J. T. Hightower into a murderous rage. I met the cattleman that afternoon when he exploded into the jail and marched over to my cell. Hightower was red faced and wrathy, snorting like an old bull, and I knew before he said a word that *he* didn't like me very much either.

"I'm J. T. Hightower," he said. "So you're one of the damned sons o' bitches that held up the bank and stole my money."

"That's what they tell me."

"You're the one we caught, by god," Hightower said. "We killed the fuzz-faced bastard in the mountain man coat. Guess we'll be killin' you, too, when your trial is over, unless . . ."

"Unless?"

"Unless you'd care to tell me where my money is, and who else was in on the robbery."

I shook my head. "I don't guess I'd care to."

"I could take you out of that cage and beat the truth out of you."

"You could try."

Shackleford had walked into the room behind the cowman. When he spoke, his words were respectful but firm. "I can't allow you to threaten my prisoner, Mr. Hightower," he said.

Hightower was still on the prod. "*You* can't allow? You wouldn't even *be* town marshal if it wasn't for me. I'm the one who pays your damn wages!"

Shackleford's answer was respectful, but firm. "Yes, sir. You pay me thirty a month to keep the law in Blue Rock, but the law ain't partial. That prisoner is not guilty until he's proved so in a court of law. Until then, the boy has his rights."

Hightower's face turned a deeper red, and his mouth became a bitter line. His clenched fists opened and closed at his side. It was obvious he wasn't used to being talked to in such a manner. The cowman glared at Shackleford for a moment, then, without a word, he strode past the marshal and stormed out the door.

Shackleford may not like me, I thought, *but I'm beginning to like him.*

My pa was a great one for giving advice, even though he seldom practiced what he preached. Pa used to tell me "haste makes waste," and then get in a big hurry himself that left disaster in its wake. He would solemnly recite "moderation in all things" just before going off on a drunken spree that left him sick, sober, and sorry for a week. And in every calamity that befell our family, he would solemnly declare that "every dark cloud has a silver linin'" and tell me I should "look on the bright side."

Being locked away in a jail cell in Blue Rock, Wyoming was about as dark a cloud as I could think of. Not only was I in prison for bank robbery—a crime I *did* commit—I was charged with murdering a bank teller—a crime I did *not* commit. As for silver linings, my jailer was a decent man who treated me well. Marshal Shackleford was a man of principle, committed to enforcing the law, and refusing to allow the abuse of a prisoner in his charge. He was polite, despite the gravity of my misdeeds. He was humane, even though I had been part of a robbery that had harmed the town's citizens and him personally. He had even hired deputies to help guard me, men like himself.

As for "looking on the bright side," I took comfort in little things. I had read of prisoners driven to despair as they watched and heard the construction of a gallows just outside their cell window. My cell had no window. No one was building a gallows for me. Blue Rock was too poor for that particular luxury.

Shackleford seemed to grow more harried each day. He was kind enough to keep his concerns to himself, but I knew. Sometimes, as he left the jail, I heard the angry mutter of men outside in the street. It was not hard to guess their intent; they were not inclined to wait for the circuit judge. A mob was forming, and it was growing in numbers. *Every silver lining,* I thought, *has a dark, dark cloud around it.*

I wish I could tell you I was not afraid. I wish I could say the threat of a lynch mob didn't concern me. I wish I could say those things, but I don't reckon you would believe me if I did. I was worried, and no mistake. As the voices in the street grew louder, my worry grew with them. I paced my cell. I couldn't sleep. Most telling of all, I was no longer interested in food.

On the evening of my fourth day in the Blue Rock jail I told my concerns to Marshal Shackleford. He had brought my supper as usual, and he was surprised when I told him I couldn't eat it.

"It's the men out yonder," I said. "I keep wonderin' when they'll kick the door in and take me out of here."

"They're all talk, so far," Shackleford said. "If they

123

come for you, they'll have to go through me and my deputies. We don't intend to let them have their way."

"I believe you," I said, "but they're like kids playin' with matches. One of these days they'll get a wildfire goin'. When that happens, it will take more than good intentions to turn 'em back."

For the next two days I saw nothing of the marshal. His deputies brought my meals and stood guard outside my cell. Twice, as they were leaving the jail, I heard the angry voices of the men in the street. The mob was not going away. It was growing *larger.*

On the evening of the seventh day, I lay on my bunk and stared into the darkness. Across the room the deputy on guard dozed in his chair, a shotgun cradled like a baby in his arms. Above him the hanging oil lamp cast black shadows thick as molasses. All was silence except for the pinging of the coal stove and the buffeting wind outside.

I recalled a passage of scripture my mother had taught me, from Psalm 121: *I will lift up mine eyes unto the hills from whence cometh my help.* From whence indeed, I thought. Where was George? Had he abandoned me to my fate? He had the money from the robbery. Would he care what happened to the men who got it for him? Not for a moment, if I knew George Starkweather.

And what of Ridgeway? He had heard nothing from me since I left Dry Creek. Had he learned of the shooting in Columbus and my supposed death? Tested by George and closely watched by Pronto, I'd had no chance to report to him. Did Ridgeway have any idea where I was? Did he even know I was still alive?

Suddenly, above the howling of the wind, there came a muffled knocking on the outer door. The deputy stood up and walked quickly out of the room. I heard him lift the bar, heard the door swing in. The howling of the wind was suddenly louder. I heard men stamping their feet, and then Shackleford and a second man entered the room and moved quickly toward my cell.

Both men were covered with snow, their faces ruddy in the lamplight. Shackleford was a man in a hurry. "I'm takin' you out of here while there's still time," he said, unlocking the cell door. "Most of the mob is off the street because of the storm, but the jail's still bein' watched."

The second man, about my size and age, shrugged out of his heavy sheepskin coat, and I saw his badge reflect lamplight. "This is my deputy, Tommy Fenton," Shackleford said. "Put his coat and hat on and come with me. Keep your head down, and they'll think you're him. It's time to move you to somewhere safe."

Quickly, I did as I'd been told. The sheepskin was a perfect fit. Tommy's hat was a little big, but I wrapped his scarf about my ears and pulled it down snug. "You said somewhere safe. Where, Marshal?"

"A place I know. You'll be all right there until the circuit judge hits town. I'm not about to let a damned lynch mob take a prisoner from me."

• • •

Outside, blowing snow swept the street and drifted deep against the buildings. Across the way, men stood in the light of the saloon's front windows. At the hitch rack in front of the jail, two horses waited, enduring the storm with stolid patience. Shackleford untied one, gestured toward the other, and swung into the saddle. I stepped in close, brushing snow from the saddle, and recognized Roanie!

Shackleford smiled. "We took *him* prisoner, too," he said. "I figured you might as well ride one of your own."

Glad to see the big roan again, I mounted quickly. With Shackleford leading the way, we rode south out of town with the wind at our backs.

An hour later we drew rein at a cabin in a grove of cottonwoods. Lamplight glowed behind its window. In the cabin's lee stood a sturdy carriage horse hitched to a sleigh piled high with blankets. "This is it," Shackleford said. Stepping down from his horse, he reached into his saddlebag and took out a holstered six-gun and cartridge belt. Even in the near darkness, I recognized the weapon—my own ivory-handled .44! Handing the revolver and gun belt to me, Shackleford said, "You're free to go, Kid. Good luck to you."

I stared at him and tried to form words that wouldn't come. At last, I said, "I don't understand, Marshal. How—"

"It seems you have a generous friend," he said. "My boy Elwood is yonder inside the cabin. We're leavin' tonight to go see that doctor in Denver."

• • •

As I rode away from the cabin, I considered my options. Now that I was free, I didn't know what to do. I thought again about trying to get word to Ridgeway, but the only nearby telegraph office I knew of was back in Blue Rock, and I wasn't about to go back there. As far as I knew, the lines were still down anyway. I was a man alone in a blizzard and had to find a place of shelter and safety. My thoughts turned to Arrowhead Ranch.

Once again, George Starkweather had saved my life; he was the only one who could've done this. He had corrupted an honest lawman with stolen money, using a good man's love for his crippled son to buy my freedom. George was a thief and a killer without conscience, but he had rescued me, and at the same time, he had answered Shackleford's deepest longing.

Of course I knew George did everything for his own reasons. Never had I known him to act out of simple kindness or decency; such motives were not a part of his nature. George *used* people. He used their better natures to gain his ends. He was my enemy. I could never trust him. And yet, even so, I turned Roanie back through the storm toward the ranch and George.

By the time I reached the canyon, the snow had lessened, but the wind continued to blow. I gave Roanie his head and trusted him to find the trail. He did not disappoint me. Eyes nearly closed and his nose mere inches from the ground, the big horse picked his way through the hidden rocks and deadfall, taking me toward shelter and a reunion.

The canyon was a strange world to me. Shrouded in darkness and two feet of snow, its landmarks had been altered by the storm. Twice I tried to turn Roanie up a side canyon in the belief I was following the main trail, but he would have none of it, and refused each time. Even when I had my misgivings, I bowed to his instincts.

The wind squalled and spat as Roanie plowed through the deepening snow and began the last steep climb to the ranch. There'd be no guards watching the trail that night, nor were any needed. Only a fool or a desperate man would be out in such weather. I reckoned I was both.

The gateway loomed before me, solid uprights framing my entrance to the ranch. I rode between them, catching the smell of wood smoke on the air. Ahead lay the scattered buildings I remembered. There was the main house, a lamp burning low in the window. Beyond lay the cook shack, dark and silent at that hour. Farther on, I could make out the bunkhouse and the blacksmith shop, barn, and corrals. Weariness fell on me like a blanket, and relief followed. I was safe. I would not die at the hands of a lynch mob. On that night at least, I would not hang from a telegraph pole in Blue Rock, Wyoming.

At the barn, I slipped clumsily down from Roanie and led him inside. Other horses were there in the darkness; I heard their breathing, felt the warmth of their bodies. Somewhere in the gloom, a horse nickered. Roanie replied, a low rumble from deep in his throat. I unsaddled the big horse, found him a stall, and tossed an armload of hay down from the loft. Standing at his side, I wiped him down with a grain sack. Roanie rubbed his head against me and fell to eating; he was glad to be back, too.

I stood outside in the falling snow, looking across the way to the bunkhouse. Within that building were comrades, not guards. Crazy Ike Mullins was there, and Pronto Southwell. Poor old Tom Blackburn might be there, I thought, if George had found a use for him.

I thought of the men who would not be there—Chickasaw Wilson, and Rufus Two Hats whose bed I had inherited. They would be nowhere in this world again, for they slept the long sleep. Dead with their boots on. Such was the nature of the outlaw's life.

The bunkhouse would be warm, the stove banked, coals glowing within its iron belly. The only sound would be of men breathing deeply as they slept. Longing to be there with them, I stepped out of the barn into the deep snow. One step. Two steps. Three.

I stopped. The bunkhouse could not have been fifty yards away, but it seemed like fifty miles. My feet were numb from the cold. My fingers felt stiff, wooden. I fought to keep my eyes from closing, then swayed where I stood and stumbled back inside the barn. In a manger near the back, I made a nest in the hay and covered myself with horse blankets. Still wearing my coat, chaps, and boots, I burrowed into my makeshift bed. Longing for the society of men, I fell asleep in the company of horses.

"Good mornin', Bodacious."

The voice broke into my sleep and nudged me toward wakefulness. It came in a deep, rasping tone that seemed at first to be part of my dreams but destroyed them instead. I fought its call, unwilling to awaken, but the voice had done its work. I turned toward the source and opened my eyes.

George Starkweather looked down at me and smiled. He wore his buffalo coat and the high-crowned black hat, and his yellow eyes seemed to glow in the barn's dim light. "You put me in mind of a Christmas pageant I saw once," he said, "layin' there in the manger like baby Jesus. How are you, son?"

I was stiff, bleary eyed, and chilled to the bone, but that's not what I told George. "Just fine, Cap'n," I said. "Snug, cozy, and glad to be alive." That last part was true, anyway.

George laughed, offering his hand. "Well, get the hell up then," he said. "Let's go on over to the house and palaver some."

I took his hand and let him help me out of the manger. I couldn't stop shivering and wondered if I'd ever be warm again. "S-suits m-me, but I'm not sure I can make it. I think my feet might be froze."

"Lean on me, Kid," he said. "There ain't no hurry. We'll just take our time."

The world was a blanket of white under a sky so

deep and blue it made a man's eyes hurt. Sometime during the night the storm had passed, and the day had dawned cold and brilliant. Undisturbed by wind, wood smoke from the stoves of the ranch buildings rose skyward to catch the early light. With George's help, I limped through the drifted snow until at last we reached the house and stepped up onto the porch. George opened the front door and pushed me inside.

"Take a seat there by the fire," he said. "I'll have Wang Lee rustle up some grub." Flames blazed behind the fireplace screen, and I leaned back in the easy chair, closed my eyes, and felt the fire warming my face, my arms, my legs. The heat was mighty welcome, but it wasn't all pleasure. It also brought a fierce pain to my feet, ears, and fingers, and I was afraid they were frozen. But they weren't. I pushed my chair away from the fire a bit and continued to soak up its heat.

I must have dozed off, because next thing I knew, George was shaking me by the shoulder and the smell of Wang Lee's cooking struck my nostrils. "Wake up, Kid," George said. "Take on some of this wolf bait and join the livin'."

The T-bone steak lay atop a double helping of beans and hung over the edges of the plate. Wang Lee bent to place the food before me and then poured coffee into a china mug. It wasn't until that moment I realized how hungry I really was. My appetite had returned with a vengeance. I sat up, told the old cook much obliged, and fell to eating like it was the first time that year. I picked the T-bone clean, polished off the beans, drank three cups of hot black coffee, and felt better than I had in weeks.

George grinned. "You've got your color back, Bodacious," he said. "I believe you're goin' to live."

"I'm startin' to think so, too, Cap'n," I said.

George pulled his chair close to mine and studied me in silence for a moment. "All right, son," he said. "Tell me about the bank."

He slouched in his chair, his pose careless and relaxed, but his yellow eyes were fixed on mine in a hard stare.

"I reckon you know most of it," I said, and then I told him all I could recall. I spoke of my capture by city marshal Shackleford and my stay in the Blue Rock jail. I told him of meeting J. T. Hightower and of the cattleman's anger. I recalled how I heard the lynch nob forming, growing in numbers each day. I did not, of course, tell George how scared I had been, but I reckon he knew.

"When Shackleford came last night to take me away, I thought my time had come," I said. "Then we rode out to the cabin in the cottonwoods. The marshal gave me my gun back, wished me luck, and set me free. I turned my horse out on the trail through Arrowhead Canyon, and he carried me here to the ranch.

"I don't know whether it was ridin' through the blizzard that way or the pure relief of makin' it back in one piece, but by the time I took care of Roanie, I was too tuckered to make it to the bunkhouse. I bedded down in the barn and slept until you woke me this mornin'.

"I reckon that's all of it, Cap'n," I said. "Did you get the money all right?"

George nodded. "I did," he said. "I was talkin' to Hightower when you boys hit the bank. He like to have shat a ring around himself when he heard about it. His hired guns rode out like hornets from a nest, chasin' Haynes and Morris."

"Did the boys get away?"

"Yep. They changed horses twice and, come sunup, had left that posse behind like a bad dream. I paid them off that evenin', and they quit the country."

"How about Pronto and Ike?"

"They rode in a little later. Pronto told me about Chickasaw. Said he figured you'd been killed or captured."

I fell silent then, and turned my eyes away from George to watch the flickering flames beyond the hearth. I thought about all the hard-working folks who had their money in the Blue Rock bank. I remembered Shackleford's face when he told me about his son's clubfoot and the savings he'd lost in the robbery. At length, I turned back to George.

"I'm obliged to you for buyin' my freedom," I said. "It must have cost you plenty."

George laughed. "Hell, Kid," he said. "I just gave Shackleford your share of the loot."

"That's fair. But I can't help wonderin' why you did it. I knew the rules goin' in. Gettin' killed or captured are the chances a man takes."

"I told you, son. I'm givin' up my wicked ways.

From here on out I'm just George Shannon, cowman. But I do need a foreman to help me run this outfit. I need you."

I made no reply. What was the old bandit up to? I had long since learned never to take George's words at face value. Truth was a changeable thing with George. He would say anything he thought would serve his ends. And yet—was it my imagination, or had there been a desperate tone to his words? Could it be he really was sincere this time?

"It has to do with this new trail I'm fixin' to ride," George said, "and the reason for it. Last month I got a letter that changed everything. Turns out there is one good thing in my life, somethin' I never expected."

George stood up, walked over to the window and looked out. When he spoke again, his voice was touched with wonder. "It seems," he said, "that I have a daughter."

CHAPTER 9

A Letter and a Lesson

George could not have surprised me more if he'd said he was studying for the priesthood. I just sat there trying to think of something to say. When I finally came up with a reply, it was a poor one, and lame. "You have a daughter, Cap'n?"

For what seemed a long time, George stood there at the window looking out at the drifted snow. When at last he turned back to me, his hard, mad eagle eyes had grown soft. "So it would appear," he said.

"I met Sally Weems in Kansas City durin' the spring of '63. She was pretty as a June mornin', with merry blue eyes and auburn hair. I was a good-lookin' Jayhawker, bold as the brass buttons on my uniform, and I was drawn to Sally like lightnin' to a mountain peak. Until my company left town three days later, Sally and me were never apart. When I rode off up the cobbled street with my regiment, I took the smell of her with me and the salt taste of her tears, but I never saw Sally again.

"I thought about her, though, from time to time. Truth is, Sally Weems was about the only decent woman I ever had anything much to do with."

He cleared his throat. "Slippery Mayfair came to visit me while I was in the pen," he said. "I'd been thinkin' about Sally, and I asked Slippery to see if he could maybe track her down. Said I didn't care what it cost; I just wanted to find her. Slippery said he'd try. He hired a private detective and put him on the case."

"That was a year ago," George said. "Meanwhile, I broke out of the pen at Deer Lodge with a couple other fellers. Slippery helped me get set up here at Arrowhead, and I went back to stealin' cows and robbin' banks. I still thought about Sally from time to time. Now and again, I wondered if the detective was makin' any progress at findin' her, or if I'd just throwed my money down a rat hole.

"About a month ago, Slippery came up to take delivery on some cows we'd rustled. He brought groceries, supplies, and a letter from Kansas City." George opened a book that lay on the table beside him and removed a folded sheet of paper. "This letter," he said.

Unfolding the paper, George held it close to the lamp and read:

Dear Mr. Mayfair,

This is to advise you that my mother, Sally Weems, passed away from pneumonia nearly four years ago.

Mother never married. She raised me with love, working long hours as a seamstress to make ends meet. Over the years she spoke often of my father, the man you call George Shannon. She often wondered what became of him and whether he survived the war. She would be pleased to know that Mr. Shannon is alive and prospering in the cattle business. I am pleased as well, and dare to hope I might meet him some day. Please present him with my affectionate regards.

Your obedient servant,
Abigail Weems

Carefully, George refolded the paper and returned it to the inside cover of the book. He lowered his eyes, and I figured he was looking back twenty-three years. "Accordin' to the detective," George said softly,

"Abigail Weems has merry blue eyes and auburn hair."

I didn't know what to say. Nothing I knew about George Starkweather—or George Shannon, as he called himself now—had prepared me for such news. The man had lived his life with nary a trace of kith or kin, or any need for such. It was hard for me to even imagine George having a mother or father—it would have been easier to believe he'd been manufactured by a gunsmith.

Finally I found my voice. "Well, if that doesn't beat all!" I said. "Learnin' after all these years that you have a daughter!"

"Yes," George said. "Thing is, I've answered her letter. I sent her money for the train and stagecoach, and I've invited her to come here for a visit. What do you think?"

I gave him the answer I thought he wanted. "Why, that's fine! I expect it will be good for you and her to get acquainted."

George smiled a shy smile. "I appreciate you sayin' that, Kid," he said. "I surely do."

He was obviously pleased by my comment, and I found that so unusual, it was almost scary. To the best of my knowledge, George Starkweather had never before cared what *anyone* thought.

Suddenly, George cleared his throat and stood up. For the first time since I'd known him, he had let his guard down. He'd allowed me to see his softer side, and I hardly knew what to think. He stepped over to my chair and squeezed my shoulder. "You did well with that bank job," he said. "I'm glad you're back. Now get out of here and let a man get back to his plannin'!"

The bunkhouse was empty when I opened the door. At the room's center, the Sunshine stove putting off dry heat had turned the space into an oven. Water stood puddled on the floor where snow had been tracked in, and the wood box was heaped with freshly split lengths of pine. I changed into dry clothes, pulled on a pair of new wool socks, and lay back atop my bed.

Everything had seemed so simple. I'd do the job Ridgeway had given me to do. The grateful citizens of Dry Creek would pat us on the back and praise our courage and dedication. Our heads would swell up until our hats wouldn't fit, and we'd all live happily ever after.

Oh but I'd found George, all right!—or rather he'd found me. And he'd muddied the waters by saving my life . . . for the third time. Now he had helped the marshal and his crippled son—with stolen money—and in the process, he'd corrupted an honest lawman. He'd loved a woman and found his daughter, and now he'd capped it all off by letting me see his heart, and it did not seem as black as I had imagined. Still and all . . .

Giving up on sleep, I swung my legs over the side of my bunk and stood up. I needed a long talk with a good horse. That may seem peculiar to you, but it always helps me. I dressed for the cold and set off for the barn to talk with Roanie.

• • •

Outside, I squinted against the sun's glare on the white snow and plodded through the knee-high drifts. I had just reached the barn when I saw the horsemen coming. Shading my eyes, I recognized Pronto and Ike Mullins riding stiffly down from the tree line. I kicked snow away from the corral gate and swung it open and waited for them.

Pronto, the first to reach the gate, drew rein and looked down at me from the saddle. "So you're back," he said. Even from where I stood, I could smell the whiskey on his breath. Beneath the flat brim of his hat, Pronto's eyes were hard. There'd been no welcome in his words or his tone, just the cold observation that I had returned.

"The chief said he paid more than three thousand to get you free," Pronto said. "What makes you so damn special?"

Pronto was on the prod, and no mistake. I grinned, trying to turn his anger aside. "Beats me," I said. "You'd have to ask the chief."

He frowned. "He don't let me in on his thoughts much these days. Not since *you* came."

Ike had ridden up now, and he nodded by way of greeting and sat his horse, watching. Pronto opened his coat, his hand an inch away from his right-hand gun.

"I still think you're soft," Pronto said. "Soft, with a yellow belly. What do *you* think?"

"*I* think you're a little drunk," I said.

"You know what else I think? I think maybe the chief

139

has took a fancy to you, if you get my meanin'. Is that it, Bodacious? Are you George's punk? His Nancy-boy?"

Fire flared up inside me from the bottom of my feet to the tips of my ears and the crown of my head.

Pronto was off balance, his body turned in the saddle to look down at me. I caught his left leg just above the ankle with both hands and heaved upward. His eyes widened, and he reached for his gun even as he plunged into the snow on the off side.

Startled, the gelding took a step backward as I ducked under its head. Pronto floundered, trying to bring his revolver to bear. I kicked it out of his hand and caught him full on the nose with a hard left hand. He was reaching for his other gun when I hit him with a right cross and put him down. I picked up his second gun and threw it out into the snow.

Blood was streaming from Pronto's nose as he struggled to get up. I stepped around him, waiting until he gained his feet. "Let's just make this a friendly fight," I said, "without guns. That way, we can tell better who's soft and who's yellow."

He swung and missed as he came up. I hit him again and dropped him to his knees. "You've about run out of weapons," I taunted. "Don't you maybe have a knife or somethin'?"

Pronto lunged at my legs, arms grasping, hands clutching, hoping to throw me to the ground. I held the back of his head and brought my knee up into his face, then jerked him to his feet and hit him just below his ribs with a left that took his breath. I caught him with a hard right hand to the head, and he fell gasping back into the bloody snow.

Rage twisted his face. Crouched on hands and knees, he fought to breathe again. I took a step back. "I'm in no hurry," I told him. "Take your time. Just let me know when you've had enough."

I glanced at Ike, still seated on his horse. I opened my hands as if to ask him if he wanted cards in our game. He grinned and shook his head. I turned back to Pronto.

"Damn you!" Pronto choked. "If I had my guns, you'd be a dead man!"

"Oh, I expect you'll find 'em when the snow melts," I said, "but if you ever pull a pistol on me again, six men will be carryin' you to a hole in the ground."

Pronto was still on his knees in the snow.

"Well?" I asked. "Are you gonna fight or just hunker there and bleed?"

"You win," he said. "*This* time."

"You still figure I'm soft? Yellow? The other?"

Pronto pulled out a bandanna and tried to stanch the blood from his nose. His left eye was red and puffy where I'd struck him. It would be black by morning. "I take it back, goddammit," he said. "Where'd you learn to fight like that?"

I offered my hand, and he took it, and I pulled him to his feet. "The schoolyard at Dry Creek," I told him. "I was the youngest boy in my class, and the smallest."

Behind us, Ike dismounted and led his horse through the gate and into the barn. He made it a point not to look at us as he passed, and kept his expression neutral.

Pronto leaned against the corral gatepost. "You could have gunned me down back there," he said, "Why didn't you?"

Good question, I thought. *For all my tough talk, I don't know if I could have.*

"I didn't figure talkin' trash was worth a killin'. I don't go to the gun as quick as you."

Pronto nodded. When he spoke again, his voice was steady, but I could hear the stifled rage behind it. "Yeah," he said. "Well, today I'm glad you don't."

I had started to walk back to the bunkhouse when Ike caught up with me. "You sure cleaned his clock, Kid," he said. "Sum'bitch had it comin'."

I made no reply, and Ike fell in beside me.

"The chief sent us out yesterday to check on his steers," he said. "We didn't find all that many, and them we did find was humped up and poorly. We camped out in a willow grove last evenin'. Pronto was in a bad temper the whole time, spoilin' for a fight. You gave him one."

" 'Seek and ye shall find,' the good book says."

"Yeah. Good book also says turn the other cheek, but I don't expect Pronto'll do that."

"He'll be all right. Prospectin' the snowdrifts for his barkin' irons will give him time to cool off some."

"Maybe. I'm just sayin' watch your back. Pronto used to be George's right-hand man. Now he figures you've took his place."

I thought, *If he knew who I really am, that would be*

the least of his worries. What I said was, "Thanks for the warnin'. I'll keep it in mind."

Pronto didn't show up for supper that evening, but nobody remarked on his absence—at least not in my hearing. When Tom, Ike, and me came back to the bunkhouse after chuck, we found him sitting on his bed, cleaning and oiling his guns by lamplight. He neither looked up nor spoke as we came inside but continued his work in silence. At last, apparently satisfied with the condition of his weapons, he reloaded them, slid them into their holsters, and made ready for bed.

His expression put me in mind of a thundercloud on a summer afternoon—dark, gloomy, and dangerous. No one spoke to him, and he spoke to no one. Apparently, Ike and Tom decided it was the better part of valor to regard Pronto Southwell as temporarily invisible. They played a few hands of pitch, talking low to each other as though they were attending a funeral. Finally, they turned in too.

I lay awake for a while, reading from a book on Greek myth George had loaned me. When at last I drifted off to sleep, there was no sound in the darkened room save the occasional pinging of the stove and the deep breathing of the men. I can't be sure, but I believe I was the only one there that night that slept with his hand on his six-shooter.

The week that followed was cold and clear with bright sunlight reflecting off the snow. Temperatures fell to ten and fifteen below during the days and dropped to forty below at night. George set Pronto, Ike, Tom, and me to sawing firewood. We smeared lamp black beneath our eyes to prevent snowblindness, and we bucked logs into stove-length sections with a crosscut saw from morning to night.

On Friday of that week, clouds gray and heavy as lead moved in and filled the skies. By mid-afternoon, heavy snow had begun to fall. By late afternoon, a north wind was driving the flakes scattershot across the plain and against the ranch buildings.

"Quittin' time," George told us. "Time to stop sawin' that wood and start burnin' it." We took him at his word, holed up in the bunkhouse, and fed the stove as we listened to the howling of the wind outside.

During the next two days, the storm continued, stopping only at brief intervals. We took advantage of those periods to shovel off the bunkhouse porch and clear the doorways to the buildings. We fed the horses from the dwindling supply of hay and waited for the snowfall to begin again.

George was troubled. He came down to the bunkhouse one morning and stood at the woodstove warming his hands while he told us his plans. "We're runnin' short of grub and supplies," he said. "I figure to take a pack string through the canyon to Blue Rock and stock up. I'll take old Tom with me.

"Some of those citizens down there have long memories," he said. "Tom's the only one of you boys who wasn't in on the bank job. That's why I'm takin' him."

For a moment, he was silent, and then he turned to Pronto and Ike. "I want you boys to look after things while I'm gone. Keep Wang Lee supplied with wood. We're runnin' short of hay for the horses. Take the saddle stock out and find 'em what feed you can. When the weather breaks, maybe we can bring some hay in from Wyoming by bobsled."

Finally, he turned to me. "That leaves you, Bodacious. I want you to take a pack outfit and check on my steers. I'll draw you a map of the range where I think they are, but it's likely they've drifted some. Try to get me a rough head count. I want to know how my cattle are makin' out."

He turned and walked to the door. Placing his hand on the latch, he turned back to me. "And," he said, "whether I'm still in the cow business at all."

Come morning, we all went our separate ways. The skies had cleared, and although the day continued cold, there was something about seeing the sun again that lifted our spirits. No longer did we spend our days cutting firewood; now we were back at the barn and working with horses.

I dressed for the weather in two suits of underwear, my light wool and my heavy wool shirt, two pairs of wool socks and my knee-high Dutch socks, choppers mitts with liners, a black silk scarf, my sheepskin coat, and my Scotch cap. A man could most always find some kind of shelter and wood enough to build a fire, but if he lost his horse or broke a leg, he would surely freeze to death if he wasn't dressed warm enough.

I combed the ice out of Roanie's mane and tail and curried him from poll to hindquarters. He was in prime condition, in part because I'd given him a measure of oats nearly every day since we'd been at Arrowhead. I had slept with my bridle the night before to keep the cold bit from hurting his mouth. I like to think Roanie appreciated the gesture, but with horses you never know.

I rode him out to the catch pasture below the barn and cut out a bay gelding to serve as packhorse. The bay was everything a good packhorse should be—short-backed and thick-bodied, with well-muscled and sturdy legs. His backbone was prominent, his withers were on the high side, and his chest and barrel were well defined. I led the animal back to the barn, curried him, and put a pad and packsaddle on him.

Wang Lee fixed me up with grub and a camp outfit, and I packed and balanced the panniers. When I had all my plunder on the bay, I stopped at the bunkhouse and topped off the load with my bedroll. Then I cinched the outfit down with a diamond hitch, and I was ready to ride out.

It may have been cold outside that day—and it surely was—but I was plenty warm. By the time I had my horses ready for the trail, I was sweating like a fat lady at a polka contest. All those winter clothes were good for riding horseback in cold country, but they were a mite burdensome for working from the ground.

George and Tom were ready to leave at just about the

same time I was. George rode his blood-bay stud and led the four-horse pack string. Old Tom brought up the rear, clad in a good blanket-lined overcoat, mittens, and sealskin hat. The clothes were borrowed, no doubt, but I was pleased to see the old-timer dressed for the weather. Apparently, he was happy, too—his toothless grin showed his pleasure and laced his face with wrinkles. If he'd had a tail, I'm sure he'd have wagged it.

George drew rein, waited for me, and when I rode up, he took a folded piece of paper from an inside pocket and handed it to me. "A rough map of my range," he said. "Takes in the foothills and valleys between Layout Creek and the Bighorn. Most of my steers wear the Circle Eight brand, but if you find a critter wearin' a different mark, he's mine, too."

I laughed. "A mite greedy for an honest cowman, aren't you, Cap'n?"

Watching me, his eyes bright, George shrugged. "Well, you know," he said, grinning. "Finders keepers. Waste not, want not. Take care of yourself, Bodacious."

I transferred the map to my shirt pocket. "I will, Cap'n," I said.

I felt a brief pang of guilt as I rode away toward the tree line, but I turned it aside. I'd agreed to check on the condition of George's steers, but I had plans of my own.

CHAPTER 10

A Message for Ridgeway

I rode north, keeping to the high ground whenever I could. Snow lay deep in the coulees and on the shadowed slopes, but wind had mostly blown the hilltops clear. Riding the ridges gave me a good view of the country and offered grazing for the horses.

During the time I'd been at Arrowhead, I had lost track of the days, but near as I could figure, Christmas couldn't be far away. I thought about Pandora back in Dry Creek and fell to missing her. Did she believe I'd killed Glenn Murdoch and turned outlaw? Everyone back home must believe it, I thought; that was the official story. Only Glenn, Ridgeway, and me knew the truth.

Maybe word had reached Dry Creek that I was dead, killed by Horace Comfort back there on the streets of Columbus. Maybe Pandora had already grieved my passing and turned her thoughts to life without me. Whether she believed I was dead or not, I figured she had likely set her mind on forgetting me. Trails we'd ridden together, sweet nights beneath a summer moon, long walks along the river in the fall—all would fade away like summer snow drifting from the cottonwood trees.

The way of a peace officer is hard, I thought, especially when it's undercover. I was doing what I set out to do, and now I had hope that I could get word to

Ridgeway. If I could, the truth would finally be told, and I could have my life back. That couldn't happen soon enough to suit me.

All that first day, I rode the broken country between Layout Creek and the Bighorn River. Drifting west toward the Clark's Fork, I counted two hundred head of George's steers, all of them the way Ike described them, humped up and poorly. As I regarded the animals, I wondered how many more had drifted before the storms only to pile up in snow-covered coulees and draws.

Passing an aspen grove, I came on seven more steers, six dead. The sole survivor, gaunt, tottering, and pitiful, watched me dully as I approached, its eyes glazed and lifeless. As I drew near, it bawled a mournful rebuke and fell silent. Long after I had passed, I could sense its eyes staring at me.

There was no question. The winter had scarcely begun, and George Starkweather—or George Shannon—was in danger of losing most if not all of his cattle. Cowmen all over the territory were likely in the same boat. Few, if any, of the big ranchers had put up hay for winter feed, and the grass beneath the snow was beyond the reach of their cattle.

Cattle will not paw down to the grass below the snow as a horse will. A steer can be standing in a foot of snow above a carpet of grass, and yet perish of starvation. Every year, many did, but the winter that lay ahead promised to be the daddy of them all. I turned Roanie west toward the Clark's Fork and tried to put the image of dying cattle behind me. I was not altogether successful.

I made camp that night in a lodge pole patch beside a frozen stream. There was plenty of standing dead timber back among the trees, and I built a fire and cooked myself a good supper. Afterward, when the horses had cooled out some, I found a loose boulder and busted a hole through the ice at the little creek so they could drink. Then I staked out the ponies, unrolled my bed, and settled in for the night.

I woke up in the dark. The fire had long since died out, and the sky was peppered with stars, more than a man could begin to count. Now and then a comet would streak across the sky and disappear. There was no wind. Only the sound of the horses scuffling for grass broke the stillness. I drew the bed tarp over my head and slept until sunup.

The second day was much like the first. I was up with the dawn, building a morning fire on the ashes of the previous night and cooking a breakfast of fried spuds, bacon, and onions. I watered the horses, fed them a bait of oats from the panniers, and repacked my outfit. When the sun broke over the mountains, I was ready to meet the day.

I left George's range about midmorning but saw more hungry cattle throughout the day. By late afternoon, I had crossed the Clark's Fork and was making my way to the top of the bench that looked down on the town of Red Lodge.

At the crest of the hill, I drew rein and let the horses

blow. Below in the valley lay the scattered tents and cabins that made up the settlement. Wood smoke drifted upward from a dozen stoves and fireplaces and the ice-covered Rocky Fork continued its journey down from the mountains, carving its way north to the Yellowstone. The camp had changed but little since I'd seen it last, except that deep snow now covered the sagebrush-studded flat.

I turned the horses downhill, crossed the creek, and made my way to the big cabin that bore the hand-lettered sign "Cowpuncher's Retreat" where three saddle horses stood tied in the trampled snow at the hitch rail. Firewood lay stacked in rows against the cabin's wall. In the field nearby, workers manhandled logs from a bobsled, bucking the wood into stove-length sections with crosscut saws. The smell of sawdust and wood smoke from their fires was in the air. The men looked up from their work as I approached the cabin, curiosity plain on their faces.

John Webber stood in the doorway watching me as I drew rein and stepped down. "I remember you," he said. "You're the deputy sheriff from Billings. Welcome back."

He offered his hand and I took it. "You have a good memory," I said.

"Sometimes. Say, did you ever find that big half-breed you were lookin' for?"

Recalling the night I found Rufus Two Hats's corpse near the aspen grove caused me to lose my smile. "I found him," I said. "How have you been, John?"

Webber shrugged. "Can't complain. I have the only eatin' place within forty miles. Somehow, the cowhands from the local ranches find me. I expect I'll be a rich man if I make it through the winter."

Inside, the restaurant was as I remembered it; the big caboose stove consuming fuel like a forest fire, half a dozen men wolfing down the special of the day. As before, the aroma coming from the kitchen range put an edge on my hunger. "What's on the bill of fare?" I asked.

"Venison stew and biscuits," Webber said. "Probably the same as when you were here before. This hash house aspires to quality, not variety. Can I bring you an order?"

"Soon as I take care of my horses," I said. "Is there a livery barn in town?"

"Not yet, but there's been some talk of buildin' one. Jim Virtue claims to operate such an enterprise, but his place is just a barb wire fence around a snow bank."

"Nevertheless," I said, "I need to look to my ponies. Is there someplace nearby I can corral them?"

Webber walked with me to the door and pointed toward a ramshackle structure across the flat. "Just joshin' you, Deputy," he said. "Virtue's place isn't fancy, but he'll take care of your animals. Meantime, I'll save an order of that stew for you."

I looked back, reluctant to leave. "Better save me a *double* order," I said.

Jim Virtue's "livery barn" turned out to be an open air enclosure with an attached corral and a haystack, a shanty with rickety stalls where saddles and harness were draped over a raised log. Trampled snow, muddy and yellowed by horse piss, made up the flooring.

A slender man in knee-high gum boots was cleaning stalls with a manure fork as I led the horses up to the corral. He straightened from his labors and smiled.

"Jim Virtue?" I asked.

"Guilty as charged," the man said, "but virtue, as they say, is its own reward."

I returned his smile. "So I've heard. Cleanin' house, are you?"

"Cleanin' *horse*," he said. "What can I do for you?"

"I need to put my ponies up for tonight. Maybe longer."

He nodded. "Four bits, each. Six bits, with grain. I know that's high, but guests at *this* horse hotel get first class service."

"Big talk for a stable without a roof," I said. "At four bits a day you should tuck them in and read 'em a bedtime story."

Jim Virtue didn't bat an eye. "I can do that," he said, "but it will cost you extra.

I gave the rickety structure a rueful glance and dug in my pocket. "Oh, I'm sure it would be worth whatever you charge," I said, "but these horses are just plain old country ponies. I wouldn't want to spoil them."

Back at Webber's restaurant, I found myself a table near the stove and peeled off a layer of clothes. By the time I went through a double order of stew, six biscuits, and a quart of strong coffee, I was feeling almost human again. John Webber came by with my bill and cleared the table.

"Well, deputy," he said, "I see by the shine on the crockery that you either found my stew to your likin' or you were half starved when you came in here."

I grinned. "I reckon both answers are correct," I said. "Two more questions. First, does Red Lodge have a post office?"

"Sure does. Post office came first, back in '84. It's in a cabin on the east bank of the Meeteetsee Trail where the road crosses the Rocky Fork. You need to send a letter?"

"I need to write one," I said, "and send it. You reckon the office is still open?"

Webber laughed. "Postmaster lives there. If he's at home, the office is open."

"How often does the mail go out?"

"Depends on the weather. It's forty-three miles from here to the N.P. main line at Laurel. In fair weather the stage comes through maybe once a week. It's been ten days since the last one."

"I need to get a report out to the U.S. Marshal in Helena. Legal business. You wouldn't have paper and pen I could borrow, would you?"

"You bet," Webber said. "Be right back."

When Webber brought writing paper and pen and ink, I spent the next hour composing a letter to Ridgeway, telling him what I had learned of George's operations and the outlaws who rode for him. I related everything from my "death" on the streets of Columbus right up to my deliverance from the lynch mob in Blue Rock, including the story of George's newfound daughter, Abigail. Finally, I drew a careful map of Arrowhead and the surrounding area, and closed by saying I'd wait for Ridgeway and his deputies at the ranch. I signed my name, placed the folded pages inside an envelope, addressed it to Ridgeway at Helena, and sealed it.

Outside, dusk had fallen, but the skies held on to the light. I trudged through knee-deep snow to the post office and found the postmaster at home. Minutes later, I had paid the man and committed my letter to the U.S. mails.

I spent that night with six other men in a one-room cabin that passed for a hotel but, overcome by a heaviness of spirit I could not explain, found it hard to fall asleep. I suppose I found it easier to practice deception than to take pride in it.

By first light the next morning, I had breakfasted at the Cowpuncher's Retreat, packed the bay and saddled Roanie, and was on my way back to Arrowhead. The weather had turned warmer overnight, and the snow was heavy and wet. The hungry cattle I'd seen would welcome the thaw, but when the next freeze came the drifted snow would harden and leave the animals worse off than before. In their constant roaming in search of food, they would scrape and cut their legs each time they broke through the crusted snow. Life wasn't easy for a cow critter in the winter time.

I made camp that night alongside a fast-flowing

stream maybe fifteen miles from the ranch. The warmer weather had caused the snow to retreat from the hilltops, and I picketed Roanie and the bay on a patch of good grass below a limestone outcropping. I had seen a few more dead cattle during the day, and others that were poorly but still holding on; none of it good news for the cowman. Winter still had a good three months to go.

There was neither sunset nor stars that evening. Low, slate-colored clouds filled the sky and crept below the treetops as fog. Darkness came on in stages until night had fully settled in, and the only light in all that lonesome land was my small, brave campfire. I ate a light supper, looked to my horses, and turned in. Coyotes warbled in the distance, sounding first close, then far away, and I listened to their lonesome music until I fell asleep.

When I threw back the flap on my bed tarp next morning, a double handful of fresh snow struck my face and I awoke with a gasp. New snow had fallen during the night, building to a depth of four inches or so, and was continuing to fall. I shrugged into my coat and trudged uphill to where I'd staked out the horses. Twenty minutes later when I had saddled and bridled the roan and packed my camp outfit on the bay, sweating from the effort, I swung a-straddle of Roanie, took the bay's lead rope in hand, and struck out for Arrowhead.

The wind picked up, driving the snow before it, and the morning turned colder. I gave my back to the storm, huddled into my sheepskin, and gave Roanie his head. Just before noon, I reached the low hill above the ranch and began my descent through the trees that led to the barn and corrals. It felt good to be back . . . but different somehow.

"That you, Kid?" The voice sounded close. I pulled Roanie up, twisting in the saddle to look for its source. There, not forty feet away, sat Crazy Ike Mullins beneath the spreading branches of a big pine. He stood up, watching me as I approached, his rifle held at the ready.

"Yeah, it's me," I said. "Has George got you standin' guard again?"

Ike shook his head. "George ain't here," he said. "He brought back grub and supplies from Blue Rock, then rode out again, this time with Pronto. Didn't say where he was goin'.

"Ain't nobody on the place except Wang Lee, old Tom, and me. Got tired of listenin' to Tom prattle on. Rode out here to find me a little peace and quiet."

Ike fished a tobacco plug out of his shirt pocket and offered it to me. I shook my head no, and he bit off a chaw for himself. I watched as he worked the quid, thinking how much he reminded me of a cow chewing her cud. Finally, he asked, "What kind of a tally did you get on George's steers?"

"Counted two hundred and sixteen head. Like you said, they're humped up poorly."

"About what I figured," Ike said. "There'll be hell to pay for cowmen this winter."

I waited while Ike led his horse out of the trees. He kicked the snow off his boots, put a foot in the stirrup, and swung into the saddle. Together, we rode down through the north gate and headed for the bunkhouse.

With Ike's help, I unpacked my bed and rolled it out on my bunk. Then I left the grub and cook outfit with Wang Lee and rode back over to the barn. Ike rode with me, and together we unsaddled and turned our horses out.

"I'm glad you're back, Kid," Ike said. "I ain't had nobody to talk to except old Tom. The Chinee cook don't savvy my lingo, and I damn sure don't savvy his."

Ike frowned. "I've had a belly full of cuttin' wood and waitin' for the rest of my money from the bank job," he said. "George ain't doin' right by us boys."

"Don't tell me," I said. "If you've got a grievance, talk to George."

"George ain't the same these days. I never hired on to be no damn ranch hand."

"Like I said, tell him."

Ike frowned. "Yeah. Well, maybe not. But I still say he ain't doin' right."

Ike leaned against the doorway of the barn and stared out across the snow-covered plain. For a long moment he just stood there in a kind of sullen silence. Then he asked, "You recall Haynes and Morris? The boys who rode with us on the Blue Rock job?"

"Sure," I said. "The boys with the hot-blooded horses. The ones who decoyed Hightower's deputies so we could take the bank."

"Well," said Ike, "They came by here last night. Just passin' through, they were."

I waited for the rest of it.

"They told me there's a stagecoach comin' to Blue Rock a week from Friday," he said. "Bringin' twenty thousand in gold and greenbacks to the bank."

"Some coach," I said.

"Haynes and Morris figure to intercept the shipment. They asked me to ride with them. What do you think, Kid?"

"That's your business, Ike."

"Yeah. Thing is, I ain't sure how George would take my leavin'. You reckon he'd mind?"

I thought of George giving up the outlaw life, replacin' the hard cases who rode for him with cow-punchers and ranch hands. On the other hand, George ran a tight ship and took a dim view of his men taking independent action.

"I don't know," I said.

Again, Ike fell silent for a time, looking out across the snow to the trees beyond. At length he turned to me. "What about you, Kid?" he asked. "You want in? Equal shares."

"Much obliged, Ike," I said, "but I reckon I'll pass."

Snow crunched underfoot as we walked together from the barn to the bunkhouse. Ike seemed relieved, his mind already on the stagecoach job. As for me, my thoughts turned to the letter I'd sent Ridgeway.

The Starkweather gang seemed to be breaking up, its members scattering. Rufus Two Hats was dead. So was

Chickasaw Wilson. As far as I knew, Shorty Benson was still holed up at the relay ranch on the Yellowstone. Only Ike, Toni, and Pronto Southwell remained, and now Ike was planning to light out.

When would Ridgeway come? I had no idea. It could take a week or more for my letter to reach him at Helena. He would have to raise and outfit a force of deputies. As always in Montana, the weather was an unknown factor. Already the skies had turned gray and dark again, and a cold wind was blowing out of the north.

And what of George? Would he be at Arrowhead when the posse came? Or would he sense the danger and slip away? George was a trailwise renegade, trap shy and careful.

Lamplight glowed in the bunkhouse window as we drew near. Inside at the table, old Tom was reading a newspaper, his mouth moving and his bony finger tracing the printed words line by line. Just as we reached the door, I looked back at the darkening skies. It was snowing again.

I awoke to gray light. Inside the bunkhouse, the air had grown keen with cold. My bed tarp was wet from my breathing, and the fire in the Sunshine stove had burned down to dead ashes during the night. I closed my eyes again, listening to the scrape of the stove lid and the rattle of kindling being added to the firebox.

I slept later than I'd intended. From the thin light that brightened the bunkhouse window, I guessed the time to be nearly seven-thirty. Turning away from the wall, I saw old Tom bending over the stove, bare of foot and clad only in a ragged union suit. The old man shivered in the frosty air, his hands trembling as he struck matches on the stovetop and tried to relight the fire. He muttered to himself, his breath visible white vapor in the gloom.

At last, the kindling caught. Tom returned to his bunk with a bound and burrowed deep into his blankets. For several minutes the only sound was the pinging of the stove as the fire grew. Tom raised his head and looked around.

"G-good mornin,' Kid," he said. "Reckon I was asleep when you come in last night."

I took my own inventory of the room. Only Tom and me occupied the bunkhouse. Ike had rolled his bed and gone. I figured he rode out early with his mind on the Friday stage and its twenty thousand dollar cargo.

"Glad you're back," Tom said. "It's been lonesome as a graveyard around here with you gone. Just me and Ike, mostly. Wang Lee, too, but he ain't all that sociable."

"George say when he'd be back?"

"Not to me. I rode down to Blue Rock with him for supplies the day you left. We'd no sooner got back when he changed horses and rode out again—with Pronto the second time. He ain't been back since."

I sat up. The stove was taking the chill off the room. I dressed in a hurry and pulled on my boots. "You build a good fire," I told him. "What's George had you doing since I left?"

"Takin' care of the horses, mostly. Shovelin' snow. Keepin' the cook shack supplied with wood. Ike hates doin' chores and such-like. I wonder where he went."

"I expect he's quit the outfit and moved on. Like you say, Ike don't much like hard work."

Tom swung his legs over the side of his bunk and stood up. He dressed quickly and pulled his boots on. "Just between you and me," he said, "I sort of like doin' chores and such. I'm gettin' too long in the tooth to run with the young dogs."

He rubbed a circle in the frost of the bunkhouse window and peered out. "Snowed again," he said. "I'll need to do some shovelin' and find feed for the horses."

"I'll give you a hand. But first, let's fill Wang Lee's wood box and see if he'll feed us."

Wang Lee nodded his approval when we showed up at the cook shack with our arms filled with wood. He pointed to the box beside the stove, nodded as we tumbled the split wood inside, and pointed to the long table and its benches. "You sit," he ordered, then poured us each a cup of coffee and busied himself at the stove with skillet and pots. Minutes later, he produced a platter of hotcakes, bacon, and fried potatoes, placed the platter before us, and we set to forking it in with a will.

Old Tom and me spent the next three days shoveling snow, sawing and splitting wood, and tending to the horses. We played rummy and knock poker in the evenings, and I read some more in that book George had loaned me on Greek myth. Later, when Tom had fallen asleep and the bunkhouse was quiet, I'd lie there in the dark and in my mind, go over my back-trail.

Sometimes the old dream of Ed Hutchins—more memory than dream—returned to haunt me. In the dream I am standing again in the tall grass of the meadow, my eyes straining to see movement inside the cabin. Gunsmoke drifts in the sunlight. In the stillness it almost seems I can hear the grass grow.

Suddenly, Hutchins explodes out of the cabin, gun in hand. He is pale, his hair lank, and his beard stubble blue against the pallor of his skin. My thumb draws the hammer of my .44 back to full cock. "Drop it!" I shout. "Drop the gun!"

Hutchins' face turns sly. His mouth twists, forms his reply. "No," he says. "I don't believe I will." He lowers his arm, aiming his weapon at me. I fire, see my shot take him in the chest. He staggers, and then brings his gun to bear on me again. I fire a second time, and Hutchins is down and dying in the grass. Rushing to his side, I take his gun from his hand—and find it empty!

I feel again my anger and my guilt. "Why?" I ask him. "Why did you make me shoot you?" His answer comes, seven cold words: "Ain't . . . goin' back . . . to that . . . damn prison." He falls back, and breathes his last. Hutchins has used me to end his life.

I awoke in the darkness. My heartbeat hammered in my ears, and my blankets were damp with sweat. In the dream as in life Ed Hutchins, escaped convict and murderer, had died at my hand. I'd given him every chance. I had fired only when I believed I had no other choice. I could not have known his gun was empty. Even so, the feeling of guilt remained.

When Ridgeway and his posse showed up, there was sure to be a showdown. When it came, could I do my part? I burrowed down into my blankets and closed my eyes. The truth was, I didn't know.

CHAPTER 11
To Meet the Stage

By the following Thursday, we had run out of hay to feed the remaining horses, and I took them out in search of grass. The cold was bitter; flurries slashed my face and probed my vitals. Snow squalls had continued to blow in, but the wind had cleared some hilltops and ridges, providing places where the animals could graze. I was bringing the ponies back to the corral that morning when a shrill whinny caught my attention. I looked over at the barn and recognized George's blood-bay stud.

I ran the horses in and closed the gate. As I turned around to lead Roanie to the barn, I saw George wave to me from outside the corral. He wore his heavy buffalo coat and the high-crowned black hat that was his trademark. He smiled as I walked toward him.

"Evenin,' Bodacious," he said. "Appears you've took good care of the horses. What about my steers?"

"Your steers aren't doin' so good," I said, "and I have a feelin' they're goin' to do a whole lot worse."

George's smile faded. He nodded. "That's no surprise. There's been too much snow and too much cold. What's my tally?"

"I counted two hundred and sixteen head. A few may have drifted off your range, but my best guess is you've lost nearly half your herd. Unless the weather breaks, you're goin' to lose a lot more—maybe all of them."

George shrugged. "Well," he said, "easy come, easy go. There's plenty more where they came from."

I guess for George it really was that easy. He would simply steal more cattle from honest men, or use stolen money to restock his range in the spring. George felt nothing for others' cares and sorrows, and less than nothing for the suffering of the poor, dumb animals.

I remembered the dying steer I'd seen on the way to Red Lodge, and the others, some starving and some already dead.

"I don't see it that way," I said. "I figure it's wrong for a man to own stock he can't take care of."

"Wrong?" George said. "Hell, kid—there ain't no 'wrong'! There's only weak and strong, win and lose."

"*I* figure it matters *how* we win," I said. "A man has to live with his conscience."

"Conscience!" George snorted. "There ain't no damned *conscience,* either! 'Conscience' is only what somebody *tells* us we should feel. Good and evil, right and wrong, moral and immoral—they're all just notions! Sure, there are laws against killin'—there's a by-god *commandment* against it! But when a war comes along, guess who puts guns in our hands and sends us off to kill as many of our fellow men as we can! Seems like the only time killin' is wrong is when society don't approve!"

I didn't like listening to that, but George wouldn't let it drop.

"And stealin'? Stealin's wrong, too, they say. But what if a man's kids are starvin'? What if he has to steal to feed 'em? Is that wrong? And what if the railroad wants a man's land, and he won't sell? The damn railroad takes his land anyway and calls it eminent domain! Say a man is abusin' his dog or his horse, and the law takes the animal away to protect it. Is the *law* stealin'? Doin' wrong?" George shook his head emphatically. "No. There ain't no 'wrong,' son. There's only what we do."

Behind George, Pronto Southwell stepped out of the darkness and into the light. He had stripped the saddle from his gelding, and was swinging the rig up onto the corral's top rail, watching me all the while. His gray eyes glittered, but his face bore no expression I could read. He neither spoke nor nodded, but I knew he still hadn't forgotten our scuffle in the snow. For a full minute, it all hung there in the cold, quiet air.

It was George who broke the silence. He smiled his cold smile, his strong white teeth bright against the darkness of his skin. "Come on up to the house," he said. "I've got news."

I nodded. "I will, Cap'n. Soon as I put up my horse."

Pronto led George's thoroughbred and his dapple gray into the barn and hung up their saddles and bridles. I did the same with Roanie, putting the big gelding in a stall by himself. Neither Pronto nor me spoke but went about caring for the horses as if the other man wasn't there. We kept our movements casual and easy and our hands away from our guns. I watched Pronto without seeming to, out of the corner of my eye, and he did the same with me.

It was like one of those days in summer when a storm is building and the air is fairly crackling with electricity. The hair on the back of my neck stood up, and it wouldn't have surprised me if I'd been struck dead on the instant. Turning my back on Pronto as I walked away from the barn was the hardest thing I'd do all day.

At the main house, I stomped snow off my boots and knocked. George was waiting for me. He swung open the door and stepped aside to let me in. "Come in, Kid," he said. "I had Wang Lee build a fire and set out the brandy. Like I said, I've got news."

I followed George into the parlor. Beyond the hearth, flames danced. Two leather-bound easy chairs faced the fireplace, a bottle of brandy and two glasses on a table between them. George gestured toward the chairs, and I settled into one of them. We seemed to be alone in the house. Only George's footprints had marked the new snow at the front door, and I had seen one set of fresh tracks leaving the house by way of the back door—Wang Lee's, I supposed.

George poured three fingers of brandy into a glass and handed it to me. I inhaled the fumes and felt the vapors clear my head. George filled his own glass and corked the bottle. I'd never had brandy before, but I figured it would be strong, like whiskey, only more so. My first taste told me I was right.

I thought again about Ridgeway and wondered if he'd got my letter and when he might be coming for George and the boys. Much had changed since the bank robbery at Dry Creek. Of the six men who rode with George that day, only two remained. Wang Lee cooked for the outfit, but I didn't figure he'd be on Ridgeway's wanted list. Wang Lee had done his time and been released.

A wild notion struck me. There might not be a need to wait for Ridgeway. With only Tom and Pronto on the place, I just might be able to take George in by myself. All I had to do was pull my pistol and say, "George Starkweather, you are under arrest for bank robbery, murder, rustlin', and for escapin' from the prison at Deer Lodge. Come with me, if you please."

Wild as the thought was, I seriously considered it for a moment. Then the doubts came, and the questions. What if George drew on me—could I shoot him if I had to? And if I was able to arrest him, how could I get him away from the ranch? One word from George would bring Pronto a-running. Maybe Tom and Wang

Lee, too. Could I best Pronto in a gun battle? Would I be able to use deadly force at all?

As quickly as the idea had come to me, it faded and fled. The fear of death raised the bet, and I was reluctant to call. I looked at my hole card and tossed in my hand. The moment passed. I was sweating, but it wasn't from the blaze in the fireplace.

I glanced up. George was looking at me, his yellow eyes steady. He had said something to me but I hadn't heard him.

"Uh—what was that, Cap'n?"

George cocked his head to one side like a dog hearing a train whistle. "I asked you," he said, "where Crazy Ike is. His horse ain't at the corral, and his saddle is missing."

"Ike quit the outfit almost a week ago," I said. "He told me Haynes and Morris stopped by here while I was gone. Said they told him about a stagecoach carryin' gold and greenbacks. They wanted Ike to help take it down."

George, raising the brandy glass to his lips, stopped suddenly and stared at me for a moment in silence. Then he asked, "Stagecoach to where?"

"To Blue Rock, Ike said. Accordin' to Haynes and Morris, it's comin' in tomorrow."

The hand that held the glass jerked so sharply that brandy splashed over the top. George still stared at me, his eyes wide, but the color had drained from his face.

His hand trembled as he carefully set the glass on the table. "My daughter," he said. "She accepted my invite. She's comin' to meet me—tomorrow, on the stage to Blue Rock!"

In four long strides George reached the front door and threw it open. Across the way, Pronto was about to enter the bunkhouse with an armload of firewood. "Pronto!" George shouted. "Saddle fresh horses! We're headin' down country, and we're leavin' right by god now!"

Pronto dropped the kindling where he stood and started for the barn at a jog-trot. Like a prairie dog popping up from its hole, Old Tom's whiskered face appeared at the bunkhouse doorway. "Me, too, Cap'n?" he asked.

"No, Tom," George said. "Not this time—I want you to help Wang Lee while we're gone. He'll tell you what's needful."

George was already shrugging into his buffalo coat. Turning to me, he said, "I need you and Pronto to ride with me," he said. "This news about Crazy Ike and the boys has forced my hand for sure."

I followed Pronto's lead. Stepping off the porch, I made a beeline through the crusted drifts and headed for the barn. My guess was we'd have a hard ride ahead of us, and I hoped to pick out a good mount for the trail. Roanie would have been my first choice, but he'd already had a hard trip and needed time to rest up some. I recalled seeing a tough little grulla in the string that put me in mind of my Mouse horse, and I figured he might do if Pronto didn't get to him first.

When I reached the corral, Pronto had already cinched George's saddle on the leggy Morgan George called High Pockets and had caught his own sorrel. I shook out my loop and turned my eyes to the grulla.

"I wondered which of them culls you'd choose," Pronto said. "That grulla ain't much bigger than a dog."

I wasn't about to put up with Pronto's bull. "He's like me," I said, "small, but mighty. I figure he'll still be goin' when that goosey sorrel of yours has laid down and quit."

Within moments, I had saddled the grulla and led him outside the corral. Once there, I untracked him, took a short hold on the reins, and swung up onto his back. I touched him with my spurs, and we lit out for the house at a lope. Pronto was close behind me, leading High Pockets.

We had scarcely reached the house when George stepped out dressed for the trail and loaded for bear. He wore a pair of belted revolvers and carried a Winchester carbine. Taking the Morgan's reins from Pronto, he slid the carbine into its scabbard and stepped up into the saddle with a grunt. "Got to quit ridin' these long-legged sons o' bitches," he said. "Like climbin' a damned mountain." Then he led out at a quick trot with Pronto and me close behind.

Pronto pulled around me and fell in behind George to be closer to the chief. I didn't mind; fact is I was glad. I had no wish to make the long ride down Arrowhead canyon with Pronto Southwell at my back.

I don't believe any three riders could have made the trip faster than we did. George knew the territory well, and he led the way with haste and skill. When deadfall or drifts blocked our path, George quickly found another way. Time and again he sensed a problem ahead long before he could have known about it. At such times he would hesitate for the briefest moment, then quickly choose a new route that took us safely past the obstacle. In any case, our pell-mell descent called for quick eyes and reflexes. It was no pleasure ride, and it did not allow for mistakes.

Twice on our way down the canyon, George drew rein, making a brief stop to let the horses blow. On those occasions, Pronto and me took the opportunity to get down and stomp the stiffness from our legs, but George did not. Instead, he sat his saddle huddled inside his buffalo coat and waited in silence until the horses were ready to move on again. Because George said nothing at those times, neither did Pronto or me. I don't know what we would have had to say to each other anyway.

Finally, late in the afternoon, we cleared the canyon and rode out onto the rutted road that led to Blue Rock. George skirted the hill that overlooked the town and then turned east. Ahead, the plains stretched away forever in the flat, gray light. Behind us, a chill wind dogged our heels and pushed us along on our way.

It was maybe an hour later that George left the road and turned down into a grove of cottonwood trees. Ahead, in the fading light, a sod-roofed cabin and a scatter of outbuildings came into view. There was something about the scene that seemed familiar, although at first I couldn't say what. Then, as we rode up to the cabin's door, I remembered. This was where Marshal Shackleford had taken me when he spirited me away from the Blue Rock jail.

George drew rein and spoke at last. "We'll stay the night here," he said, "and move on tomorrow at first light. You boys put the horses up at the barn yonder while I get a fire started." Stiffly, George slid out of the saddle to the ground. For a moment he leaned against his horse, his right hand gripping the saddle horn, his face drawn and haggard with pain. Looking at me, he said, "Old wounds, Bodacious. The wages of sin."

"The bullet Kiowa John put in your hip back in eighty-two."

George stepped away from High Pockets. His face was strained, but he grinned his old go-to-hell grin and nodded. "Close up and personal, and like you said once before, with a Spencer rifle. You helped me doctor that wound when blood-poisonin' set in. I wish you'd done a better job."

"I never claimed to be an expert," I said, remembering. "I can't even cut hair."

Pronto rode his sorrel over, picked up High Pocket's reins, and led the animal away toward the barn. I turned the grulla after him and followed.

It was full dark by the time we returned to the cabin. George had built a fire in the cook stove and had set the coffeepot on. A coal-oil lamp burned low atop a table near the door. The cabin was small but neatly kept, and I wondered who owned the place. Answering my unspoken question, George said, "Cabin belongs to a friend of mine. Used to be a top rope-and-ring man till he got married and took up this homestead. Him and his missus appear to be away for a day or two."

The coffee reached a rolling boil, and George pulled the pot off the stove and added cold water to settle the grounds. He poured us each a cup and fixed us with his cold gaze. "We'll camp here tonight," he said. "Then tomorrow we'll see if we can't head off a stagecoach robbery."

Pronto frowned, and looking at George, waited for more.

"Ike Mullins has quit the outfit," George explained. "He's joined up with Haynes and Morris. They're fixin' to hold up the Blue Rock stage tomorrow." He looked from Pronto to me. "Trouble is," he continued, "my daughter, Abigail Weems, is on that stage. She's come all the way from Kansas City to meet me.

"The last stop before Blue Rock is the Sand Coulee stage station, twenty miles from here. I figure Ike and the boys will hit the coach some time after it leaves the station. Most likely spot would be either Hay Creek Crossing or Cooper's Hill. Those are the two places the team has to slow to a walk."

George fished the stub of a cigar from his shirt pocket and struck a match on the stovetop. He lit the stogie, staring at nothing. For a moment he was silent, seeing the land in his mind, I supposed.

Finally he said, "Hay Creek crossin' is twelve miles east of here. Cooper's Hill is three miles closer. Come mornin' we'll go find them boys, and I'll ask 'em to change their plans."

Pronto took a sip of coffee and looked at George. "What if they won't?"

George's expression didn't change. "They will," he said.

George cooked up a supper of side pork and fried spuds, then we ate and turned in for the night. "I'm takin' the bed," George said. "You boys can roll out your blankets there by the stove. We'll be ridin' before first light."

Pronto chose to spend the night sitting up in the homesteader's rocking chair. Wrapped to his eyes in a comforter and with his Winchester cradled in his arms, he fell asleep almost at once. Or, leastways, he seemed to.

I built up the fire and shut down the damper to hold the heat in. Then I blew out the lamp and curled up on the floor beside the wood box. I was wide awake for some time, thinking about the coming morning. Hot as the stove was, it didn't stay that way for long. It may have been cozy up near the ceiling, but it was cold as a wedge down where I was.

Stretching out on a cold, hard floor in total darkness near a man who'd just as soon kill me as not, might seem an unlikely way to get some shut-eye, but durned if I didn't drop off right in the middle of my fussing and fretting.

I awoke to the sound of George Starkweather rattling stove lids and stoking up the fire. I was cold as a carp and stiff as a rake handle, but I was glad to be alive. "Daylight in the canyon, boys," George rasped. He produced a pint whiskey bottle from his coat pocket and took a long pull. George made a face, and then offered the bottle to Pronto and me. "If you don't like whiskey, breakfast is over," he said. "Time to saddle them ponies and ride."

Pronto took the bottle and drank, but when he passed it to me, I just shook my head and handed it back to George. "Maybe later," I said. "I make it a rule not to drink whiskey until I'm awake."

The sky was black velvet, studded with stars. A fingernail moon cast its pale glow upon the land, and the morning was still as a millpond. Pronto and me followed our own tracks to the barn, combed and brushed the horses by lantern light, and saddled them. By the time we led them back to the cabin, George had reheated the coffee. Lifting the pot from its place on the stove, he poured us each a cup. My cup caught most of the grounds, but the coffee was hot and strong. I drank it down to the dregs, grateful for the eye opener.

Outside, George used an old packing crate to step up onto his long-limbed Morgan. "Go to buckin' if you've a mind to," he told the horse, "but I don't aim to let you throw me. Hard as it is for me to get in the saddle, I don't plan to leave it for a while."

The Morgan tossed its head and rolled its eyes some,

but it made no move to pitch. "Much obliged for the good behavior," George said. "I owe you, High Pockets." Pronto and me got horseback ourselves. George touched the Morgan with his spurs and we jogged out to meet the day.

Ahead, the sky faded and turned to dusty rose. Stars winked out and disappeared. Only the clatter of our horses' hooves on the icy roadway broke the stillness. The land around us commenced to take form out of the gloom until I could make out hills and coulees, rim-rocks and ridges, and an occasional stand of cotton-woods huddled together in the low places.

Then the sun broke out atop the far ridge and flooded the plains with light. Brightness painted the hilltops and dazzled the eye. Even though I knew that dawn in winter is oft-times the coldest time of the day, I somehow felt warmer just seeing the light.

We reached the crest of Cooper's Hill watching for Ike and his partners but saw no trace of them any-where. We turned down the steep grade braced for action and tense from the watching. Nine miles farther on, we reached Hay Creek crossing. Again, there was no sign of the coach nor of the men we hunted—no movement, no tracks, and no smoke from a warming fire. We watered the horses at Hay Creek and scanned the country through George's binoculars, but to no avail.

"What now, Cap'n?" I asked. "You reckon the coach broke down somewhere?"

For a moment I thought George hadn't heard me. He

raised his head toward the rising sun, eyes narrowed, sniffing the air. Finally, he answered me. "Damned if I know," he said. "You sure them boys figured to hold up the stage today?"

"That's what Ike told me."

Again, George fell silent. He shaded his eyes, looking down the road and into the distance. He shifted his weight, turning in the saddle to face Pronto and me. "We'll go on ahead," he said. "Chances are we'll meet the coach comin' this way. If we don't, we'll ride on to the Sand Coulee station. Could be the driver had trouble with the team, or maybe the coach broke down. The station keeper might know somethin'."

George reined High Pockets back onto the road and sunk spur. Pronto fell in behind him and I brought up the rear again. Just before George turned away from me, I saw something in his face I'd rarely if ever seen. George was worried. He was worried as any father would be. He was worried about a daughter he'd never met and about a future he'd never expected to have. He was concerned about someone other than himself, and that was a rare thing for George Starkweather. Somehow it made him seem vulnerable and more human than he'd ever seemed to me before.

By the time we reached the station, the wind had picked up and the day had turned colder. We'd seen no riders on the road or any sign of the Blue Rock coach. George, edgy and restless, was pushing the big Morgan to its limit. Keeping up with George had taken its toll on the other horses, too. Pronto's sorrel was nearly spent, and my little grulla was tiring as well.

The station consisted of a weathered barn, pole corrals, and a low log building that housed the station keeper and a couple of hired men. A top buggy and a square body sleigh were parked in the lee of the barn, and I saw a half-dozen good-looking saddle horses in the round corral. The animals raised their heads, watching our approach.

Smoke billowed from the stovepipe atop the station's roof and blew away in the wind. A buck-toothed kid I took to be the hostler was splitting wood at a chopping block. Seeing us rein up, he paused to take our measure.

"Mornin'," George said. "Lookin' for the station keeper. He around?"

The kid squinted up at George. "That'd be Rance Finley. He's inside. Get down and go on in."

"Obliged," George said, and stepped down. Pronto and me followed suit.

I watched as George made his way to the front door. He was hurting, though he tried not to show it. Only the stiff, tight way he carried himself tipped his hand. George opened the door, and we went inside.

At first I could see nothing. After the bright sunlight, the room seemed dark as a mineshaft. It was warm, too, and while the heat was mighty welcome, I think I appreciated most just being in out of the wind. As my eyes grew accustomed to the light, I could make out a spacious kitchen and a long plank table. Beyond, at the far side of the room, an older, bald-headed man removed a coffeepot from atop a big Sunshine range. He looked up as we came in.

"Rance Finley?" George asked.

"That's right," he said. "What can I do for you boys?"

George nodded at the coffeepot. "Give us a cup of that coffee and a moment of your time," he said. "We're lookin' for the stage to Blue Rock."

Finley took three mugs from a cupboard and filled them from the pot. "You and me both," he said. "Ben Holloway's drivin' today—one of the best whips on the line. He should have been through here two hours ago. Damned if I know what's keepin' him."

He gestured toward the table. "Take a seat, boys," he said. "Warm up some. It's colder'n a witch's teat out there."

George nodded, warming his hands on the mug. "Obliged for the coffee," he said, "but we can't stay. I'm George Stark—that is, I'm George *Shannon*—from up Arrowhead Canyon way. Fact is, I'm some worried. I believe my daughter is on that stage."

Finley looked up sharply. "Hell you say. Well, you're more than welcome to wait here till she comes in."

George pulled a buckskin pouch from an inside pocket. Loosening the strings, he poured a dozen double eagles into his other hand. The sound of those gold coins clinking together got the station keeper's full attention. "Appreciate the offer," George said, "but I believe we'll ride on and see if we can find that coach. There is somethin' we do need, though."

"Name it."

"Our horses are pretty well wore down. Could you lend us some fresh mounts?"

"Uh—well, our livestock is property of the stage line. I ain't authorized—"

George poured the coins back into his pouch. "We'd be helpin' to find the stage line's property. Be happy to pay for the use of the horses."

"Oh. Well . . . I'm afraid that might be rather expensive. Stage line don't usually lend its livestock—"

George pocketed the pouch. "I'll pay ten dollars. Each."

Greed was plain on Finley's face. "Oh . . . I couldn't possibly lend them for that, Mr. Shannon. I'd need twenty dollars a head, at least."

Turning to face the man, George drew back the tails of his buffalo coat to reveal the butt of his revolver. His voice was flat when he spoke. "You should have took the ten," he said. "Offer now is five and goin' lower. I'd advise you to take the five."

Color drained from the station keeper's face. His eyes went wide. He stammered when he spoke. "Uh . . . sure, mister," he said. "I—I never meant to rile you none. I'll send Wilbur over to the corral with you. He'll help you catch your mounts."

"Obliged," George said. He handed the man one of the double eagles. "There's an extra five there to take care of our horses till we get back. Cool 'em out. Give 'em some water. Maybe a little grain."

Finley's hand trembled when he reached for the

money, but he took it. "You bet," he said, smiling. "We—we'll be plum' glad to do that for you."

"That's good to hear," George said. "I thought maybe you weren't *authorized*."

Down at the corral, the young hostler called Wilbur showed us what saddle stock the stage company had. George hadn't lost his eye for horseflesh. He picked out the three best horses in their string, and we put our saddles on them. Minutes later, we were back on the road, leaving the stage station behind us.

CHAPTER 12
Meeting Miss Abigail

The road snaked through low hills and coulees across a broken, sagebrush-studded plain. We scanned the distance as we rode, but the land ahead lay colorless and flat in the pale sunlight. We saw no trace of the coach or its passengers.

Then, a little past noon, we drew rein atop a wooded ridge to study the country below. We dismounted to rest the ponies, and I managed to stamp some feeling back into my feet. A cold wind blew up from the valley, but there was no other sound save the heavy breathing of the horses. George lowered the binoculars, his expression marked by a growing concern. We mounted and made ready to ride on again.

That's when we heard—sharp and clear in the stillness—three gunshots, evenly spaced, from someplace just ahead. Our horses raised their heads, listening. George, Pronto, and me held our breaths, staring in the direction the sound had come from. We waited a full minute but heard nothing more. George shifted in the saddle, looking at Pronto and me. "You boys hear that? Pistol shots, close by."

"Somebody's in trouble," I said. "Three shots, deliberate and spaced. One, two, three."

"Fan out, boys," George said. "We'll ride up to the top of that next hill. I've got a feelin' we'll find whoever fired those shots just on the other side."

We rode out of the trees and down the slope, feeling the jarring of the horses' stiff-legged descent. At the bottom, we slipped our Winchesters from their scabbards and spurred our mounts into a gallop. The animals lunged uphill, kicking up crusted snow, and carried us to the top. At the hill's crest we drew rein and looked down. There, in a brushy wash a hundred yards from the road, lay the Blue Creek stage, the coach sprawled on its side, the four-horse team tangled in the traces. A traveling bag, several boxes, and a small trunk lay scattered on the ground. The trunk had been opened, and articles of female clothing were strewn about.

We had started down toward the coach when we heard the man's voice. "Over here, fellers," he shouted. "I'm over here!"

I turned in my saddle and saw him. He was a big man, sprawled in the snow just off the road. He struggled to rise to a sitting position, but settled back. He held a Colt revolver in his right hand, and in the snow nearby, empty cartridge cases glinted in the sun. The snow was bloody where he lay.

The man's eyes told us how glad he was to see us. He was pale and shaky, and I was afraid he was going into shock.

"I'm Ben Holloway. I was drivin' the coach to Blue Rock this mornin'. About two hours ago, three outlaws wearin' masks jumped me," he said. "Told me to throw down the strong box. I wasn't carryin' a strong box this run, and I told them so. I was supposed to, but the company bosses changed their mind at the last minute. Hell, I didn't even have a shotgun guard along. Figured I wouldn't need one."

Holloway tried to sit up again, winced and lay back. "One of 'em—mean sum'bitch in a hair coat and black hat—said I was lyin'. Told me I'd better throw the box down or by god he'd shoot me. I told him again I wasn't carryin' a strong box, and by god he shot me!

"Bullet took me in the thigh," he said, his fingers touching the wound. "I believe it broke my leg. Can't walk on it."

George bent over the man. "What happened then?" he asked.

"Horses bolted. I fell off the coach. The team stampeded over yonder till they piled up in that washout."

"Your *passengers!*" George said. "What happened to your passengers?"

"Only had one. Young lady goin' to Blue Rock. I guess she's still inside the coach. Couldn't get over

184

there to help her. Called out several times, but she never answered."

George swung back into the saddle, his eyes on the coach. "Stay with the driver, Bodacious," he said. "Do what you can for him."

Turning to Pronto, he said, "Gather some wood and start a fire. There's a dead cottonwood back yonder below the road." Then he was gone, covering the hundred yards to the stagecoach at a brisk trot.

I watched as George dismounted and climbed atop the overturned coach. He bent, opened the door, and lowered himself inside. A minute later he reappeared. "She's alive," he shouted. "Hit her head when the coach upset, but she's comin' around."

With my knife, I slit open Holloway's pant leg and found the wound—a bullet hole swollen and ugly. The slug had broken the man's thigh bone, but it had missed the artery. "Looks like the bullet's still in there," I said, "but I'm not going to probe for it. I'll leave that for a doctor."

"What I will do," I continued, "is rinse the wound with whiskey and bandage it. George has whiskey in his saddlebags. Then I'll put a splint on the break."

Pronto rode up pulling a load of cottonwood branches behind him. He stepped down and began to clear a space in the snow for a fire. I looked at Holloway. His eyes were closed, his arms and legs beginning to tremble. "Stay with me now," I said. "We'll have a fire goin' in a minute. That'll warm you some."

I glanced back at the coach. George had lifted the girl

up through the stage's doorway and then pulled himself up. He took her in his arms, stepped down into knee-deep snow, and put her on his saddle horse. I could see she hadn't come out of it yet and couldn't help him any. Swinging up behind her, he held her with his right arm and now was riding back toward us.

The fire caught in the dry wood and soon swelled to a roaring blaze. Pronto fed the fire, building it higher. Then George drew rein and stepped down with the girl in his arms.

"Boys," he said, "meet my daughter Abigail."

The girl, dressed in a black wool skirt and a fur-trimmed jacket, looked helpless and frail as George lifted her from the saddle. Auburn curls framed her heart-shaped face, and her nose was small and dainty. Beneath a small hat decorated with ribbons and feathers, an ugly purple bruise marked her right temple.

Still holding her with one arm, George untied his blanket roll from behind the cantle of his saddle and spread it on the ground. Gently, he laid the girl down. "She's a pretty little thing," he said. "Helpless as a new calf, but I don't believe she's hurt too bad."

The girl's eyes were still closed, but her lashes fluttered, and her lips moved as if she was trying to speak. Then she trembled and opened her eyes. "C-cold," she said. "So *cold*—"

George took off his buffalo coat and spread it over her. "Don't you worry none," he said. "Everything's all right. You'll be warm soon."

I turned my attention back to the driver. Holloway was trembling, his face ashen. "Let me have that whiskey from your saddlebag, Cap'n," I said. "I need to set this feller's leg."

"Take it," George said, his eyes still on the girl.

I stood and retrieved the bottle, then kneeling at Holloway's side, poured whiskey onto the wound and every muscle in his body went tense; you could see the pain in his face. I finished bandaging it and handed him the bottle. "Take a drink. A big one." He nodded. I didn't have to ask him twice.

Bending over him, I took the woolen muffler from his throat, removed his belt, and picking a couple of sturdy sticks from the wood pile, handed one to my patient. "Somethin' to bite on," I said. "You're gonna need it."

I took hold of his leg and drew it straight, lining up the broken ends of the thigh bone. The driver arched his body, trembling. Eyes wide, he bit into the stick with a will, but he didn't moan or cry out. Using the other stick as a splint, I wrapped it tight with strips torn from his muffler. Then I used his belt to bind his injured leg to the other. It wasn't perfect, but it got the job done, and I figured it would hold him until we got him to a doctor.

I turned away to find George kneeling by his daughter and watching me intently. "Where'd you learn to do that?" he asked.

"Growin' up with my pa back in Dry Creek. Pa and me had a partnership goin'—he'd get himself hurt breakin' horses and fightin' in town, and I'd patch him up. I had a lot of practice."

George nodded. "Good job," he said.

He turned again to the girl. She was sitting up on George's blanket roll now, leaning against him, and she seemed to be trying to get her bearings. Her gaze returned to the overturned stagecoach and then to the injured driver lying by the fire. In turn, she looked at George, Pronto, and me. When her eyes met mine, I saw they were a pretty shade of cornflower blue, candid and intelligent. I smiled to reassure her. She held my gaze for a moment, and then turned her face back to George.

"If your name is Abigail Weems," he said in a tender voice I'd never heard from George before, "you're the young lady I have come to meet. I'm George Shannon, and I believe I'm your daddy."

For a moment she was silent. She studied George's weathered face as if to memorize its every feature. Then she said, "Mr. Shannon? Father? How did you—?"

"I couldn't wait to see you," George said. "I set out early this mornin' with two of my . . . cowboys to meet the stage. When we reached the Sand Coulee station and found out it was overdue, we rode on ahead to find you."

"I'm so glad you did," she said. "Those masked men, they held up the coach. They shot the driver."

Clumsily, George patted her shoulder. "I know, darlin'," he said. "Don't you worry. Everything's all right now."

She was looking at me again. She was a small girl, a few inches over five feet tall. Her manner was shy and demure, but her gaze was cool as a card sharp's. I would have expected the girl to be plumb skittish after what she'd been through, but she seemed calm, even serene.

George saw her looking at me. "Meet Merlin Fanshaw, Abigail. He's foreman on my spread. My right hand man."

She smiled. "I am pleased to meet you, Mr. Fanshaw."

I touched my hat brim and returned her smile. "Miss Abigail."

Turning to Pronto, George said. "And this is Pronto Southwell, one of my top hands."

"Mr. Southwell," she said.

Pronto acknowledged her greeting with a nod, and then looked down at the ground. "Miss," he mumbled. Beneath the shadow of his hat I could see his jaw muscles working. He glanced at me, and his eyes were hot. He didn't like what George said about me being his right hand man. I thought, *The hell with him.*

It took some doing to get the team straightened out. It might have gone easier if we had been able to use our customary horse-talking vocabularies, but Miss Abigail's presence caused us to restrain ourselves. Eventually, we managed to untangle the harness and get the horses back on their feet and lined out again. Except for a few scrapes and bruises, they looked none the worse for wear.

While Miss Abigail watched from her blanket by the fire, George, Pronto, and me put our lariats on the overturned coach. With our saddle horses pulling together, we soon had it upright and on its wheels again.

When we turned our attention back to Miss Abigail, she was gathering up the clothing and personal items that had been scattered by the holdup men. "They even looked for money among my things," she said wistfully. I turned to help her, picking up her trunk and some of the boxes and placing them in the boot.

George rode up to me. "Can you drive a four-up, Bodacious?"

"You bet, Cap'n. I can drive a six."

"I'll bear that in mind if we ever have us a six-horse hitch to deal with. Right now, we need somebody to drive this outfit back to Sand Coulee station. You're elected."

George looked back toward the fire. It had nearly burned out. The driver still lay on his back near the smoldering embers, watching the smoke climb into the sky. "We'll put him in the coach," George said. "Abigail and me will ride with him. Tie my horse and yours on behind."

"What about me, Chief?" Pronto asked.

"Once we get that driver on board, I want you to ride on ahead. Let the station keeper know we're bringin' his coach and driver in. Tell him the driver needs doctorin', and a lady passenger needs a quiet room to rest in. Then tell him to get supper on. He's got five hungry people to feed."

Pronto nodded. Then we turned our attentions to the driver.

As gently as we could, we lifted Holloway up and placed him inside the coach. His body stiffened with pain as we eased him onto the seat, but he didn't cry out. Miss Abigail sat beside the man, holding his hand, and George sat across from her.

"Much obliged, boys," George said. "Take us to Sand Coulee station, Bodacious."

I climbed into the box, took up the reins, and eased the team out onto the road.

The sun had set by the time we reached the station. The day's last light still lingered in the west, but darkness was crowding in fast. Scattered stars appeared, and lamplight glowed warm in the windows. I caught the smell of wood smoke and of something cooking inside the station, and my belly reminded me of how long it had been since I'd sat down to a meal.

Pronto was waiting in the shadows, watching as I turned the coach off the road. Rance Finley, the station keeper, rushed out through the front door to greet us. Wilbur, the hostler, and another station hand followed quickly right behind him.

Seeing me in the driver's seat, Finley asked, "Where's Holloway? Your man told me about the holdup. Is he all right?"

"He's alive," I said. "He took a bullet through the thigh. Broke his leg, but I managed to get a splint on him."

George opened the coach's door and stepped down. It was his nature to take charge. "Some of you boys help get him inside," he said. "He's cold, hungry, and hurtin'. He ain't had a real good day so far."

The station hands took hold of Holloway's makeshift litter and lifted him out of the coach. "Put him in the back room," Finley said. "There's a spare bed in there. Go easy with him now!"

As the boys carried the wounded driver inside, George helped Abigail down. Clinging to George's arm, she offered Finley a shy smile. "This here is my daughter Abigail," George said. "I expect she's had better days, too."

Finley reached up to tip his hat and suddenly remembered he wasn't wearing one. Instead, he smoothed his thinning hair. "Uh, howdy, Miss Abigail," he said. "Come on inside and set by the fire. I'll ready a room for you, and you can freshen up some. We'll be servin' supper d'rectly."

I wrapped the reins around the brake handle and stepped down from the coach. The evening had grown suddenly colder with the setting of the sun, and I looked forward to the shelter of the station. George was right; it had been quite a day.

Once again, I had helped the very man I was supposed to bring to justice, and once again I found myself feeling troubled and guilty, somehow. I suppose I might have spent more time considering the moral questions of undercover work, but at that very moment the smell of fresh stew and biscuits drifted out the open door, took me by the nose, and drew me inside. My appetite always seems to have first claim on my attention.

We ate together that night at the long table in the station's kitchen, one big happy family—more or less. Rance Finley played the genial host, freely helping himself to a whiskey jug as he lavished praise on George, Pronto, and me for bringing in the coach and its driver.

He was considerably less jovial when he talked about the desperados who had held up the coach. Inspired by the contents of the jug, he spoke at length of what he considered their shortcomings. He offered some speculation as to their parentage, which he opined was either fatherless or canine.

Miss Abigail, of course, was the center of attention. Seated at the table's head, she responded to each compliment that came her way with a smile and lowered eyes. Wilbur and the other stable hand couldn't take their eyes off her, but they were tongue-tied by her presence. Their conversation was mostly limited to such remarks as "that stew is mighty tasty" and "pass them biscuits."

The cook at the stage station, like Wang Lee back at Arrowhead, was Chinese. He took some stew on a tray to Ben Holloway's room and stayed to make the man as comfortable as possible. I looked in on Ben myself after supper, but found him asleep. I eased the door shut and cat-footed back to the others, but I was glad; I figured sleep would help the man more than anything.

Finley's monologue continued all the while. He talked about taking the stagecoach on to Blue Rock the following morning; he'd drive it himself, he said, and he'd take Ben to town so the local sawbones could treat his wounded leg. Also, he would telegraph the head office from Blue Rock and tell his bosses about the holdup. Miss Abigail, of course, would ride along and thus complete her trip.

"My daughter and I will not be going into Blue Rock," George said. "We have business elsewhere. I wonder if I might ask a favor of you."

Finley's gratitude was apparent. "Why, of course, George," he said. "After what you and your men did for the line, I can hardly refuse you anything."

"Thank you, Rance. Mighty generous of you. Well, you see, I need to take my daughter along with me, but I can hardly expect a genteel young lady like her to ride astride of a saddle horse."

Finley took another pull from the jug and wiped his mouth with his sleeve. "Of course not," he said. "Wouldn't be fittin'."

"Exactly. Well, the thing is, I noticed when we rode in this mornin' that you have an open-top sleigh parked beside your barn. I wonder if you might rent me that rig and a good team."

The word "rent" seemed to stir up Finley's greed. Eyebrows raised, he studied George in silence, as if he was preparing to begin the bargaining process. George, too, said nothing. He simply regarded the station master with his yellow, mad eagle stare and waited.

Finley broke. "I couldn't charge you, George," he said. "Take the sleigh and welcome to it. It's little enough thanks for bringin' the coach and driver back. Keep it as long as you like."

"That's mighty neighborly," George said. "I am obliged."

George turned to Abigail. "Excuse me a moment, my dear," he said. "I need to talk with Merlin and Pronto."

Leaving his place at the table, George led Pronto and me to a corner of the big room and turned to face us. When he spoke, his tone was low. "We're leavin' in the mornin', but we're not goin' to Blue Rock. I'm takin' Abigail with me in the sleigh, and I want you boys to ride along and lead my High Pockets horse."

Pronto frowned. "You takin' that sleigh back to Arrowhead?" he asked.

"No," George said. "We're not goin' back to Arrowhead, and we're not goin' through Blue Rock. We're movin' to new country."

"New country, Cap'n?" I asked.

He nodded. "I've sold the old place to a cow man from Blue Rock. Bought me a new spread next to Slippery's place, out of Wolf City."

George's announcement caught me off guard. I had no time to put on my poker face, and I reckon I must have shown my surprise. George was watching me intently. Beneath the shadow of his hat brim, his hard yellow eyes seemed to glow. A slight smile played at the corners of his mouth. I glanced at Pronto and was relieved to see he looked as dumbfounded as I felt.

Pronto frowned. "We—we ain't goin' back to Arrow-head?" he asked.

"No, we ain't," George said. "We're goin' straight to the new spread. I never have liked to stay too long at any one place."

Including territorial prison, I thought. *You're a clever old fox, George Starkweather.* What I said was, "What about our gatherin's, Cap'n? I still have some clothes and my bedroll at the bunkhouse."

"I left Wang Lee and Old Toni to gather up our personals," he said. "They'll haul them out by bobsled and meet us at the new place."

My assignment slipped through my fingers like sand. The letter I'd sent Ridgeway told him he could find George and his men at Arrowhead ranch. If he led a posse there now, he'd be too late. Once again, an assignment that seemed simple and clear in the telling turned out to be complicated and muddy in the doing.

"I sold the cattle with the ranch," George said, "whatever is left of them come spring. Didn't tell the buyer where I was goin'. None of his damned business."

Across the room, Abigail reigned at the supper table like a queen. Far as I could tell, she neither put on airs nor resorted to her feminine wiles, but every man at the table tried to outdo the others in attending to her needs. It was almost comical. No sooner did she take a dainty sip from her cup than the Chinese cook scurried over with the coffeepot to fill it up again. Wilbur and the other stable hand stared at her like they'd been hypnotized, and Finley sucked in his belly and plied her with flattery.

She answered each effort with a sweet smile and a grateful glance, but her eyes kept turning to where George stood talking to Pronto and me. At length she caught his eye, and George ended our conversation. He strode over to the table and pulled out her chair as she stood. "We're obliged for your hospitality," George said, "but my daughter has had a long and tryin' day."

"Yes," she said. "I feel suddenly quite fatigued. If someone would be kind enough to show me to my room—"

Finley like to have broke a leg, jumping up from the bench where he sat. "Why, of course, Miss Abigail," he said. "Please, follow me."

George offered his arm, and Miss Abigail took it. Together, they followed the station keeper down the hallway. Just as she passed Pronto and me, she looked into my eyes and smiled. No doubt about it. There was power in that smile.

CHAPTER 13

A New Ranch and Some Old Business

Morning broke clear and cloudless over Sand Coulee station and found me ready to ride. After breakfast in the station's kitchen, I walked with Pronto down to the barn where we saddled our horses. By the time we led them out into the sunshine, Wilbur the stable hand had hitched a handsome pair of Morgans to the sleigh. He grinned at us, nodding toward the horses.

"That's a good team," he said. "The mare's name is Delilah and the geldin' is—"

"Samson," I guessed. "And next you're gonna tell me that horse wasn't a geldin' till he teamed up with Delilah."

Wilbur grinned. "Well, that's the way the story goes, ain't it?"

With a shake of the reins, he drove the sleigh out over the drifted snow toward the station, and Pronto and I rode alongside.

George and his pretty newfound daughter were waiting at the door as we rode up. Abigail had on the fur-trimmed jacket and hat she'd worn during the holdup. A woolen scarf covered her ears and throat, and her small hands were nestled inside a fur muff. She looked rested and eager and gave no sign of the misfortunes she'd endured yesterday.

Wilbur stepped out of the sleigh, loaded Abigail's trunk and traveling bag in back, and George took the reins. When Abigail had settled herself and had the lap robe close about her, George gave the horses their heads, and we struck out over the hard-packed snow on the road to Wolf City.

Pronto and me rode along behind the sleigh, Pronto leading George's horse. We had nothing to say to each other, which suited me just fine. George's leaving Arrowhead ranch for a new spread, and Abigail's arrival, made me take a hard look at my plans. He'd dealt me new cards, and I needed to think how best to play them.

We crossed Sand Coulee, headed north. The road showed signs of travel both by wagon and by sled, and the rutted thoroughfare was rough and broken from the melting and refreezing of the snow. About mid-morning, we came to a fork in the road, and George turned the sleigh off onto a trail that led west toward the distant blue mass of the Beartooths.

"Wolf City's ten miles north of here," he said, "but we're not goin' there just now. The way to the ranch lies due west. We'll make it in another hour."

We passed over ice-covered O'Hara Creek and the Clark's Fork River, and at length turned up a long slope and out onto a wooded ridge. George drew rein, allowing the team to rest, and pointed to the valley below.

There in the distance, along a narrow creek marked by aspen trees and stands of willow, stood the corrals and outbuildings of a cattle ranch. A thin thread of wood smoke spiraled up from a stone chimney at the center of a rambling ranch house. In a pasture beyond the buildings, horses watched our approach.

Abigail shaded her eyes, looking at the scene below. "Oh," she said. "Is that your ranch, Father?"

George nodded. "That's our *home,* Abigail."

Starting the team again, George turned the sleigh downhill into the valley.

It was Slippery Mayfair himself who welcomed us to George's new spread. The fat man appeared in the front door of the ranch house and stood squinting in the sunshine. He wore a long black overcoat and a slouch hat, and he looked every inch the prosperous banker. His own open sleigh, a Portland cutter, was parked nearby.

"Good afternoon," he said in that formal manner of his. "I've been expecting you."

George stepped out of the sleigh, extending his hand to Abigail. "We made good time," he said. "Abigail, this is my friend and business associate, Obadiah Mayfair. Obadiah—my daughter, Abigail."

I don't believe George had ever called Slippery by his proper name before, but if it surprised the old scoundrel, he didn't show it. Bowing slightly, he doffed his hat and lowered his eyes. "Delighted to meet you, Miss Abigail," he said. "I trust you had a pleasant journey."

"Not as pleasant as I might have hoped," Abigail said. "I'm afraid my father and these gentlemen had to rescue me from a rather distressing situation. But I'm sure Father will tell you all about that in due time. I'm pleased to meet you as well, Mr. Mayfair."

Abigail let George help her from the sleigh. The chill air had colored her cheeks and the tip of her nose a rosy red. Strands of her auburn hair had crept from beneath her scarf, glowing like copper in the sunlight. As she stepped down, she smiled, and the hope I saw in her eyes suddenly troubled me.

I was thinking, *Your father is a thief and a killer. Not a blessed one of us is who you think he is. If you knew the truth about this outfit, you'd go back to where you came from fast as ever you could. You shall know the truth, says the Good Book, and the truth will make you free. Well, I reckon that's true, but sometimes it'll also break your heart.*

I guess I was lost in my thoughts, because I suddenly realized George was talking to me. Flustered, I turned to face him. "Uh, what were you sayin', Cap'n?"

Abigail had stepped up onto the gallery, and Slippery was escorting her inside. George stood beside the sleigh looking up at me. "I *asked* you to bring Miss Abigail's trunk and traveling bag inside. You want to stop wool gatherin' and take care of that, Bodacious?"

I stepped down from my horse. "Sure, Cap'n," I said. "Right away."

George turned to Pronto. "Take the horses over to the barn yonder. Cool 'em out and give 'em each a flake of hay and some oats. I'll talk to you boys later on."

Pronto nodded. Leading George's horse and mine, he rode away toward the barn.

When I carried Abigail's trunk and traveling bag inside, I saw that the furnishings from Arrowhead were all in place at the new house. Navajo rugs gave color to the puncheon floors. George's easy chairs were grouped before the fireplace. His books were arrayed on shelves and atop the mantel. Even the piano he had bought for Abigail had been hauled down and now stood beside the big windows at the far side of the room. Its polished wood gleamed in the afternoon light.

George took my arm and pointed me down a long hallway that led off the big room. "Abigail's room is two doors down," he said. "Take her things in there."

Abigail's room turned out to be a pleasant bed-chamber on the south side of the house. Its pale yellow wallpaper was printed with blue morning glories. Sunbeams slanted in through the room's one window, and a new brass bed piled high with pillows stood alongside an oak table that held a painted vase lamp. A dresser, washstand, bowl and pitcher, a small heating stove, and a large oak wardrobe completed the furnishings. A braided rug in shades of blue lay on the floor beside the bed. George had done his very best to provide a pretty room for his daughter.

Back in the main room, Abigail sat near the fireplace with George and Slippery Mayfair—drinking tea, of all things, porcelain cups held by thumb and forefinger with the pinky finger up. Wang Lee, who was pouring, glanced up at me with hooded eyes, then returned to his tea service.

"Wang Lee tells me there's coffee in the cook shack," George said. "Help yourself. I'll be along d'rectly."

I had just poured myself a cup of Wang Lee's strong coffee when the door of the cook shack opened and Tom Blackburn walked in. When he saw me, he grinned, and his face lit up like a Mexican dance hall. "Well, howdy, Kid," he said. "It's good to see you!"

I gave him his grin back. "It's good to be *seen*," I said. "How you doin', Tom?"

"Better, now that you're back. Ain't had nobody to talk to but the Chinee cook, and he mostly saves his breath for breathin.' "

I took a sip of my coffee. "Looks like you and Wang Lee have been busy," I said. "You pack out everything from Arrowhead by yourselves?"

"Packed out the grub and fixin's from the old cook shack and bunkhouse. Slippery Mayfair's men took out the rest. His riders even brought the horses down."

I nodded. "I thought I recognized some of our ponies out yonder. Saw my Roanie horse for certain."

Tom nodded. "I made sure they brought him, Kid. I know you set a heap of store by that big geldin'."

"Obliged, Tom."

Tom fell silent then. He walked over to the cook shack window and stood there looking out at the snow-covered hills. I knew Tom well enough to know he had something on his mind, and I waited for him to unload it.

After a long pause, he said, "I was the last man to leave Arrowhead, Kid. But I had visitors just before I pulled out. Crazy Ike came by with Haynes and Morris. Said they'd held up the Blue Rock stage, but the robbery hadn't panned out."

"That's a fact," I said. "The coach wasn't carryin' a strongbox after all. Driver said he told the boys that, but they shot him anyway. The team spooked and ran, piled up in a washout and upset the coach.

"Trouble is, the coach had a passenger—Miss Abigail, George's daughter. She wasn't hurt, but she might have been. She's over at the house now."

Tom frowned. "It's a good thing Ike ran into me instead of George. The Chief might have took things personal."

George's voice came from behind me. "What is it I might have took personal?"

I turned. George stood in the doorway. He stepped inside and closed the door behind him. He nodded at the coffeepot. "Pour me a cup of that mud, Bodacious. Wang Lee's tea is a little short on body."

I filled a crockery mug and passed it to George. He bowed his head, sipped, and drank deeply. "More like it," he said. Lifting his head, he fixed Tom with his cold stare.

"I'm waitin', Tom," he said softly.

"Uh, I was just tellin' the Kid, Chief, seen Ike Mullins up at the old place day before yesterday. Haynes and Morris were with him. Ike said they tried to hold up the Blue Rock stage, but it went bad."

George's voice was calm, controlled. "You figured I might take the holdup personal?"

"Well, I—that is, I know you don't like the boys to go off on their own without your say-so, Chief. That's all I meant."

"That's true. But it ain't personal. It's more like . . . a *policy* matter."

George drained his cup and set it carefully down on the table. Then he lifted his gaze to Toni again. "Those boys didn't happen to say where they're camped, did they?"

Tom was sweating now. He couldn't meet George's eyes. "Uh . . . well . . . yes. Seems like they did. Ike kind of mentioned they were holed up in that old trapper's cabin down on Arrowhead Creek."

George reached out and gripped Tom's shoulder. He looked for all the world like a man praising his dog. "I appreciate you tellin' me," he said. "Means a lot to know I can depend on you."

He stopped beside the stove and tapped the wood box with the toe of his boot. "Bring in a little stove wood, will you, Tom? Wang Lee's gonna need it to cook supper."

Toni nearly raced to the door. "You bet," he said. And then he was gone, the door closing behind him. *Good dog,* I thought.

George turned to me. "I'll be ridin' out with Pronto this evenin'. I expect we'll be gone for a day or two," he said.

"You're goin' after Ike and the boys," I said. It was not a question. George nodded. "Sometimes a man has to take measures."

"Are you 'taking' measures' because those boys went off on their own? Or because they put Abigail in danger?"

George's eyes seemed to glow. When he spoke again his voice was soft but laced with menace. "You're walkin' on thin ice, Bodacious. Be careful, son."

I heard the threat behind the words, but I was nobody's dog. "Tom was right, Cap'n," I said. "You're takin' that botched holdup personal. Those boys didn't know your daughter was on that stage."

"If they'd cleared the job with me, they would have."

"She wasn't hurt."

"She could have been."

We stared at each other across the table. Outside, the wind had picked up. Gusts moaned lonesome against the cook shack and swept away over the snow. George wore a wild-eyed look that told me further talk would do no good.

I shrugged. "All right," I said. "What do you want me to do?"

"Look after Abigail while I'm away. Show her around the place. There's a ladies' sidesaddle in the barn. If she can sit a horse, take her ridin'. Hell, I don't know—*talk* to her some! You *can* talk to a girl, can't you?"

George was nervous! It occurred to me I had never seen him nervous before—about anything. I couldn't help it. The idea of George Starkweather being fidgety because of a young female made me smile. Seeing my smile, George smiled, too, and the tension between us passed.

"Yeah," I said. "I guess I can talk to a girl."

"I'm obliged, son. Take supper with us up at the house this evenin'. Pronto and me will be ridin' out afterward."

"I will. Right now I'm goin' to settle in over at the bunkhouse. I'll shave and see if I can find a clean shirt. I've noticed talkin' with girls goes better when a feller's clean."

We sat together that evening at the big oak table in the main house—George, Slippery Mayfair, Abigail, and me—over coffee and a dessert of Brown Betty pudding. Wang Lee had cooked up a boiled dinner of corned beef, potatoes, turnips, and squash, and he had done a first-class job.

Talk ran easy there in the candlelight, with Slippery holding forth on western life in that ponderous, solemn manner of his, and Abigail asking questions and marveling at the answers. I did my best to entertain her with tales of hunting mustangs as a youngster and working as horse wrangler on the roundup. George said little, but his eyes spoke for him—he looked at Abigail with open admiration.

There were times that night when he seemed distant, as if he was thinking of something else. I knew what that something else was. His thoughts were fixed on three desperados in a cabin over on Arrowhead Creek and on his own stern code.

Abigail stifled a yawn as the cabinet clock atop the mantel struck nine. She smiled shyly and placed her napkin on the table beside her plate. "It has been a long and exciting day," she said, "but I fear the fresh air and fine supper have made me sleepy. If you gentlemen will excuse me . . ."

George pushed back his chair and stood up. "Why, of course, child," he said. "Go to your room, by all means. The truth is, I've got to leave, too—overnight business trip. Pronto and me will be ridin' out d'rectly.

Mr. Mayfair will be here while I'm gone, and Wang Lee'll be at your beck and call."

George gestured at me. "And Merlin will be makin' an inspection tour of the ranch tomorrow. You may wish to accompany him, if the weather permits."

Her blue eyes met mine and she favored me with her bright smile. "Why, yes," she said. "That might be very nice."

"Good night, gentlemen," she said. "Thank you for a lovely evening." With Wang Lee carrying a lamp to light their way, Abigail walked up the hallway to her room.

Outside, the wind had died down. The sky was a scatteration of stars, cold fire lighting the heavens. Across the way, a lantern glowed orange in the bunkhouse window. I turned up the collar of my sheepskin, stepped off the porch of the ranch house, and made my way through the drifted snow toward the light.

Warm air met me as I stepped inside. The bunkhouse was laid out like most, built of logs and made up of a single room with double-decker bunks for eight men. Like the bunkhouse at Arrowhead, it was heated by a rusted woodstove that popped and pinged as it turned wood into warmth. I recognized my bedroll on a bunk near the back wall and figured Old Tom had laid it out for me. I crossed the room and sat down on the bunk.

Old Tom, the room's only occupant, lay sound asleep and snoring in a bunk near the window. He was a loyal follower of George Starkweather, faithful as a hound but long past his prime, a young outlaw turned old. I hoped he was young again in his dreams.

At the sound of hooves breaking crusted snow, loud in the stillness, I went to the window and saw Pronto ride up to the house across the way, leading the horse George called High Pockets. The front door opened and George stepped out dressed in his buffalo coat and a sealskin cap. Starlight glinted on the barrel of the short-barreled shotgun he carried. He mounted High Pockets, settled himself, and the two men rode away into the night.

I added wood to the stove and turned down the damper. Then I blew the lantern out and slid between the soogans. I lay there in darkness, reflecting on the events of the past few days. I needed to work out a plan of action, but my mind was in no mood to cooperate.

Instead, my thoughts went to a girl with eyes of corn-flower blue and a smile that could brighten the darkest day. I found myself anticipating the coming day and our tour of the ranch together, and so I drifted off to sleep with Abigail on my mind.

Beyond the bunkhouse window, daybreak dawned clear and still with cloudless skies stained red above the ridges. The fire in the woodstove had long since burned itself out, and the room was cold as a hangman's heart. I turned my bed tarp down and watched my breath turn to vapor in the chill air.

Across the room, Old Toni huddled deep in his blankets. His snoring had ceased, and I assumed he was still asleep. However, it might not be safe to make such an assumption about a feller his age, so I called out to make sure. "Mornin', Tom," I said. "Rise and shine, pardner."

The canvas mound moved. "Rise and shine your own self, Kid," Tom mumbled. "I ain't leavin' these blankets till spring."

Somewhere nearby a rooster crowed. "Hear that?" I asked. "I thought George was buyin' a cow outfit. Sounds more like he bought a chicken farm."

The bed tarp moved again, and Tom's balding head appeared. "Slippery brought them chickens over. Wang Lee told George he wanted 'em."

I put my hat on and sat up. "That's good. Now we'll have eggs for breakfast, maybe chicken an' dumplin's sometimes. And with that rooster on the job we won't need the alarm clock."

"If that cocky-doodle sum'bitch wakes me up once too often, he'll *be* chicken an' dumplin's," Tom grumbled.

I wasted no time getting dressed. My boots were cold and stiff as boards. I knew they wouldn't limber up until they borrowed some warmth from me. Tom commenced to get dressed, too, shivering like a wet pup. I was about to open the door and head over to the cook shack when I heard him clear his throat serious-like and say, "Kid."

Something in the tone of his voice made me take a closer look. Tom sat at the edge of his bunk, staring at his hands. When he met my gaze, I saw worry in his eyes.

"You reckon George aims to *kill* Ike and the boys?"

"I don't know, Tom. That might be his intent."

Tom stared at his hands again. "Damn, Kid! I feel like I helped bring killin' on those boys. It was me told George where they're holed up."

"Go easy on yourself. You only answered George's question. You can't help what he does with what you told him."

"Maybe not. But still, it seems like my tellin' makes me part of whatever happens. I don't feel good about it."

I opened the bunkhouse door. "Let it go. Let's have some breakfast."

Slowly, Tom got to his feet, shrugged into his coat, and moved toward the open door, but his face still held its troubled look.

"Damnedest thing," he said, "I was hungry when I first woke up, but somehow I ain't any more."

Wang Lee met us at the cook shack door, scolding us in what I took to be a mix of English and Chinese, and handed us a broom to sweep the snow off our boots. Once we'd broomed ourselves to his satisfaction, he let us inside, and Tom and me sat down to a hearty meal of pork sausage, biscuits, and gravy.

If, as George said, Wang Lee's tea was a mite short on body, his coffee was not. I drank two cups of that hearty brew during breakfast and a third cup afterward. Tom said little and barely picked at his food, still brooding about telling George where Ike, Haynes, and Morris were camped.

After breakfast, I left Tom to his chores and walked over to the ranch house. Slippery Mayfair answered the door.

"Good morning, Bodacious," he said. "Miss Abigail is expecting you. Come in, please."

Wang Lee's earlier scolding had its effect. I stomped the snow off my boots and stepped inside. As I did, Abigail came out of the kitchen, pretty as a sunrise.

She wore a high-necked white shirtwaist and the black woolen skirt I'd seen at the stage wreck. Her hair was pulled back into a bun and tied with a blue ribbon. She smiled when she saw me, and I felt my face grow warm.

"Good morning, Merlin," she said. "I've been waiting for you."

Too late, I remembered to remove my hat. I snatched it off and held it with both hands before me. "Uh, good mornin', Miss Abigail," I said. "Like your daddy said last evenin', I'm ridin' out to look the ranch over today. You said you might like to come along."

"Yes," she said. "I *would* like to, if it wouldn't be a bother."

I grinned. "No bother at all. I'd be plumb tickled to have you."

Her laugh was my reward.

"Do you ride?" I asked. "If not, we can take the sleigh."

"Actually, I do ride a little. I used to ride sometimes back in Kansas City."

"Then we'll ride," I said. "Your daddy tells me there's a ladies' sidesaddle in the barn—I'll saddle our horses and meet you back here."

Abigail touched my arm. Her eyes were wide, earnest. "Please," she said. "Mayn't I go to the barn with you? I'd love to meet the animal I'll be riding."

"Why, sure," I said. "That's a good idea, Miss Abigail."

She placed her small fists on her hips and scolded, "I do have one request. You must stop calling me Miss Abigail. I'm sure you and I shall be friends, and my friends call me Abby."

"It's a deal," I said. "Let's take us a ride . . . Abby."

CHAPTER 14
Lunch at the Al Fresco Café

I ran the horses into the big corral and put a loop on Roanie. The gelding hadn't put on any fat since I'd left him, but he seemed none the worse for our time apart. Abby watched as I combed and saddled him, and I have to admit I showed off a little when I swung up and rode him back through the remuda.

I had my eye on a *dilsey*—a small bay saddle mare I figured would make a good mount for Abby. I'd seen the animal up at the Arrowhead and figured her for a rocking-chair horse, smooth gaited and sensible. When I found her, I dabbed my rope on her with a hoolihan throw and led her back to where Abby waited.

"She's beautiful," Abby said. Her face fairly glowed. "What's her name?"

I grinned. "I don't think she has one," I said. "I reckon you get to name her."

Abby looked thoughtful as I bridled and combed the mare. "She's smaller than most of the other horses," she said, "and she has a prim and proper look about her. I think I'll call her 'Little Miss.'"

I found the sidesaddle in the barn. I was no expert on the sidesaddle, but no respectable eastern lady in those days would ride any other way. When I worked at Walt's Livery back in Dry Creek, it had been part of my job to saddle horses for the female customers, and I'd learned how best to fit the rigs for the comfort of both mount and rider. I drew the cinch up snug, but not tight, and led the mare out through the gate to Abby.

Slippery Mayfair had drawn a rough map of the ranch, and Wang Lee had provided us a lunch wrapped in a flour sack. Carefully, I placed the lunch in my saddlebags and tucked the map away in the pocket of my sheepskin. I helped Abby into the saddle, untracked the mare to be sure there was no buck in her, and stepped up onto Roanie.

The ranch had three good-sized pastures, all three fenced so that a man could bring his stock in off the range and feed them during the winter. There were a couple of haystacks, also fenced, and it occurred to me that the former owner—and now George—was better off than most of the cowmen in that country. Ranchers turned their stock out on the open range after calving and gathered them in the fall. Hardly anyone bothered to put up hay, figuring that losing stock to winter kill was just a normal part of doing business. The trouble was that the winter of 1886 was far from normal.

We left the hay meadows and turned our horses uphill. The skies were cloudless, brilliant blue above the drifted coulees and draws, and the sun's bright reflection was hard on the eyes. Riding the ridges made for easier traveling and offered a good view of the valley, but the wind was bitter and caused us to huddle deeper within our clothing.

Abby seemed to be experienced at riding aside, and she sat squarely with her hips lined up with the mare's hips and shoulders. As for the mare, the animal proved to be bridle wise and moved easily to the touch of the reins upon her neck.

"You ride well, Abby," I told her. "You must have had plenty of practice back there in Kansas City."

"Mostly bridle paths in the city parks, I'm afraid," she said. "But I enjoy riding. I took lessons at a stable there."

We rode together in silence for a time. Above the valley floor, the wind whipped the naked hilltops and raised welts on the morning. Abigail rode up beside me and spoke again. Raising her voice so as to be heard, she said, "The land seems so open—and barren. Does the wind always blow like this?"

"Pretty much," I said. "As for the land, you're not seein' it at its best. When winter ends, this whole country comes alive. There are springs and creeks, birds and flowers, and a sea of grass from here to tomorrow."

She looked out across the range, her eyes squinted against the brightness. She was trying to imagine the green, rolling grassland and the warmth of a spring day, I suppose.

"It all seems so lonely—so *empty*," she said.

"Only seems that way," I said, drawing rein. I pointed at the sky above us where a red-tailed hawk circled slowly on the rising currents. "That hawk's huntin' his dinner," I said. "And notice the tracks in the snow as we ride; mule deer in those brushy draws, white-tailed deer in the bottoms. Down in the valley yonder, there's a pair of coyotes on the prowl for field mice. This country's full of life, even in winter."

I took my field glasses from my saddlebags and handed them to Abby. Below, on the valley floor, the coyotes trotted across a broad, sagebrush-studded flat, one ahead of the other. They moved easily, bushy tails almost horizontal behind them. Their heads were held low, their eyes on the crusted snow.

As Abby watched through the glasses, the lead coyote checked its pace and leaped high into the air. A mouse broke from cover and scurried past and behind the coyote, dashing for safety. Waiting and alert, the second coyote snatched up the mouse in midflight and consumed it. Scarcely pausing, the coyotes resumed their hunt.

Twice more on their journey across the flat, the coy-otes repeated the performance and then changed places. The lead coyote who had flushed the mice became the catcher, and its partner took the lead.

Abby lowered the field glasses, her eyes still on the scene below. "I see what you mean," she said. "The country is full of life. And speaking for the field mice, also full of *death.*"

There was a hint of mockery in her smile as she handed the glasses back to me, but I took it in stride. "Life and death," I said. "The way of the world."

We continued to ride the hilltops in silence. I had seen no livestock throughout the morning. For all my talk about the valley being full of life, only the coyotes and the lone red-tailed hawk seemed to share the vast open country with us. Abby huddled within her coat, her head lowered into the wind. The gusts grew stronger, icy blasts determined to find a way through our defenses.

Overhead, the sun reached its high point and turned toward sundown. I signaled to Abby, pointed to the lee side of the hill, and turned Roanie off the ridge. Abby smiled a quick smile of gratitude and followed.

Carefully, the horses picked their way down along a well-worn cattle trail, plodding through crusted snow and ice. Minutes later, we broke out onto the valley floor, and I led the way across a broad meadow toward an aspen grove. Below the trees, a narrow stream meandered across the meadow, its few patches of open water nearly black against the bright snow. Reaching the grove, I drew rein and stepped down.

I spoke to Abby. "Thought we'd have lunch here," I

said. "I'll build a fire, and we can thaw out some."

Abby nodded, and I took the reins of her mare while she dismounted. "Stamp your feet," I said. "Move around some. It'll warm you."

I tied the horses to a bush and gathered dry branches from the grove. Abby seated herself upon a log, watching as I laid out the wood and lit a fire. Once I had a blaze well started, I turned back to her. She was watching me, curiosity in her bright blue eyes.

"How long have you known my father?" she asked.

It took me a moment to frame my answer. "I met him four years ago," I said. "Rode with him for a time in the fall of '82." I lowered my eyes and turned back to tending the fire. "He . . . moved away . . . for a while after that. I worked at other jobs here and there, then hired on with him again."

"He seems to think highly of you."

"I've learned a lot from him."

Abby held her feet out toward the fire, looking into the flames. "I know so little about him," she said. "Only his name—George Shannon—and that he is a cattleman. He seems to have led a hard life."

"He . . . has always been a leader of men," I said. "Makin' a business succeed can be hard."

"Yes. But now, it seems, he has. This new ranch—"

"Yes," I said, "and your visit. He sure has looked forward to meetin' you, gettin' to know you."

"I look forward to that, too," Abby said. "I'm sorry he had to be away on my first day here."

"I expect he'll be back this evenin'," I said. "What

do you say we see what Wang Lee packed for our picnic?"

Abby smiled. "Yes," she said. "Let's."

Taking the bundle from my saddlebags, I opened it and spread its contents on the log beside Abby. At first glance, it seemed that old Tom's early morning threat against the ranch rooster had become fact—our lunch was chicken fixins and corn dodgers with pan dowdy for dessert. I boiled coffee in a can over the fire, and Abby and me fell to eating and drinking with appetites made greater by the morning's ride.

I was relieved. For a while at least, Abby asked no more questions about George—or me. Instead, she praised the food and joked about the fine restaurant we had found in the aspen grove. She said its name was the Al Fresco Café, and I didn't understand her jest until she told me *alfresco* was an Italian word for dining in the out-of-doors. She was full of compliments for Wang Lee's cooking, and I agreed with her. For an ex-convict who, according to George, had poisoned at least one of his former employers, Wang Lee was a first class bean master.

When we had eaten our fill, I wrapped the remnants in the flour sack and returned them to my saddlebags. Abby scattered a handful of crumbs over the snow—"for the mice," she said—and I kicked snow onto the embers of our fire. I had to smile. Abby seemed to root for the underdog—or undermouse, in this case. Seeing those coyotes hunting mice out on the flat had made quite an impression on her. "Mice are such helpless little creatures," she said. "Somebody needs to take their side."

"Maybe so," I said, "but it seems like their purpose in life is mostly to be food. They're a mainstay of hawks, eagles, bobcats, snakes, owls, and coyotes— just to name a few."

"All the more reason to give them their due," Abby said.

We watered our horses at an open place in the stream and turned the animals toward home. I led the way with Abby following. Because the snow was deep and crusted on the flat, we took to the hilltops again and found the wind there had not abated. Gusts swept the snow from the drifts along the ridges and moaned through the sagebrush like a sad song played on a violin.

I don't know whether it was the mournful sound of the wind or simply that it was hard for us to hear each other, but Abby and me didn't talk much on the way back. Instead, we faced into the gale, occupied with our thoughts, and allowed the horses to just carry us along.

I smiled, remembering Abby's sympathy for field mice. Somehow, it put me in mind of my boss, U.S. Marshal Chance Ridgeway. Four years before at his office in Silver City, the marshal had explained his passion for the law to me. He had done so with a story from his childhood.

He said he had grown up on a Kansas homestead

with his folks. Their house was sod, and the highest point for miles around in the flat, open prairie. The family was poor as Job's turkey, he said, but they had one special possession—a young cottonwood tree nearly eight feet tall. It was Ridgeway's job as a shirt-tail kid to water that tree.

One spring, when he was about nine, a pair of robins built a nest in the little cottonwood, and the mother robin laid her eggs. Because the tree was little more than a sapling, the nest was pretty close to the ground, but it seemed to suit the robins. Besides, it was the only tree around.

Ridgeway said he was excited as a pup in a butcher shop as he waited for the baby robins to hatch. He carried water to the tree every day and checked on the nest every chance he got.

Then one day, he heard an awful commotion coming from the direction of the tree. The robins were fluttering around, chirping and chattering and throwing a regular conniption fit. Ridgeway said he came running from around back of the soddy to see what all the fuss was about and discovered the source of the uproar. A big bull snake had crawled up the trunk of the little cottonwood and was eating the robins' eggs.

Ridgeway said the sight plumb outraged him. He took hold of the snake and tried to pull it away from the tree, but it was wrapped tight, and he couldn't budge it. He ran to the house, took down his pa's shotgun and rushed back outside.

"Them eggs were that snake's last meal," Ridgeway

told me. "My first shot blowed him out of the tree, and the second killed him as dead as a snake ever gets."

His pa scolded him. He said bull snakes were a farmer's friends, and that the snake was only doing what came natural. But Ridgeway didn't care about that. His only regret was that he'd been too late to save the eggs.

"From that day to this," he told me, "I have made it my life's work to keep the snakes from doin' harm to the robins. I still see things in terms of right and wrong, of good and evil, and I *never* cut evildoers any slack."

That was Ridgeway all right. Marshal Chance Ridgeway—my boss, my teacher, and my guide for as long as I'd known him. He was a man who never wavered in the performance of his duty. He suffered no doubts regarding evildoers. A lawbreaker was a lawbreaker; never mind his reasons. Never mind that Starkweather seemed now to want to change, to live out his days as an honest rancher and a family man.

George Starkweather was an escaped convict, a thief, and a murderer. He was a wanted man who stole cattle and horses from honest men. He had robbed banks in Dry Creek and Blue Rock—and was responsible for the killing of bank tellers in both towns. It was my job to bring him and the men who followed him to justice. I knew that Ridgeway's way was the right way. More than that, I knew it needed to be *my* way. And yet . . .

Why did I waver when I thought about dealing with George? I knew the man for what he was, and still my feelings betrayed me. Some part of me wanted his approval. I had felt pride when he told Abby I was his right-hand man. I was grateful to the man. Twice since I left Dry Creek, he had saved my life. In spite of all his crimes and treacheries, God help me, I *liked* him. What was wrong with me?

Damn it! I would do what I came to do. Somehow I would bring George in. I would deliver him, Pronto Southwell, and Old Tom to a court of law and let a judge and jury decide their fate. I would do it in spite of my feelings and my failings. I *would* do my duty!

This argument with myself took place entirely within my mind, of course. But somehow—maybe in the way I held the bridle reins—I must have communicated my peevishness to Roanie. He tossed his head, broke his stride, and cast a baleful glance back in my direction. I could almost hear him say, "Hey, watch it! You jerked the reins, and the bridle bit hurt my mouth! What is the matter with you?"

The wind was blowing too hard for Abby to hear me, and she wouldn't have understood if she had, but I apologized to the big horse then and there. "Sorry, Roanie," I said. "As for what's the matter with me, I was just wonderin' that myself."

As we came in sight of the ranch buildings, I saw George's horse standing alone in the round corral. The long-legged Morgan raised his head and nickered at our approach, and I saw the animal had been ridden hard since I'd seen him last. His hair was matted by sweat where the saddle had been, and there were fresh spur tracks on his flanks.

Pronto stepped out of the barn as we passed by, his face hard as flint. Abby smiled at him and raised her hand in greeting. Pronto didn't return her smile. He nodded, touching his hat brim, turned, and went back inside the barn.

"Daddy must have returned from his business trip," Abby said. "Didn't he say Pronto was going with him?"

"I believe so," I said. "Let's ride over to the house. I'll take your horse back to the barn afterward."

We drew rein at the steps that led to the open porch of the ranch house. I noticed that Slippery Mayfair's sleigh was no longer parked out in front, and I guessed that he'd returned to his own ranch or to the bank in Wolf City.

Dismounting, I turned to help Abby down. "Thank you for a wonderful day," she said. "I especially enjoyed our lunch at the Al Fresco Café."

I grinned. "It's a good restaurant," I said, "but it does seem the management might have turned up the heat a little."

Abby's smile was warm. "Perhaps they will have the boiler repaired by the time we visit there next time."

The front door swung in, and George stepped outside. He looked haggard and wind-burned, but his eyes glowed as he looked at Abby. "Appears you enjoyed your tour of the ranch," he said. "What do you think of our spread, girl?"

"It seems enormous," she said, "and a little bleak this time of year. But Merlin assures me it will be alive with green grass and wildflowers when spring comes."

"We didn't cover it all, Cap'n," I said, "but from what I saw, I'd say you've bought yourself a handsome spread."

"I appreciate you showin' the place to Abby," he said. He offered her his hand as she stepped up onto the porch. "Come on inside and tell me all about your day, darlin.'"

Riding Roanie and leading the bay, I returned to the barn. Pronto stood just outside the open doors, watching me through hooded eyes as I drew near. He leaned against the building, a half-empty whiskey bottle in his hand, and his lip curled in a sneer that told me his opinion of me hadn't changed all that much.

I dismounted and opened the corral gate. Pronto took a step toward me, swayed, and slumped back against the wall. I could see he was more than a little drunk, and I knew that made him even more dangerous than usual.

"So," he said. "The boss finally found somethin' you can do—play nursemaid to young girls."

He raised the bottle and drank. Wiping his mouth with his sleeve, he grimaced. His face was flushed, and his eyes held a wild and haunted look. "Tha's all right, little Mary," he said, slurring his words, "Don't matter a damn if you ain't got the balls for men's work. The boss and me'll take care of it."

I ignored his taunting. "Did you find Ike and the boys?" I asked.

A spasm passed over Pronto's features. His face seemed suddenly drained of color. "Oh, yeah," he said. "We found 'em. My god, we *found* 'em, all right!"

Pronto stared vacantly into space, remembering. When he spoke again his voice was hushed. I had the impression he was no longer talking to me, that he had forgotten I was even there.

"We got to the cabin just after sundown. There was smoke from the chimney, a light in the window. Crazy Ike came out to meet us. He looked nervous. Behind him, so did Haynes and Morris. Guess they weren't sure how George might feel about them goin' out on their own.

"Turns out the way George felt was *bloody*. The boss never said a word. Just walked straight up to Ike and shot him in the chest! Haynes and Morris were plum' surprised. They fell all over themselves, tried to pull their guns, but they were too late. I dropped both of those boys where they stood, gunned 'em to doll rags.

Pronto slumped down on a straw bale, bottle still in his hand, a great weariness in his face.

"Dragged the boys back inside," he went on. "Boss found coal oil and splashed it around—on the beds, the table, and on the boys. Haynes was already dead as yesterday's hash. But—my god!—Ike and Morris were still alive.

"Before I knew it, the cabin was afire, and we went

outside and watched 'er burn, Ike and Morris screamin' all the while."

Pronto closed his eyes, hunched his shoulders, and shivered. "I can hear 'em yet, and I can still see a burnin' man crawl out through the doorway. It was Ike. Poor bastard was plumb wild! He rolled in the snow, tryin' to put the fire out, but he was still smokin' and still screamin'."

Pronto raised his bloodshot eyes to me.

"Would you believe it? The boss walked over to him—I thought he was goin' to put him out of his misery—but he never. He put him into his misery. Took hold of Ike's collar and dragged him back to the cabin, flung him inside, and shut the door! He done it in a hurry, for it was a blast furnace by then, an' the heat made us back away. Loud as the fire was, I could still hear the boys yellin'—leastways, I thought I could.'"

I'm not certain, but looking at Pronto as he talked, I thought I saw a bitter tear on that hard man's cheek.

"Then, after a while, I couldn't hear 'em any more. All I could hear was the roar of the fire and the cabin fallin' in on itself."

Pronto fell silent then, his eyes wide and staring now. He seemed to remember I was there, and turned to look at me like a man coming out of a dream. "Yeah," he said. "We found 'em all right."

Pronto's hand shook as he raised the bottle and drank the last of the whiskey. "Now get the hell away from me," he said, "before I 'find' you, too."

Stepping unsteadily away from the barn, he threw the empty bottle far out toward the willows that lined the creek and pulled his gun in a blur of speed. His shot echoed across the flat, but the bottle fell unbroken to bounce and slide on the crusted snow.

Strange as it sounds—and even now, I don't know why I did it; rage I guess—I drew my .44 and fired. The bottle that a split second ago was still sliding fifty feet away, shattered in an explosion of glass.

"Is that what you were tryin' to do?" I asked.

Pronto jerked unsteadily to face me, gun still in his hand, eyes wide.

I was feeling wrathy, tired of his bull, furious over the cold-blooded killing of Ike and the boys.

"Put that pistol away or use it," I said. "I've had a belly full of your sass and swagger!"

Surprise was stamped on Pronto's face like a brand. I saw hatred in his eyes, and something else. For the first time, I saw doubt beneath his bluster—doubt and fear. Through the whiskey that fogged his mind, I saw him trying to decide which way to go. Then his gun hand trembled; he lowered the weapon, hesitated, and slid it back inside the leather.

I holstered my gun as well. "Good choice," I told him. "From now on, you'd best walk wide of me and keep a check-rein on your mouth. If you don't, George Stark-weather may have to find himself a new bully-boy."

I turned back to my horses and led them inside the barn. As I passed Pronto, I hoped I seemed cool and confident to him, but that was not my state of mind. In that moment I felt the way a man does when he's run a bluff in a high-stakes poker game and won. I was relieved, light-headed, and more than a little surprised I'd brought it off.

Once again I had come up against Pronto Southwell, and once again he had folded his cards and let me rake in the chips. Still, I knew the game wasn't over. There would be other hands dealt, other bets made and called. The final hand was yet to be played.

CHAPTER 15
Mending Fences

The following week, George seemed determined to spend as much time with Abby as he could. He took her on walks and sleigh rides around the place, entertained her with tales of his heroism during the War Between the States and of his successful career as a hard-working cattleman. He slathered on the charm with a trowel, describing people he'd never met, places he'd never seen, and a life he'd never known.

As his intended foreman, I was twice invited to share supper with him and Abby, and I marveled at George's inventiveness. Reading all those books must have helped stir up his imagination. George's stories were fiction, and that was true to his nature. He was a deceiver, and he practiced his gift with the acquired skill of a lifetime. He was good at his lies; I'll give him that. If I hadn't known better, I'd almost have believed him myself.

• • •

After supper one evening, Abby entertained us at the piano, singing in a lively, lilting voice. George had brought the piano in while we were still at Arrowhead Ranch in the belief that all well brought up young ladies played the instrument. He was delighted to learn that in Abby's case, he was right.

But he'd neglected to order sheet music, so Abby sang and played such old songs as "Buffalo Gals" and "I'll Take You Home Again, Kathleen" from memory. Some high-class tunes, too, that she called "nocturnes" and were real pretty but had no words to go with the music.

George spoke of his plans for the future. He would wait till spring to buy cattle. The hard winter would break some of the open range cattlemen, and they'd be obliged to sell their surviving stock at almost any price. When spring came, he'd hire hay hands to cut and stack hay in the watered meadows so that his cattle could better survive another such winter if it came.

His plans, he told her, would require capital, but he was confident he could raise it. What he didn't say was that he already had the money, and that most of it had come from the bank robberies at Dry Creek and Blue Rock. The two hold-ups had brought him at least fifty thousand dollars—probably more. By anybody's guess, George was far from broke.

All of which caused me to reconsider an old question: where *was* that money from the robberies? I had thrown the money bags into the coal shed at Blue

Rock. George had said he had a key and would pick up the loot himself. I had no doubt he had done it, but if he had, *then* what?

Had he hidden the swag somewhere at Arrowhead Ranch? If so, it would certainly no longer be there. He'd have moved it—maybe to his new place.

Well then, was the cash here? Almost certainly, hidden in the main house. But where? Beneath the floorboards? Locked in a safe? Stashed in a strongbox?

The only way to answer that question would be to search the house. I decided to make that search the first time I had a chance.

That chance came unexpectedly the following Friday. George came over to the cook shack where Pronto, Tom, and me were having breakfast and announced that he and Abby were going to Wolf City to buy supplies. An amateur theatrical group was performing there on Saturday night, he said, so he and Abby would put up at the hotel and come back on Sunday.

"While I'm gone, I want you boys to ride my fence line," George said. "I'll be stockin' this spread come spring, and I want tight wire and good posts to hold my steers."

I had to smile. George Starkweather was a boss rustler. During his checkered career he had made most of his money by stealing other men's livestock. Now he was worrying about holding on to his own.

"We'll do it," I said. "You don't want to lose any of your new cattle."

George fixed me with his cold, yellow gaze. "I don't aim to lose anything that belongs to me!" he said.

Pronto frowned. "I mostly go where *you* go, Boss," he said. "Ridin' guard and coverin' your back is what you pay me for."

"Doin' what I tell you is what I pay you for," George said. "When I need you to ride guard, I guess I'll let you know."

Pronto's frown deepened. He stared down at his coffee but made no answer.

"Merlin is ramrod while I'm away," George said. "You boys will take your orders from him."

George turned to leave the cook shack. At the door, he looked back and met Pronto's gaze. "Any questions?" he asked.

"No," Pronto muttered. "Not just now."

George nodded. Looking at Tom, he said, "We'll need the sleigh d'rectly, hitched and ready to go."

Tom pulled his coat on. "You bet, Chief," he said.

We stacked our eating tools in the dishpan beside the door and followed George outside. In the east, the sky had grown lighter. The morning star was fading quickly in the brightness of the coming day. Tom made his way along the broken trail to the barn while George headed back to the main house. Pronto and me stood together, watching.

"Have you got any questions for me?" I asked.

Pronto's eyes were hot. "Like I said, not just now. Takin' orders from you galls me like vinegar, but I'll do what George says." He buttoned his coat and pulled his gloves on. "I'm not sure what it is," he said, "but there's *somethin'* about you that just ain't right. I'm damned if I know why George made you straw boss of this outfit, but he did.

"So I'll do what you say when it comes to work. But I'm a patient man. One of these days you'll slip and show your true colors. When that happens, I'll be on you like a duck on a Junebug." His locked eyes with mine. "I'll blow out your damned lamp," he said.

"Sometimes a lamp doesn't go out that easy," I said. "Meanwhile, get your fencin' tools and go to work. We've got wire to string."

Tom brought the sleigh up from the barn, driving Samson and Delilah at a steady trot. The horses swung past the bunkhouse and cook shack, sleigh bells jangling, and came to a stop in front of the main house. George and Abby appeared dressed for travel, and Tom stepped out of the sleigh and held the horses.

Abby took her place on the seat and tucked the heavy lap robe about her. She smiled at me and waved a gloved hand in farewell. Tom stood aside; George cracked the whip, and the team struck out on the road to Wolf City.

We walked to the barn where Tom hitched the work team and loaded the bobsled with tamping bar, wire stretcher, staples, and wire. Pronto swung up onto the sled, and Tom took the reins.

"Start in the hay meadows," I said. "Tighten the loose wire and splice what's broken. You won't be able to get to some places because of snowdrifts. We'll take care of those come spring. Same with rotted posts. The ground's frozen too hard to dig now. When you come to a post that needs replacing, mark it. We'll set new posts after the thaw.

"When you've worked through the meadows, move on up through the lower pastures to the boundary fence on top. I'll bring you boys coffee and grub at noon, and see you back here at supper time."

Pronto was sullen as ever. "What are *you* gonna do, straw boss?" he asked.

"I haven't decided," I said pleasantly. "Probably just sit around by the stove, drinkin' coffee and thinkin' up more work for you. Now move out—we're burnin' daylight."

Tom grinned and shook the reins. The team stepped out, briskly, pulling the sled through the crusted snow. I watched until the sled was well past the barn before I turned away and walked past the cook shack to the woodpile at the end of the building. Wang Lee watched from the half open door, and I gave him a wave as I passed.

"You need firewood?" I asked. "I'm goin' to split some for the main house."

"No wood," Wang Lee replied. "Got plenty."

I pulled the axe free of the chopping block, replaced it with a stove-length section of log, and in a few swift blows, split the section into kindling. I split several more, then sunk the axe blade into the block and gathered the wood into my arms. Stepping carefully through the snow, I carried my load across the yard and up the steps to the front door of the main house.

George had put a bootjack just inside the door, and I used it to take off my boots. In stocking feet, I carried the kindling to the wood box and dumped it inside.

So far, so good, I thought. I had established a reason for entering the house. Wang Lee would simply think George had asked me to carry in wood for the stove.

Coals still glowed amid the ashes of the fireplace. I added wood and fanned the embers with my hat until flames blazed again. I stood in the center of the parlor and looked around the silent room. Where, I wondered, would I hide my money if *I* was George?

Carefully, one room at a time, I searched the house. I scrutinized the rocks and mortar that made up the fireplace. I inspected the cupboards and drawers of the kitchen. I examined the flooring in each room, rapping the boards with my knuckles and listening for a hollow sound that might indicate a hiding place.

In George's sleeping room, I searched his wardrobe and his trunk, went through the drawers of his dresser and desk, and even looked beneath the mattress on his bed. But I found nothing—no gold coin, no bank notes, nothing.

At the back of the house, George kept a room as his personal office. The door creaked softly as I eased inside. Oak filing cabinets stood against one wall beside a big roll-topped desk and a couple of chairs. I looked through both cabinets and desk. Again, nothing.

Then, behind a folding screen, I found a small safe.

I dropped to one knee, holding my breath. The safe was painted dark green, its door decorated with painted scrollwork, and it stood on steel wheels in a corner behind the screen. Little more than two feet by a foot-and-a-half in size, it seemed too small to hold George's treasure. Besides, I thought, it was almost certainly locked, and no one but George would know its combination.

Carefully closing the office door behind me, I continued my search, walking through each room again. The silence in the house was nearly complete.

Now and again, I thought I heard footsteps on the porch outside or someone at the door. I'd stop in mid-motion, holding my breath, listening. But there was only the wind, the pop and crackle of the flames in the fireplace, and the sound of my own heartbeat. Once I stopped when I heard the buzzing of a fly, and again when, as loud as a church bell, the chime of the mantel clock startled me.

Minutes passed. I went through George's bookshelves, leafed through each volume, but found only dust and an occasional bookmark. I even searched Abby's sleeping room, feeling nervous and guilty amid the female fofarrow and fancies, like some kind of Peeping Toni.

I began to imagine I heard voices and once tiptoed into the big room when I thought I heard Abby talking soft the way she did, but it was only the wind outside. When I saw that the fire had burned down to ashes in the fireplace, I was surprised to find I'd been in the house that long.

Baffled, I sat down in one of George's leather-covered easy chairs. I had been so sure I'd find the loot hidden somewhere in the house. Where could it be? Where would George keep his money, anyway?

From nowhere, the impulse came. *Go back,* it seemed to say, *look in the office again.*

The wind had picked up, and now it gusted across the chimney top, making low moaning sounds. A tree branch rattled against a window at the rear of the house. And always, there was the ticking of the clock.

Even though I knew no one else was nearby, I had the strong impression I was being watched. Rising from the chair, I cat-footed softly up the hall, opened the door, and again entered George's office.

Squatting on my boot heels, I studied the safe. Nothing had changed. It stood heavy and solid in its place. At the center of its door, the safe's dial and locking knob seemed to mock me. I reached out, twisted the handle sharply downward—and the door swung open. It had been unlocked all the time!

Bending closer, I peered inside. A few papers— receipts and such, Abby's letter to Slippery Mayfair— lay on an upper shelf. Five hundred dollars in bank notes occupied a lower shelf. I was about to close the safe door and leave the room when I noticed a large manila envelope marked "Wolf City Bank & Trust." Inside, I found two documents, one the deed to the ranch, and the other a bank statement addressed to

George Shannon. I was about to put it back in the envelope and admit defeat when I looked at the statement more closely. It showed assets of more than sixty thousand dollars.

In that moment, I knew the answer. Of course! The money from the bank at Dry Creek and the bank at Blue Rock was hidden—in another bank! It was on deposit in George's account at Slippery Mayfair's Wolf City bank. No strongbox, no buried treasure for George—his ill-gotten gains were drawing interest in his perfectly legal, legitimate bank account, under his new name, George Shannon.

I looked at the clock—half past eleven! Where had the morning gone? Toni and Pronto expected me to bring them lunch and coffee at noon; it wouldn't do to be late. Quickly, I went through the rooms, making sure I had left no trace. Inside the front door where I'd left them, I picked up my boots and pulled them on.

Dashing across to the cook shack, I picked up a pail of coffee, fresh biscuits, and stew from Wang Lee. At the barn, I saddled Roanie and swung up onto his back. Then, carrying the chuck and fixings in a feed sack, I pointed the big horse out on the trail of the bobsled and gave him his head. I had at last learned where the stolen money was, but I had found something else as well—a perfect irony. Stealing money from two banks and depositing it at yet a *third* bank sure seemed ironic to me.

I found the bobsled and the boys near the same aspen

grove where Abby and me had our midwinter picnic. They had a fire going and were warming their hands when I rode up. Tom grinned when he saw me, but Pronto of course did not. He scowled, surly as a sore-headed hound, and said, "It's about goddamned time. A man could starve to death waitin' for you."

I stepped down and opened the sack, pulled the lids off, set the coffee and stew on a rock beside the fire, and handed out plates and cups.

"I followed the fence line, comin' up," I said. "You boys did a good job on the wire."

Tom grinned, helping himself to the stew. "It was in pretty good shape. We only found three posts that'll need replacin' come spring."

Pronto filled his cup from the pail. Steam billowed up, catching the sunlight. He made no comment, but it was plain he figured fixing fence was beneath him.

We ate together there at the grove, and I put the cups and plates back into the sack. "Work on up to the boundary fence," I said. "Go as far as you can. I'll see you this evenin'."

"We'll get 'er done, Kid," Tom said. Pronto turned his back and walked away.

That evening, Pronto seemed even more sulky than usual. He kept to himself, speaking to no one. After supper in the bunkhouse, he sat on his bed, cleaning and oiling his guns. Tom and me broke out the cards and played a game or two of rummy, but Pronto gave no sign he even knew we were there.

Then, as we were playing our last hand of the night, I glanced up and found him staring hard at me. His mouth was a thin, bitter line, and his eyes burned with a heat I could almost feel. I met his stare and held his eyes until he looked away.

There was no doubt about it. Pronto Southwell was an enemy I would have to deal with sooner or later. He had nursed his grudge against me until it had become a mania. I still didn't know whether I could ever shoot another man, but I slept with my .44 close at hand, just in case I had to find out.

The next morning dawned cold and overcast, the daylight gray and thin beneath cloudy skies. I sent Tom and Pronto back out to work on the fence line and turned my attention to the horses. Roanie had been shod with flat plates, and they needed to be replaced. I gathered the shoeing tools from the barn and snubbed the big roan's head high to a corral post. I placed the hoof nippers, rasp, and hammer in my boot top where they'd be handy, crowded Roanie against the corral post, and began changing his old shoes for new ones.

I clipped the horseshoe nails and pried off the worn and loose shoes and fit new ones in their place. To give the horse better footing in the snow and ice, I shaped heel caulks on the new shoes, bending the open ends in toward each other to protect his heels. Horse shoeing was familiar work, and it freed my mind to think about George, Abby, Pronto, and my assignment.

I could no longer wait for Marshal Ridgeway and his posse to come and arrest George and his men. If Ridgeway had received my letter and mounted a raid, he had found Arrowhead deserted or in new hands. He wouldn't know about this new place, nor that Abby had actually arrived, or about the killing of Ike, Haynes, and Morris.

Most of all, he couldn't know what I had learned about the money. I needed to get word to him— soon.

There'd surely be a telegraph office in Wolf City, I thought. Somehow, I needed to find a way to get into town alone, away from George and Pronto's watchful eyes. I was determined to complete my assignment, with Ridgeway's help if possible, but without it if I had to.

When I finished shoeing Roanie, I spent the rest of the morning straightening up the barn. I mucked out the stalls, organized the saddles, harness, and other tack, and replaced a broken hinge on the side door. By the time I finished, it was time to take the noon meal out to Pronto and Tom, so I saddled the big roan and headed for the cook shack.

Wang Lee was waiting. He'd packed fresh beef stew, cornbread, and coffee in tins and placed it all in a feed sack as before. As I drew in rein, he handed the bundle up to me.

"You bring back dish," he scolded. "Bring knife, fork, spoon, too. Not lose, like last time."

"You bet," I said. "What did I lose last time?"

"Lose *spoon*," he said. "You bring *all* dish back this time." Turning, he went back inside the cook shack.

I found Tom and Pronto two miles farther along the fence line than they'd been the day before. They had found shelter from the wind in a patch of willows and had once again built themselves a warming fire. Pronto met me with his usual scowl; I would have been surprised if he had not. Tom sat on a fallen log, huddled in his coat. He raised a hand in greeting, his face ruddy from the cold, but his smile seemed hesitant and strained.

"Dinnertime, boys," I said, dismounting. "Wang Lee sent beef stew and corn bread today. He told me to 'bring all dish back this time.' Claims we lost a spoon yesterday."

Pronto opened the coffee tin and poured himself a cup. I set out the plates and began to fill them. Tom held up his hand, palm toward me, and shook his head. "Don't dish up none o' that for me, Kid," he said. "I— I'm a little off my feed today."

Pronto blew on his coffee. "Old fart's about as useless as tits on a boar," he said. "I've been doin' most of the damned work by myself today."

I took a closer look at Tom. His lips were pulled back from his teeth in a tight grimace, and there was pain in his eyes. "What's wrong, Tom?" I asked. "Are you all right?"

"I've—been better," he said, grunting. "Likely, it's only belly gas."

I poured a cup of coffee, then bent down and handed it to him. "Drink a little of this," I said. "It'll warm you, at least."

He shook as he took the cup. Trembling, he raised it to his lips and sipped. "That's good," he said. "Much obliged."

Behind the high color in his cheeks and nose, his skin was as gray as the weather. I turned to Pronto. "How long has he been like this?"

Pronto was spooning in the stew. He swallowed, and shrugged. "Maybe an hour or so," he said. "I think the old bastard's fakin'."

"You know him better than that," I said. "Tom's more likely to hide it when he's hurtin'."

I looked at Toni again. He bent slightly forward where he sat, arms crossed and hugging himself. "You boys are quittin' early," I told Pronto. "Pick up your tools and help me get Tom on the sled. I'll go back and build a fire in the bunkhouse stove. We need to get him out of the cold and into his bed."

"Suits me," Pronto said. "I never signed on for this goddam sodbuster work anyway. But I still say you're soft—too soft to be George's ramrod."

I put the dishes and leftovers in the feed sack, stepped up onto Roanie, and struck off down the valley. Twenty minutes later I reined up at the cook shack. Briefly, I told Wang Lee about Tom, that he was feeling poorly and that he didn't look well.

Wang Lee nodded. "I take look when he comes," he said. "Give medicine, maybe."

At the bunkhouse, I stoked up the stove and refilled the wood box. I had just stepped back outside when I saw Pronto coming with the bobsled, the work team stepping high. He drove standing up, with Tom sitting on the planks beside him, one hand grasping the sled for balance. A moment later, Pronto drew rein at the bunkhouse, and I helped Tom down.

"Why don't you go to bed for a while?" I asked. "Wang Lee says he'll be over to take a look at you. He's no doctor, but he seems to know somethin' about medicines."

Tom put a hand on my shoulder and I helped him into the bunkhouse. "Maybe I will," Tom said. "My belly ain't hurtin' so much now—but I could use me a little rest."

Inside, he pulled his boots off and slipped between the soogans of his bedroll. "More'n likely, it's just somethin' I et," he said. "I'll be all right d'rectly."

Wang Lee was as good as his word. A moment later, he shuffled across from the cook shack with a basket filled with various powders and nostrums. He drew back the quilt that covered Tom and peered at his face. "Not to move," the cook said, "I look-see what makes you sick."

Swiftly, Wang Lee conducted his examination. His slender fingers gently pushed up Tom's eyelids, and Wang Lee studied his eyes. He looked into the old outlaw's mouth, manipulated Tom's fingers, and laid his head on Tom's chest, listening. At length, he straightened and took a small brown bottle from his basket.

"Old man hurt more than he say," Wang Lee observed. "I give laudanum for pain."

He filled a cup from the bucket on the washstand and added twenty drops from the bottle to the water. Helping Tom sit up, he pressed the cup to his lips. "You drink," he said. "Drink *all*." Obediently, Tom drank the mixture and lay down again.

Wang Lee picked up his basket and looked at me. "Later," he said, "I come back, make mustard plaster for chest. I think, maybe so, Old Tom have *heart* problem."

CHAPTER 16

Fast Ride to Wolf City

A little after four that afternoon, George and Abby came up the road from Wolf City and turned in at the gate, the Morgan team trotting in unison and the sleigh bells jangling. George drove the horses up the lane and reined to a stop in front of the house.

Abby smiled as I approached the sleigh, her cheeks rosy as a painted doll's. George put the whip in its socket and gave me his familiar one-eyed squint. "You're just in time to help Abigail take her packages inside," he said. "We like to have bought out all the shops in Wolf City."

"Don't listen to him," Abby said, laughing. "I just bought a hat and one or two items of clothing."

"I believe we might have room in the house for it all," George said, "if we add on a wing."

Holding Abby's hand, I helped her down from the sleigh. Her blue eyes searched my face, her smile fading. "Is something wrong, Merlin?" she asked.

"No," I said. "Everything's fine. Old Tom was feelin' poorly at noon, but I sent him to bed. He seems to be doin' all right now."

Abby began to hand me packages from beneath the lap robe. They were more than "just a hat and one or two items of clothing" but not enough to require adding a room to the house.

George stepped out of the sleigh and stretched. He looked rested, relaxed. "We had a fine time," he said. "We ate oysters on the half shell, drank champagne and brandy, and took in the theatrical. I laughed till I thought I'd bust a gut."

"The play was a comedy," Abby said. "Very amusing. All about a backwoods boy meeting his sweetheart's pompous family. After the play, an actor recited Mr. Poe's poem, *The Raven*."

Having loaded my arms with packages, Abby led the way to the front door and opened it, and George and me followed her inside. "Just stack them in the parlor," she said. "I'll sort them out later."

Inside, I saw that Wang Lee had built a fire in anticipation of George and Abby's return. Coals glowed dull red amid the ashes within the fireplace, and the room was warm.

Abby removed her coat, hat, and woolen scarf, and freed her hair with a toss of her head. She turned and took the last packages from me. "Thank you, Merlin," she said, smiling. Then concern clouded her eyes. "I do hope Mr. Blackburn is all right," she said.

For a second I couldn't think who she was talking about. *Mr. Blackburn?* I thought. *Who's that?* Then I realized she meant Tom. No one ever used Tom's last name. Since I'd been with George's outfit the only names I'd heard him called were "Tom," and "Old Tom."

"Oh," I said. "I'm sure he will. Wang Lee's been doctorin' him some. My pa had a case of devil's grip once. Caused him pain in his lower chest for a week or two and then went away by itself. Likely, that's what Tom has."

George doffed his hat and hung it on a peg inside the door. "Go along now," he told Abby, "and put away your pretties. I need to talk business with Merlin."

Abby smiled. "Of course, Daddy," she said. Her arms laden with packages, Abby strolled away in the direction of her room.

George walked over to the fireplace and stirred the coals with a poker. He added wood and watched as the flames rekindled, then sank into his favorite chair and, with a nod, invited me to take a chair facing his.

"Talked to some cowmen in Wolf City," he said. "They told me starvin' cattle are dyin' all across the plains. The critters even come into town huntin' food. They beller, bawl, and die at the town folks' front doors. Hell of a note. Many a cowman'll go belly-up this winter. I'll be able to stock the ranch come spring for next to nothin'."

247

I nodded. "I reckon so. Still, it's a hard thing to profit from other folks' misery."

"Like hell it is. The strong survive and the weak go under. That's just the way of it."

George stared into the fire and fell silent. In the stillness, the only sounds were the occasional snap of burning wood and the ticking of the mantel clock. Recalling Pronto's account of the killings on Arrowhead Creek, I wondered. Was George remembering that other fire and the lives he took? Did his conscience trouble him? Knowing George, I decided it did not.

He turned to me. "How did the fence work go?"

"Good. I put Pronto and Tom to work the day you left. They marked the rotted posts and tightened wire all the way to the boundary fences on top. There's more to do, but they made a good start.

"While they were doin' that, I put a set of shoes on my roan and mucked out the barn. Organized the saddles and harness a mite."

George nodded. "Good," he said.

Again, he fell silent, his eyes on the flames beyond the andirons. Then he turned back to me again and asked, "This thing about Torn. How bad do you think he is?"

"I don't know, Cap'n. You know Tom. He's loyal as a hound, and he doesn't complain. Whatever's botherin' him, it's bad enough to make him take to his bed in the middle of the day. Wang Lee thinks it could be his heart."

George looked troubled, and that surprised me. He rarely showed concern for anyone. After a brief pause he stood up and looked me in the eye. His hard, mad eagle stare seemed softer, more open somehow.

"There's a sawbones in Wolf City," he said. "Doc Whittier. Lives in a blue house at the edge of town. Take the sleigh and get old Tom in to see him."

Again, I was surprised. "Sure, Cap'n," is what I said. What I thought was, *Are you becoming human, George Starkweather? What happened to* the strong survive and the weak go under?

Tom was asleep when I entered the bunkhouse. He was huddled deep within his blankets so only his face showed above the bed tarp. His thinning hair was tousled and wild, silver where the pale light touched it. Wrinkles crisscrossed his weathered skin, and his breathing was ragged and uneven.

I touched his shoulder and spoke his name. "Tom," I said. "Come on, Tom. I'm takin' you to town."

His eyelids fluttered; he opened his eyes. For a moment, the old outlaw seemed confused, still holding on to sleep. Then he looked into my face, and his confusion faded. "Kid?" he said. "Did you say somethin'?"

"You need to get up now. I'm takin' you to Wolf City."

"I ain't been fired, have I?"

"No," I said. "The boss thinks you need to see a doctor. How are you feelin'?"

He closed his eyes again. "Comes and goes, the pain does. Hurts like Billy Hell when it comes. Like a bear trap across my chest."

"Let's go, pardner."

Tom raised himself on one arm and swung his legs over the side of the bunk. "Hand me my hat, will you, Kid?" he asked. I took his battered sombrero from its peg by the door and gave it to him. Bending low, he struggled to pull on his boots. He tried not to show it, but it was plain to see he was hurting bad.

I watched as he dressed, heard him grunt with the exertion and wince when the pain hit him. I wanted to help but forced myself to wait as if we had all the time in the world. Tom's pride was more important than my impatience.

Outside, I helped him into the sleigh and got him settled in the seat. He was dressed for the weather in his blanket-lined coat, angora shaps, and elk hide mittens, with a wool muffler covering his ears and throat. By the time I was ready for the road, I had the old man wrapped up like a mummy. I took the reins, swung the coach about, and drove the team out for Wolf City at a fast trot.

The road was rutted by travel and mostly clear, except for some low spots where wind had blown the snow hard-packed across the track. There the drifts were crusted and unyielding as sand. When the sleigh's runners struck one of those spots at speed, the jolt was nearly enough to bounce us out of our seats. I tried to watch ahead and rein in the horses before we reached those places, but sometimes a drift appeared out of the blue, and I couldn't slow up in time.

We were about five miles from town when we slued

around a corner and plowed into a big drift that shook the sleigh and rattled my teeth. Beside me, Tom clutched his chest and cried out, his teeth bared and his face twisted by pain.

I pulled the team in and turned to help Tom. He was half out of the sleigh, his body a rigid arc, his eyes wide and staring.

"Damn, Tom, I'm sorry," I said. "I saw that drift too late to stop. Are you all right?"

Tom made no answer, but sat absolutely still. Sweat beaded his forehead and he seemed not even to breathe. After a moment, he groaned and began to tremble. "God a'mighty, Kid," he said. "Feels—like I'm bein' tore up inside! The pain's a-runnin' up my arm, clean to the shoulder! I . . ." Abruptly, he gasped and fell back into his seat.

I opened his coat, my hands on his chest. His skin was cold and clammy to the touch, but his chest rose and fell with his breathing. His heartbeat, though wild and irregular, seemed strong. Tom was unconscious but alive.

I covered him hurriedly and turned the team out on the road at a run. Whether we hit the drifts no longer mattered—Tom was beyond feeling the shock. I had to get him to the doctor as fast as I could. The crack of the buggy whip above the horses' ears gave them the message.

I saw the heat rising from the stoves of Wolf City before I saw the town. I drove the team hard along the roadway, circled the base of a low hill, and burst upon the outskirts of the settlement at a dead run. Wood smoke rose from every chimney into the still, frigid air. Steel rails gleamed under the setting sun. Alongside a depot at the far end of town, a locomotive chuffed white steam and black smoke. Ahead on my left, I saw the blue house George had described. It was a small, frame residence, set inside a white picket fence, and to my relief, lamplight showed in a front window.

I hauled back on the reins, trying to stop the Morgans. They slowed, straining against the bit as they broke from their dash back into a trot. Fighting to keep their footing on the icy roadway, they plunged into the deeper snow beside the doctor's house and stumbled to a stop. Their foam-flecked sides heaved with their breathing, the heat from their bodies steaming, but they had brought us in. It was not the first time I was grateful to horses.

Almost before the sleigh came to a stop, I had leapt out and dashed to the other side. Tom was unconscious, his face deathly pale. I gathered him in my arms, plunged through the snow to the open gate, and strode toward the house. The front door opened and a slender man in shirtsleeves stepped out.

"I hope you're Doc Whittier," I said, "because this man sure does need a doctor."

"I am," the man said. "Take him inside. My office is straight ahead, beyond the parlor."

I was only half aware of the parlor as I carried Tom in—but I had the impression of a neat and orderly room, simply furnished with divan, rocker, and parlor chairs. I passed a heating stove and a bookcase, crossed the room, and entered the office.

The doctor pointed to a raised examination table. "Put him there," he said. A brass lamp hung from the ceiling overhead. Drawing it down, the doctor struck a match and lit the wick. Gently, I laid Tom on the table. I remember feeling relieved that I had got him there, and surprised; until I put him down, I hadn't realized how heavy he was.

"What can you tell me about this?" the doctor asked.

"I ride for George Star—George *Shannon,* up the road a piece. Old Tom here started complaining about pain in his belly and chest yesterday. Our cook gave him twenty drops of laudanum in water, and we put him to bed. He was worse this morning. Shannon told me to bring him in to you.

"On the way here he had some kind of attack. Said he felt like he was bein' torn up from the inside. Said the pain ran all the way up his arm to his shoulder. Then he passed out."

"You did well, cowboy," the doctor said. "There's coffee on the stove in the kitchen. Help yourself while I have a look at your friend."

Like the parlor, the kitchen was clean and tidy. I took a heavy china mug from the cupboard and filled it from the pot. The windows above the kitchen table looked out upon the buildings that made up Wolf City, and I stood and watched the lights go on as the sun dropped behind the hills.

As I lifted the coffee to my lips, I was surprised to see that my hand was shaking, and suddenly I felt as tired as if I had run a long race. "You're entitled," I told myself. "Runnin' a race is just what you've done."

Again, the idea of irony returned to mind. A few days ago, George Starkweather had shot and burned to death three men who had ridden with him, and now here he had rushed another burned-out old outlaw to the doctor in order to save his life. But that wasn't all. Old Tom was a member of a gang I had been sent to arrest, capture, or kill. But now I was worried about him like he was my grandpa. Yessir, I found the whole thing ironic.

I'd just finished my second cup of coffee when Doc Whittier walked into the kitchen. "Your friend is sleeping comfortably," he said. "I gave him an injection of morphia to relieve the pain. He'll need to remain here overnight."

"I'm obliged, Doc," I said. "Will he—will he be all right?"

Doc Whittier shrugged. He lifted the coffeepot from the stove and poured himself a cup. "Hard to say. He has angina pectoris, but that's a symptom, not a disease. And you already *know* about the symptoms. Almost always means a serious disease of the heart or the aorta. I won't know specifically which disease until I examine the man further."

The doctor took a sip from his cup and made a wry face. "My coffee gets pretty rank by the end of the day," he said. "I apologize."

"I've had worse," I said. "Besides, I didn't come here for the coffee."

Behind his gold-rimmed spectacles, Doc Whittier's eyes were friendly and kind. "No," he said. "Of course you didn't."

He smiled. "You look a bit weary yourself, cowboy. Why don't you rent yourself a room over in town? Get some sleep. I should know more about your friend's condition in the morning."

"Maybe I will," I said. "I'll need to take care of my horses first."

"Bob Fraley's Livery is on this end of the street. Tell Bob I sent you. There's a hotel a few doors farther down—the Sherman. Reasonable rates and clean."

I stood and offered my hand. "Much obliged until you're better paid. I'll see you in the mornin'."

"In the morning," he replied, and we shook hands.

Outside, the night sky was clear and cloudless. A broken moon cast its pale light on the town, and stars glittered in the blackness. From somewhere in the distance, I heard the lonesome wail of the locomotive. The horses stood hitched where I'd left them, vapor from their breathing catching the lamplight from the doctor's house. I stepped into the sleigh and turned them toward Wolf City.

Bob Fraley was in the stable office when I drove up, but when he heard me stop, he came out to meet me. He was a short, stocky man in his late forties, dressed in a winter coat and gum boots. He held a lighted lantern high, watching as I stepped down from the sleigh.

"Evenin'," he said.

"Evenin'. Would you be Bob Fraley?"

"Not if I could help it, but I have no choice. Yeah, I'm Bob Fraley. Somethin' I can do for you?"

"I need to put my horses up for the night. They could use a dry stall and feed."

Fraley stepped closer, still holding his lantern aloft. "Yes, they could," he agreed. "They could also use a brushin' and a scoop of oats. Good-lookin' team."

"Yes, they are. The gelding is Samson and the mare is Delilah. A match made in heaven."

Fraley's laugh was a deep chest rumble. He put his hand on Samson's neck. "Yes, indeed," he said. "I see no sign she's gave him a haircut, and he still looks like he could pull down a good-size temple."

"I'll pay in advance," I said. "What do I owe you?"

"Room and board for the happy couple, and a good brushin' to dry their hair. Call it a dollar six bits."

"Make it an even two dollars," I said, handing him a brace of cartwheels. "Put 'em up in the bridal suite. They've earned it."

Fraley guffawed. "The *bridle* suite, huh? It's a deal, mister. I'll even serve them breakfast in bed."

"Obliged," I said. "I'll be back for them in the mornin'."

"They'll be here," Fraley said, "unless they elope or somethin.'"

Three doors down the street, I found the Sherman Hotel. It was a white-washed two-story building set apart from its neighbors by a vacant lot. Snow was piled high along both sides of the street, even covering the hitch rails in some places, but the hotel veranda and the stairs leading up to it from the street had been shoveled and swept clear.

Inside, oil lamps turned down low lighted the lobby. Two wing chairs and a divan clustered around a big parlor stove whose hot sides glowed dull red. Potted ferns stood on plant stands near the chairs, and the mounted heads of deer, elk, and pronghorn stared glassy-eyed from the walls. The desk clerk looked up as I approached. "I need a room for tonight," I said.

The clerk leaned across the desk and craned his neck. "Sure, mister," he said, "but you'll have to pay up front. No luggage, you understand. Hotel policy."

"How much?"

"I've got a nice single upstairs facing the street. It'll run you a dollar and a half."

"It's a deal," I said. "It cost me more than that to put my horses up for the night."

He turned the hotel register around toward me and handed me a pen. I looked at the page for a moment, thinking how I was a wanted man. I dipped the pen in the inkwell and wrote "Charlie Jones," and gave my address as general delivery, Lander, Wyoming. It was not, I was sure, the first time a man signed a false name to a hotel register.

The clerk read what I'd written. "From Lander, eh? How's the weather down there?"

"Same as it is here," I said. "Same as it is everyplace this year—cold as a miser's heart, with snow hump-deep to a buffalo."

The clerk's face turned grim. "Yeah," he said. "This is the year of the Big Die-up, sure enough."

I paid the clerk, and he handed me a room key with the number 3 stamped on it. "Thought I'd go out and look the town over before I turn in," I said. "Be back later.

"If you haven't had supper, the Roundup Café is pretty good. It's down in the next block, across the street."

"Business before pleasure," I said. "Does this town have a telegraph office?"

"Sure. It's down at the express office at the end of the street, next to the depot. Kid named Barney Foster is the agent on duty. He's usually there until seven."

When I stepped out onto Wolf City's main street, there wasn't a soul in sight. The stores and shops were closed for the evening, and only the Roundup Café and the town's three saloons were still open for business. Shaggy-haired horses huddled together at the hitch racks, asleep on their feet as they awaited their riders' returns.

The temperature had dropped with the setting sun.

258

Falling snow, fine as talcum, glittered in the lamplight. I turned up the collar of my sheepskin and set out for the express office.

As I walked in, I saw a red-haired youth I took to be Barney Foster seated behind the counter. A young woman of about the same age stood facing him, obviously caught up in conversation with the boy. He didn't look up when I came in, the young lady occupying his full attention, and I sure couldn't blame him. She was mighty fetching.

Apparently, the boy paid the girl some kind of particularly pleasing compliment, because she giggled demurely and batted her eyelashes, and he grinned and blushed until his face turned red as his hair. She must have caught sight of me out of the corner of her eye, for she cut her giggle short and looked embarrassed. Then the boy glanced my way, and the mood of the moment passed.

I felt a mite awkward myself. I had come to the office on business, but I felt like I should apologize for interrupting their flirtation. The girl backed away from the counter and lowered her eyes, and the youth on the other side put on his business face.

"Evening, sir," he said. "Can I help you?"

"You can if you're Barney Foster, telegraph agent."

"I am," he said. "What can I do for you?"

"I need to send a telegram to U.S. Marshal Chance Ridgeway, up in Helena, Montana."

Barney handed me a pad and pencil. "You bet," he said. "Just write it out."

I took the pencil, and studied the blank pad for a moment. Then I quickly wrote out my message, tore it from the pad, and handed it to the young telegrapher.

"Read that back to me," I said.

"Have found killer wolf at George Shannon ranch near Wolf City, Wyoming. Other wolves in pack killed or scattered. Bounty money on deposit Wolf City bank."

"That's fine," I said. "Sign it 'Charlie Jones.'"

Barney opened the key and rapidly tapped out the message. He waited a moment, and then the telegraph clattered briefly and fell silent.

"Message sent and received," he said.

I paid the youth and turned to leave. "So you're a wolfer, Mr. Jones?" he asked.

"That's right."

"It's none of my business, I guess, but what does a federal marshal in Montana have to do with hunting wolves in Wyoming?"

I shrugged. "Durned if I know," I said. "I guess the man just plain despises wolves."

CHAPTER 17
The Big Jump

When I left the telegraph office, I felt as though a great weight had been lifted from my shoulders. I had at last been able to get a wire off to Ridgeway, and my mind was easier because of it. All at once, I realized I was hungry enough to eat an entire buffalo, hooves, horns, and all. Without further ado, I sauntered up the frost-slick boardwalk and walked into the Roundup Café.

The café was busy at that hour. Waiters bustled about carrying trays of food and drink from the kitchen. Customers filled the tables and lined the counter, forking it in and talking. The rattle of eating tools on china was a constant din that forced the sweating cook to shout to make himself heard. It was altogether my kind of place.

A seat at the counter opened up, and I pounced on the stool before it had a chance to cool off. "Special of the day," the blackboard on the wall said, "lamb stew and corn dodgers," which sounded just fine to me. When a waiter came by, I asked him for a double order and a slice of apple pie, then waited, drinking black coffee and looking the crowd over.

Most seemed to be townsfolk, although there were cowpunchers and ranch people on hand, too. A potbellied stove at the center of the room glowed with heat, and a thin layer of smoke hung and eddied just beneath the tin ceiling. Coats and hats hung on pegs along the wall beside the door, and the whole place smelled of lamb stew, hot metal, wet wool, and tobacco.

Directly, a waiter brought my order and set it before me. The sight of that stew and those corn dodgers fresh from the oven stirred up my appetite considerable, and I fell to eating like a starving man. As I ate, I kept on looking the place over. I wasn't looking *for* anything really; just observing folks to pass the time, but suddenly my gaze met a man sitting alone at a table near the stove. He was a dapper gent in a black woolen suit and derby hat, and he was looking directly at me.

Our eyes met and held for a moment, and then he looked down at his coffee. I watched him out of the corner of my eye, but he did not look my way again. A moment later, he got to his feet, shrugged into his overcoat, and paid for his meal. Without a glance back at the crowded café, he opened the door and went outside.

I told myself the gent just happened to be looking my way, that I was not the object of his interest. To the best of my recollection, I had never seen him before. Still, I reminded myself, I was a wanted man and couldn't afford to be careless.

When I finished my pie, paid for my meal, and stepped out into the cold evening air, the man in the derby was nowhere in sight. I walked back toward the hotel, casting an occasional glance back over my shoulder. Once, I thought I heard the sound of footsteps behind me, but when I turned around, the street was deserted. A moment later, I entered the hotel and crossed the lobby. The desk clerk was not at his station. I took one last look back and climbed the stairs to the second floor, unlocked the door to my room, and went inside.

Sleep didn't come easy that night. My thoughts kept returning to Tom across town at Doc Whittier's place. If Tom pulled through, any prison sentence was likely to be a life sentence.

I thought of George. He *appeared* to be different,

softer somehow than the George I knew, kinder and more human maybe. Abby seemed important to him; no doubt he had hopes of becoming a family man, living out his days as a doting father—and maybe even a grandfather. But there was the money, and there were the killings. No. George was still bad to the bone.

But Abby. Ah, yes, Gentle Abby. It was hard to think of her learning the truth. What would that do to her? No doubt, she too had dreams of family life—dreams that would soon die. Would the news break her heart?

As for me, my assignment was nearly at an end, and I could go back to Dry Creek, and Pandora would learn I was neither killer nor outlaw.

So the last thing on my mind before I drifted off was Pandora Pretty Hawk. It was a fine way to fall asleep.

The morning dawned still and cold under clearing skies. I rubbed a clear patch on the frosted window near my bed and looked out on the world. New snow covered the old drifts and dusted sidewalks and awnings. Smoke and vapor rose again from the chimneys of Wolf City, catching the early light.

I dressed in a hurry and washed my face in cold water at the room's commode, then closed the door behind me and took the stairs down to the lobby. A different clerk behind the desk smiled and bade me a good morning, which I hoped it would be. I gave him back his greeting, left the key on the desk, and stepped out onto the street.

Wolf City looked different in the daylight, bigger than last night. In addition to the saloons, I counted two groceries and a mercantile, a hardware, a drugstore, a barbershop, and a feed store. I was a little surprised at the number of people out and about at this early hour.

Already, saddle horses lined the hitch rail in front of the Roundup Café. A few doors down, a stocky gent in an apron was sweeping the walk in front of a dry goods store. Directly across the street, built of native stone and solid and substantial as a fort, stood Slippery Mayfair's bank. A sign above the front door read "Wolf City Bank & Trust. Obadiah J. Mayfair, President." I was willing to concede the place was a bank, all right, but knowing that that institution was the repository for George's stolen loot and other ill-gotten gains, as for the "trust" part, I had my doubts.

A man's nickname tells a lot about him. People called President Lincoln "Honest Abe" because he was honest. They called Obadiah Mayfair "Slippery" because, well, because he *wasn't* honest.

I ate breakfast at the Roundup and walked back up the street to Fraley's livery stable. Fraley helped me harness Samson and Delilah and hitch them to the sleigh. Having paid my bill last night, I had only to take up the reins and strike out for Doc Whittier's place.

"I'm sorry."

Doc Whittier stood in the open doorway, his face drawn and tired. He was in his shirtsleeves. "I did everything I could," he said, "but . . ."

"Tom's dead," I said.

"Yes," the doctor said. "When the end came, it came quickly."

A great sadness tightened my breath. Tom—poor Tom—in spite of his wayward ways, he'd been a man with the sorrowful light of an abused conscience in his eyes, yesterday my friend, now a candle blown out by the prairie wind. Almost unaccountably, I felt tears rise into my eyes.

The doc led me into the kitchen and invited me to sit. He poured us each a cup of coffee and sat down heavily across the table from me. Then for maybe five minutes, he talked of things I hardly heard or understood. Things about Tom's heart. I caught the word exudation—warts or pimples on the valves torn away by the blood, like trees on a stream bank swept away by the current, lodging in the blood vessels to the brain. Like I say, I hardly heard it, my mind on Tom's being gone, but I got the idea, anyway.

"Death was immediate," the doc said.

That brought me around, and I was glad to hear it.

"He was unconscious most of the time after you left, but just before the end, he was quite lucid and talked of you. 'The Kid's been mighty good to me,' he said. 'Most of my life I've been bossed around and kicked around, but the Kid's treated me square.'"

The doctor looked into my eyes. "Something to think about if you're blaming yourself for not doing enough."

I made no reply. The lump in my throat was too hard to talk around.

• • •

I stood beside the bed in Doc Whittier's examining room, looking at Tom's body. The old outlaw's eyes were closed, his face relaxed. He might have been asleep and dreaming of better times. I reached out and touched his cold, lifeless hand. *Well,* I thought. *You won't be going back to prison, anyway.*

At last I found my voice. "About the body, Doc," I said. "Is there somewhere I can take it until the ground thaws?"

"Wolf City has no mortuary, but Bob Fraley has an ice house down by the creek. The body would keep well enough there."

"I'm already in your debt, but I'd be obliged if you could arrange that with Bob. I need to get back to the ranch and let my boss know what's happened."

"Certainly. I will need Tom's full name for the death certificate."

"Tom—Thomas, I suppose. Thomas Blackburn."

"Mind telling me your name?"

"Uh . . . Charlie Jones. From Lander."

"I'll talk to Bob. Stop in next time you're in town."

"My boss will take care of your fee. If he doesn't, I will."

"There's no charge. I only wish I could have saved him."

Doc Whittier smiled and shook my hand. I had kept company with outlaws so long I had almost forgotten what good men were like.

Refreshed by their overnight stay at Fraley's, the

horses took to the road with a will. Heads held high and tasting the wind, Samson and Delilah broke into a smooth trot that swept the sleigh over the rutted track back to the ranch. They were a good team, accustomed to pulling together, and moved as though they were a single horse.

The places where we plowed through the hard-packed snow on the way to town were plain to see. Had that desperate ride really been only yesterday? Tom alive beside me in the sleigh and hurting bad? Again I heard him cry out when the runners struck the cross drifts, the quaver in his voice, the sudden silence. Those tortured words on the road were the last I'd heard him speak.

Now he was dead, destined to lie in storage like a side of beef until the snow melted and somebody could dig his grave. Another member of George's gang had perished, this time of a bad heart.

When I turned the horses into the ranch gate, I saw that George had visitors. Slippery Mayfair's Portland Cutter was parked beside the house, his matched team of grays asleep in the sunshine. I drove up alongside and reined Samson and Delilah to a stop.

Pronto Southwell stepped toward me out of the shadows like a guard dog coming to challenge a stranger. He swaggered up to the sleigh and craned his neck to look inside.

"I see you left the old fool in town," he said. "Did he stay at the sawbones' house?"

"His name is *Tom*," I said. "Yeah, he stayed at Doc Whittier's."

Pronto tipped his head back and looked down his nose at me. He was taller than I am and liked to remind me of it. "The boss has company," he said. "Wait here, and I'll tell him you're back."

I shouldered my way past him. "I'll tell him myself. Get the hell out of my way."

George stepped out onto the porch and his shrewd yellow eyes took in the situation at a glance. "I'm glad you're back, son," he said. "How's Tom?"

George enjoyed pulling Pronto's chain; he'd called me "son" at least partly to provoke Pronto's jealousy.

"Tom passed away last night," I said. "It was his heart."

George was silent for a moment. Then he said, "Sorry to hear it." His tone of voice made me believe him. Again, I marveled at how he seemed to have changed.

George turned, holding the door open for me. "Come on in," he said. "Slippery is here. He brought his niece out to meet Abby."

I doffed my hat at the door and walked inside. Behind me, George turned and spoke to Pronto. "Take the sleigh up to the barn and unhitch the horses," he said. "I'll be there d'rectly."

At the piano in the parlor, a blonde girl in a blue dress sat beside Abby at the piano; they were playing the instrument together. Slippery Mayfair, dressed in a dark suit and wing collar, sat in an oversized chair, leaning on his cane and beaming at the girls. He turned to look at me when I entered the room. "Bodacious," he said.

I nodded. "Mr. Mayfair."

The girls stopped playing and looked at me. Abby nodded, her smile warm.

"Permit me to introduce my brother Austin's lovely child," Slippery said. "Behold, the fair Winifred."

"Howdy, Miss," I said.

Slippery turned to the girl. "And this, my dear, is young Merlin, Mr. Shannon's foreman."

Winifred lowered her eyes. "I am pleased to make your acquaintance, Merlin," she said shyly.

My hat was still in my hands. "The pleasure is mine, Miss Winifred," I said. "Have you come to visit Miss Abby?"

"Yes. We're becoming great friends. We've been playing duets, but Abby is so much better than I am."

"Sounded mighty pretty to me," I said.

Behind me, George cleared his throat. "You girls go on a-makin' music," he said. "Merlin and me have business to discuss."

Leading the way, George walked ahead of me down the hall. "You've never been inside my office," he said, "but I figure we can talk better there. Them fillies have been pickin' out tunes on the piano, talkin' and gigglin' all mornin'." He chuckled. "Mighty pleasant, but a mite distractin' at times."

I felt a pang of guilt. I *had* been in George's office. I had visited every room in the house only the week before.

269

George opened the office door and showed me inside. "Take a chair," he said. "Now tell me about Tom."

"He was hurtin' when we left for town," I began. "Then, on the way in, the pain hit him hard, and he was out cold when we reached the doctor's house.

"Doc Whittier gave him a shot and said he'd watch over him. He told me to go on into town and come back in the morning. I put the horses up at Fraley's, ate supper, and got myself a room at the Sherman. This mornin' when I went back, Tom was dead."

George looked thoughtful. "You reckon he said anything? About the bank jobs, I mean."

"Not Tom," I said.

"You didn't use your right name in town, did you?"

"No. Said I was Charlie Jones from Lander."

George slumped back in his chair. "Good," he said. "That's good, son."

"I offered to pay the doctor, but he wouldn't take my money."

"I'll pay him anyway. What about Tom's body?"

"The ground is froze hard as iron right now," I said, "but the Doc said Bob Fraley has an ice house over on Wolf Creek. He thinks Bob will let us keep Tom's body there until spring."

"That'll do," George said. "When the thaw comes, we'll give old Tom a first-class buryin'."

For a moment George seemed to lose himself in thought. When at last he spoke again, there was something like wonder in his voice. "Damnedest thing," he said, "but nearly all the boys who rode for me are gone—

one way or the other. Now that Tom's took the big jump, there's just you and Pronto left from the old outfit.

"I've pretty well done what I aimed to," he continued. "I've bought this place, and I figure to stock it when winter's past. I'll be hirin' ranch hands and cowpunchers instead of long rope artists and *pistoleros.*

"Gettin' to know my daughter's been a fine thing; she makes me feel like a new man. I can't wait to put my old life behind me and build a new one. I don't even wear a gun anymore. Abby don't like weapons around the house."

Listening to all this, the sadness and foreboding weighed on me heavy.

"I still want you to be my foreman," he was saying, "Abby and me have talked about doin' some travelin', maybe down to Denver or even out to California. Always wanted to see the ocean.

"I need a man I can trust to run my spread. I figure you're that man."

"I-I appreciate that, Cap'n, but I'm not—"

George's voice took on a hard edge. In that moment he was once again the bandit chief I remembered.

"There is one loose end I still have to clean up," he said. "Pronto's part of the old life. I'm goin' to give him his walkin' papers."

I was surprised. "You're . . . letting Pronto go?"

"This very day," George said. "As my foreman, I want you with me when I do it."

He won't take it well, I thought. What I said was, "You're the boss."

CHAPTER 18
Out of the Frying Pan

I walked with George from the office into the parlor where Abby and Winifred continued their recital while Slippery Mayfair sat in the big chair and listened. The music was some kind of high-class music, and it sounded pretty but complicated.

George bent and spoke to Slippery as we passed. Because of the music, I couldn't hear what he said, but I supposed he told Slippery we were going up to the barn and asked him if he'd look after the girls. Still intent on the recital, Slippery replied with a nod. George and me crossed the room and walked to the front door.

On a hall tree beside the door, George's belted revolver hung next to his hat and buffalo coat. He put on the hat and shrugged into the coat, but he left the revolver behind. Outside, he gave me a wolfish grin. "Better if I'm not heeled when I give Pronto the news," he said. "He ain't as likely to pull on an unarmed man."

I remember wishing I was as sure of that as George seemed to be.

The sunshine at midday reflected off the drifted snow and caused a man to squint against the brightness. Ahead, darkness pooled in the shadows of the out-buildings. A raven soared overhead, its cry raucous and loud in the stillness. Walking behind George, I made my way along the pathway to the barn.

As we neared the big corral, I saw that Pronto had turned the Morgans out. The animals stood in the sunlight, feeding at the hayrack. Almost in the center of the corral, Pronto lounged, watching our approach. George hesitated briefly, then swung the corral gate wide and led me inside. He walked across the corral until he was maybe thirty feet from Pronto, thrust his hands deep into the pockets of his coat, and stopped.

"Been wantin' to talk to you," George said.

Pronto stared at me and frowned. Then he looked to George and said, "Well, here I am."

"This ain't the same outfit as when we started," George began.

"It sure as hell ain't," Pronto agreed. "When we started, all we needed were a few good men, our guns, and some fast horses. Now that you've turned respectable, we mostly just need a manure fork and some fencin' pliers." He smiled, as if to show he was only joking, but his smile didn't fool me.

"That's what I wanted to talk to you about," George said. "This outfit ain't a gun outfit any more. You're a loyal hand and a top *pistolero*. You've kept the back shooters off me, and you've done what I asked. But the truth is, this outfit don't need you any more."

Pronto's eyes widened and his head jerked back as if George had struck him. "You're *firin'* me?"

"I'm sayin' I don't need you anymore."

Pronto nodded at me, and then looked back at George. "But you need *him.*"

"I've asked Bodacious to be my *segundo*. This ain't no longer your kind of operation."

"So you figured you'd just tie a can to my tail and run me off?"

"It ain't like that," George said. "You've been well paid for what you've done. It's over; that's all."

Pronto took a slow step back and set his feet. "Maybe it is, and maybe it ain't," he said. "Suppose I don't *feel* like movin' on?"

"I ain't packin' a gun," George said.

"You *should* be," Pronto said.

They stood, facing each other, two proud men squaring off in a corral, neither man willing or able to back down. The cold, flat words hung in the air between them. Suddenly, I knew: Gun or no gun, Pronto meant to kill George Starkweather!

Time stopped. Pictures flashed before my eyes: George unmoving, his hands still deep in his pockets. Pronto's right-hand revolver a blur, flashing as it catches the light. My hand finding George's shoulder, shoving him aside. My own gun out of the leather and coming up.

Then Pronto, teeth bared, fires point blank. Flame stabs from the muzzle, fire and blossoming smoke. I feel the shock at my side, the impact twisting me. I hear the sound of Pronto's shot, hear my own gun answer, and then—then Pronto is down, his revolver flying free.

Hard hit, he draws his left-hand gun, shifts it to his right hand. I fire again, see the slug take him in the chest, see it slam him to the frozen earth. The revolver falls from his hand. Pronto stiffens, convulses, and lies still. Gunsmoke drifts in the sunlight.

Pronto lay sprawled in the trampled snow, blood from his chest wounds pooled and spreading beneath him. Everything had happened so fast, I could scarcely take it in. Ever since that shootout with Ed Hutchins, I'd wondered if I could ever again pull my gun against a man. Now the wondering was over. My hand had owned a mind of its own, and I had drawn and fired without thinking.

I holstered my .44. A dull pain had begun to throb just above my left hip. I unbuttoned my coat, pulled up my shirt, and touched the place. Pronto's bullet had gone through the flesh of my belly, in one side and out the other. I felt no pain, only a numb throbbing.

I turned to where George stood looking down at Pronto's lifeless body. "I had to do it, Cap'n," I said. "He meant to kill you."

"He'd have got the job done if not for you," George said. "Dumb sum'bitch just had too much mustard."

George raised his eyes to me, a kind of admiration on his face. "You're fast, Bodacious," he said. "Faster than you were."

He drew his right hand from his coat pocket—and brought a short-barreled Colt .45 out with it. "I wasn't quite as unarmed as I let on," he said. "How bad are you hurt?"

I stared at the gun in George's hand. "Not bad," I said. "Just a scratch."

"I hate to seem ungrateful," George said, "but I'm afraid I have to withdraw my job offer. I won't be needin' a foreman on this outfit after all."

He pointed the gun at my middle and eased the hammer back to full cock. "Unbuckle your gun belt, son," he said, "and let it drop. I don't want to kill a man who just saved my life, but you know I will if I need to."

My head whirled, and I couldn't do anything but stare at him open-mouthed.

"You see, Slippery has an *arrangement* with Barney Foster. Barney told Slippery about your message, and Slippery told me."

George glanced around the ranch buildings quickly, then looked back at me. "That message of yours requires me to change my plans," he said. "Looks like I ain't goin' to be no gentleman rancher after all.

"But that's all right. I've got money to last me a while, and I want to do some travelin' with Abby anyway. Slippery can manage this outfit for me . . . or sell it. Abby and me will be long gone by the time the law shows up."

My heart was pounding in my ears and in the wound in my side.

"And speakin' of the law, here's how we're goin' to play this. Like any other good citizen, I'll have to report this killin' to the Wolf City marshal. As the only witness to the shootin,' I get to make up my own version of what happened."

"Which is?" I asked as I pressed on the wound with the heel of my left hand, trying to stop the bleeding.

"There's been bad blood between you and Pronto for some time now. Today it finally came to a shootin', and Pronto went under. Trouble is, poor old Pronto wasn't armed. You gunned him down in cold blood."

"What makes you think the marshal will believe you?"

"Why, he'll have to, son! Like I said, I'm the only witness. Of course, you can always tell him a different story, but I expect he'll lean toward my version. Slippery and me pay his wages."

"So," I said, "you've bought yourself a peace officer."

"No, we just rented one. He's free to enforce all the law he wants to, long as he don't try to enforce it against Slippery or me."

A gust of wind, cold as charity, swept through the corral, dusted Pronto's body with snow, and sent his hat flip-flopping across the frozen earth. His gray eyes were open, staring at nothing.

I met George's gaze and tried to look braver than I felt. "All right," I said. "What happens now?"

"First off, you saddle three horses," George said. "One for me, one for you, and one for Pronto. Then I take you boys into town."

"What'll you tell Slippery and the girls?"

"Pretty much the same thing I'm fixin' to tell the marshal. You and Pronto got into a fuss, and you gunned him down. Pronto was unarmed, so it was plain murder. I'll say I'm shocked, but terrible things happen now and again. Then I'll leave Slippery with the girls, and take you and Pronto's corpse in to Wolf City."

So it was that within the hour three horses carrying three men left the ranch for Wolf City. I rode Roanie, George sat his blood-bay thoroughbred, and Pronto's lifeless form was wrapped in a tarp and tied facedown across the sorrel he had so favored in life.

From somewhere, George produced a pair of handcuffs and shackled my right wrist to the saddle horn. Then he set me out on the road while he rode a pace or two behind and led the sorrel and its mortal burden.

"If you're thinkin' about makin' a run for it, I wouldn't," George said. "Not only is my horse faster than that roan of yours, a bullet's faster still."

George had a way of stating the obvious.

The jail in Wolf City was a grim, ugly building of quarried stone that stood directly across the street from Bob Fraley's Livery Stable. A barred door and a single window opened onto the marshal's office in front, and it occurred to me that if a building could be an animal, the jail would be a one-eyed bulldog with the mange.

The door opened as we drew rein, and a slope-shouldered gent with a paunch like a brood mare in foal stepped into the sunlight. He squinted against the brightness, shading his eyes with his hand as he studied our three-horse procession. The man wore an old wool vest over a faded undershirt, and the nickel-plated star that was pinned to it told me I was looking at Wolf City's town marshal.

"It's me, Butch," George said, "George Shannon. There's been some trouble out at my place."

The man called Butch craned his neck, and then recognized George. "Oh . . . Howdy, Mr. Shannon," he said. "What can I do for you?"

George nodded at me. "This man is Merlin Fanshaw, also known as the Bodacious Kid. He gunned down one of my riders today. Killed the poor devil in cold blood."

"Butch" assumed an official air. "I see. Is that the victim under the tarp yonder?"

"That's him," George said. "Ripley Southwell. One of my best men."

Ripley? I thought. *Funny the way people start using a man's given name once he's dead.*

"That's *Pronto* Southwell," I said. "He was a wanted man and a killer. He was armed when I shot him, and he fired first."

"Another thing about Fanshaw," George said calmly. "He's a terrible liar." George dismounted and stepped up onto the boardwalk. He fished the key to the handcuffs from his vest pocket and handed it to the marshal. "You'd best lock this boy in a cell," he said. "I'll give you a full account of what happened. Then I'll stop by the city attorney's office and give him my deposition."

While George looked on, the marshal unlocked the cuff that bound me to the saddle horn, and I stepped down. "All right, Fanshaw," he said. "Inside."

When I feel I have been particularly ill-used, I oft-times say the wrong thing to the wrong person at the wrong time. As the marshal took me by the arm, I did so again.

"So your name is Butch, I said. "Do you have a last name?"

"Yeah," he said. "I'm Butch Wilson. *My* name is Butch, and my *Pa's* name was Butch. Does that answer your question?"

I gave him my best smart aleck grin. "Then I guess that would make you a *son* of a Butch."

His fist caught me just beneath my ribcage. The blow folded me up like a jackknife and knocked the wind out of me. The marshal dragged me inside, shoved me into a cell, slammed the door, and locked it. It was a long moment before I could breathe again, and the pain was fierce. Even so, the look on the man's face just before he hit me was worth the price.

The Wolf City jail boasted two rude cells, each about ten feet square, separated from the marshal's office by a heavy wooden door, which, when closed, pretty much cut off all sound and light from the front of the building.

A barred, narrow window high on the back wall in each cell provided what light there was, but the windows were at least seven feet from the floor. A man could see outside only by standing on something, and in those cells, there wasn't a whole lot to stand on.

There was a battered slop pail in one corner, but it looked like it hadn't been cleaned since it was new. I wouldn't have stood on that stinking bucket even in my gum boots and wearing two pair of socks.

Already the light was fading, and through the windows I could see the skies had gone to dusty rose. A cold draft crept into the cell. A threadbare blanket and a shabby quilt lay atop an iron cot at the cell's rear wall, but they wouldn't do much to keep a man warm. I was glad I still wore my sheepskin.

I sat on the cot and pulled my shirttail out. The wound on my side was swollen and sore, but the bleeding had stopped. Pronto's bullet had pierced the flesh just above my hip and had torn through to the other side, but I had been lucky. An inch or two farther to the right, and I would have been gut shot for sure.

I wondered how George would explain my getting shot by an unarmed man, but figured he'd probably tell Marshal Butch that in all the excitement, I'd accidentally shot myself. Knowing George, he'd even make it sound believable.

As darkness settled in, I lay back on the bunk and closed my eyes. Everything had gone wrong. I had played my hand close to the vest, but it was George who'd dealt the cards. As always he'd dealt from the bottom of the deck. When Abby had come, I had even found myself sympathizing with the old renegade. And this very day, I'd stood between him and Pronto's bullet. I had *protected* the man!

I was guilty—not of murder, but of stupidity in the first degree. I had failed in my assignment.

I awoke to the sound of a bolt being thrown on the door between the cells and the office, followed by the murmur of voices. Marshal Butch swaggered into the narrow corridor, a lighted lamp held high. Behind him were townsfolk I recognized: Doc Whittier, the desk clerk from the hotel, telegraph agent Barney Foster, and the gent in the derby hat who had looked me over at the café.

"Wake up, Fanshaw!" said the marshal. "There are some people here to see you."

I swung my legs over the side of the cot and sat up and, half awake, mumbled, "Mighty neighborly of 'em. You Wolf City folks know how to make a stranger feel welcome."

"I've had enough of your smart mouth, Fanshaw," the marshal said. "Stand up in the light so they can get a good look at you."

As I stood, I favored my wound, leaning a little to that side.

The marshal turned to Doc Whittier. "What about it, Doc? Is this the man who brought George Shannon's ranch hand to your place night before last?"

The doctor looked troubled at the sight of me, like I'd disappointed him. "It is," he said.

"What'd he say his name was?"

"Charlie Jones—from Lander."

Marshal Butch looked pompous. "What if I told you

282

his real name is Merlin Fanshaw, and he's a bank robber and a murderer?"

"I would have to say that that's not the impression I have of the man."

"Nevertheless, Doc, that's who he is."

Barney Foster spoke up. "He gave me that name, too. He asked me to send a telegram to U.S. Marshal Chance Ridgeway, up in Montana. Somethin' about wolf huntin'."

"That's the name he signed to the hotel register," the clerk said.

Marshal Butch turned back to me. "So! Do you admit you were usin' a false name?"

I was growing tired of the marshal's grandstanding. "No," I said. "Charlie Jones was my true and official name . . . at the time."

The marshal scowled. "Yeah? How could that be?"

I shrugged. "I gave it to myself," I said. "That made it official."

"Let me tell you what else I found out about you, smart boy," the marshal said. "You're also wanted for murder up Montana way. Seems you killed a peace officer in the town of Dry Creek and helped a known bank robber escape."

I was beginning to feel like an exhibit at the zoo; me on one side of the bars and Marshal Butch and his witnesses on the other side. Judging by all the fuss, my arrest must have been the most interesting thing that ever happened in Wolf City.

The dapper dude in the black wool suit and derby hat

was watching me intently. I met his gaze and remembered how he had studied me that day in the Roundup Café.

"I remember you," I said. "Do you know me?"

"Uh . . . no," he said. "I never saw you before that day. I'm sorry if I stared at you. You see, I'm a salesman for the Topper Hat Company, and I couldn't help noticing the hat you were wearing . . . *are* wearing."

"What about it?"

"It's the dirtiest, most disreputable hat I've ever seen."

I had to laugh. "Keeps the rain off," I said. "It has character."

Marshal Butch seemed annoyed by the interruption. There was an edge in his voice when he said, "I asked you folks here to help establish this man's true identity. Whatever hat he wears or don't wear is beside the point."

Turning back to me, he said, "Your former employer, George Shannon, also suggested I contact the marshal's office up in Blue Rock. Said a man of your description was arrested after the robbery there back in January. Apparently, you bribed an officer to help you escape."

I was growing tired of the marshal's kangaroo court. "Are you really interested in the truth?" I asked.

"That is what I'm tryin' to establish."

"All right. My name is Merlin Fanshaw. I'm a deputy U.S. Marshal on special assignment. I was sent to infiltrate the Starkweather gang, to gather evidence, and help bring it to justice.

"That telegram I sent was a coded report to my boss, U.S. Marshal Chance Ridgeway. Now that he's heard from me, I expect he's either on his way here himself or sendin' someone to straighten all this out."

Marshal Butch snorted. "From what Mr. Shannon wrote about you in his deposition and what I've learned about the bank robbery in Blue Rock and the killin' at Dry Creek, I'd say you were more likely to run *from* a U.S. Marshal than to work *for* one."

I took a deep breath and tried again. "The man you know as George Shannon is a rustler, thief, and cold-blooded killer known as Original George Starkweather, an escaped convict and the man I was sent to track down. Does that sound like somebody you'd want to believe—about *anything?*

"Look into my claims. Bring Starkweather—the man you call George Shannon—in and question him. You can do *that* at least, can't you?"

The marshal's answer came as no surprise. "Already did," he said. "Mr. Shannon gave his sworn deposition to the city attorney.

"He told me he's catchin' the northbound train with his daughter tomorrow evenin'. Said they'll be gone five or six months—and they may not come back at all."

CHAPTER 19
In the Lockup

Marshal Butch Wilson scowled. He had brought citizens to the jail to serve as witnesses, and—I suppose—to admire his handling of the murderous bank-robbing desperado he had me figured for. He'd failed on both counts.

I didn't grovel or rage. Neither broken nor bent, I gave him the truth. Even George and Abby's leaving town didn't shake my calm—at least on the outside. My inward thoughts, however, were something else.

"It's been nice talkin' to you, Marshal," I said, "but unless you've got some more dumb questions right now, I'd like to get a little rest. This bullet wound in my side is hurtin' me a good deal more than somewhat."

"Bullet wound?" the marshal said. "What bullet wound?"

I shucked out of the sheepskin coat I'd slept in to stay at least halfway warm, pulled out my shirttail, and turned where he could see the big dark red patch on my white long johns where the blood had caked and dried. "The one that 'unarmed' man I killed gave to me," I replied. I turned so Doc Whittier could see the bloody patch on my side. "Could you take a look at it, Doc?"

"Of course," he said. "I'll get my bag."

When Doc Whittier opened the office door and stepped out onto the street, I turned my gaze back to the marshal. He was standing there staring at my bloody side, gape mouthed and slack jawed.

"Why the *hell* didn't you say somethin' about that wound last night!"

"Well sir, I'm askin' myself the same question; maybe it's you just didn't seem interested in anything I had to say."

"Well, I'll be damned," he said.

To take advantage of his being suddenly off balance, I said, "Also, I haven't et since yesterday mornin'. I could use some food—if that doesn't violate your policy.

He looked uncertain. "I-I was just fixin' to send out for some breakfast," he said, his voice a mite less sure. "My wife generally cooks for the prisoners, but . . . I forgot to tell her."

He turned to young Barney Foster. "Go on over to the Roundup and fetch back some grub for this man," he said. "Tell Hank I said charge it to the city."

"I'm late for work as it is, Butch."

"That's *Marshal* Butch to you—and the only *work* you do these days is sweet talk that young Nordquist girl! Now go do what I told you!"

Barney's lower lip jutted out like a ledge, and he gave me a surly look, as if to say all his troubles were my fault. I offered him a smirk, and he moseyed out the door.

The desk clerk cleared his throat and shifted his feet. "I need to be gettin' back, too," he said. "You still need me, Butch?"

"No, no," the marshal said. "Go ahead on back, Fred."

He turned to the dude in the derby. "You, too," he said. "Thanks for comin' in.

I heard the door facing the street open and close, and even back there in my cell, felt the inrush of cold air. The marshal added wood to the potbellied stove and gave me a thoughtful look.

"That man you killed," he said. "Did he shoot you first?"

"As I recall."

He lifted a coffee pot from the stovetop. "You want some coffee while we're waitin'?" he asked. "It's yesterday's, but it might tide you over till your breakfast gets here."

"No, thanks."

"Sometimes a man gets busy," the marshal said. "He forgets others have needs." It was as close to an apology as I was likely to get.

Doc Whittier came back a few minutes later, medical bag in hand. The marshal unlocked the cell door to let him in, and turned the lamp in the corridor up high.

The doctor opened his bag and set it on the floor next to my bunk. "You want to peel out of those long johns, or shall I cut them away?" he asked.

"Cut 'em," I said. "If I try to get 'em off, I'm afraid I might open the wound and start the bleedin' all over again."

"Makes sense," he said. "Lie down on your right side."

I stretched out on my right side, studying the contents of the doe's open bag while he examined me. I saw ointments and pills, bandages, syringes and needles, a bottle of chloroform, a stethoscope, and various instruments and cutting tools I neither knew—nor wanted to know—the purpose of.

The doc took out scissors and cut away the bloody patch, and working slowly at it, got it unstuck from my hide. His touch was gentle and sure. "You're a fortunate young man," he said. "The bullet passed through the lower abdominal wall just above your left hip, and I don't think it did any serious internal damage."

He turned to Marshal Butch, who had fallen quiet. "That washbasin and water pitcher in your office," he said, "I need to borrow them if I may."

"Sure, Doc," the marshal said, and went out. When he came back, he set the water on the floor and handed Doc the basin.

I mustered nerve enough to watch while Doc Whittier mixed up some kind of a solution, carbolic acid and water, I think he said, and scrubbed his hands with it and dried them. He pulled a syringe from his bag and started rinsing the wounds—the one where the slug went in and the other, where it came out. That stung pretty fierce, and I winced, but I was curious enough to keep looking; the first was a small hole, but I craned my neck, and saw the other was torn a little bigger; the bullet hadn't mushroomed much. Then Doc poked a little clean square of folded gauze in each hole to keep them open.

"We'll need to let these drain for a day or two," he said. "When we're sure there's no infection, I'll sew them up."

He closed his bag, looked me in the eyes, and I saw kindness and encouragement in his gaze. "I'll look in on you again later today," he said. "Do you know how long you'll be here?"

I lay there letting the air get to my side. Cold as it was, it felt good. Nodding at the marshal, I said, "Ask him."

"I expect another week or two, at least," the marshal said. "I sent a telegram to the district judge last night, but I haven't heard back from him yet."

Doc Whittier gave the cell a disapproving glance. In a voice that showed he was in charge now, he said, "Clean this place up, Marshal. You can start by getting rid of that slop bucket."

Marshal Butch looked at the cell as if he he'd never seen it before. "I've been meanin' to do it," he said. "Haven't had a prisoner in here in quite a spell."

"Apparently not," the doctor said. Stepping outside the cell, he returned the pitcher and basin to the marshal and left the office.

Minutes later, Barney Foster showed up with an order of biscuits and gravy on a tray, but his mood hadn't improved much. Marshal Butch took a careful look to make sure there were no hidden armaments or high explosives lurking behind the biscuits and passed the tray in to me.

"*Now* can I go back to work?" Barney asked.

"Go on," the marshal said. "Let me know if an answer from the judge comes in."

"Oh, I surely will," Barney said, snippy-like, "if ever I get to the office."

The city attorney, Austin Mayfair, stopped by the jail to see me. He turned out to be Slippery Mayfair's brother and Miss Winifred's daddy. I might have known. Sometimes I agree with the feller who said if it wasn't for bad luck he'd have no luck at all. Learning that Slippery's brother was the local prosecutor did little to brighten my mood.

Anyway, on my first full day in the Wolf City jail, City Attorney Austin Mayfair—fastidious and neat, the spitting image of his brother, except not quite as fat—entered the jail at about half-past ten in the morning. He was carrying a bulging leather briefcase and was accompanied by a wispy gent I learned was a stenographer.

"Merlin Fanshaw," he began, "I am here to depose you in regard to the charges and circumstances of your arrest. Do you mind if I ask you a few questions?"

"Go ahead."

The lawyer took a paper from his briefcase and studied it for a moment. "You are accused of murdering peace officer Glenn Murdoch at Dry Creek, Montana, last October and of aiding and abetting the escape of a criminal held in custody there, one Rufus Two Hats.

"You are accused of taking part in the December robbery of the First Bank of Blue Rock, Wyoming, and of being accessory before and after the fact in the murder of a bank employee there.

"Finally, you are accused of the willful murder of Ripley Southwell at the George Shannon ranch earlier this week. How do you answer these charges?"

The stenographer opened his pad, produced a pencil, and waited, his eyes on me.

"Quite a list," I said. "I plead not guilty to all charges."

The attorney pursed his lips and frowned. "That is your right, of course," he said, "but do you really believe that's wise? If you admit your guilt, the judge may be more inclined to show mercy."

"You mean he'd maybe only hang me for *one* of those killin's? I'd sure like to help you out, Austin, but I can't. It's my mother's fault."

"Your mother?" He looked startled.

"She raised me to tell the truth. It wouldn't be right for me to confess to crimes I didn't commit."

"Are you saying you're innocent of these charges?"

"I am."

"I have substantial evidence—witnesses, a deposition from Mr. Shannon, and more—that contradict your assertion."

"Sorry, but that doesn't change anything. Your evidence makes you believe I'm guilty, but I have the bulge on you. I *know* I'm innocent; you only *think* I'm not."

That pretty well wrapped up our meeting. City Attorney Mayfair shook his head and picked up his briefcase while the stenographer folded his pad and put his pencil away. Both men walked through the marshal's office and out onto the street. Neither of them said good-bye.

Marshal Butch was away a good deal that day, basking in his newfound celebrity as captor of the Terrible Bank Robbing Murderer (that would be me). From the way his slurred speech and unsteady gait grew as the day went on, I deduced he was spending much of his time in the saloons, and that the Wolf City barflies were keeping him well supplied with liquid congratulations.

The truth, of course, was that he hadn't captured me at all but had merely taken delivery. That fact didn't seem to trouble him much. I guess he figured I was locked in his jail; therefore, I was his trophy. Twice that day he brought visitors in to see me. I obliged by trying to look as mean and murderous as I knew how, just to keep up my image.

Just after sundown, Marshal Butch brought in a part-time deputy to stand guard over me while he went home for the evening. The marshal was three sheets to the wind by then, and it occurred to me he could be in for a chilly reception from Mrs. Butch.

"This here is Pooch McKinney," the marshal said. "Pooch helps me out here sometimes. Sweeps up, makes coffee, and such. He might not be the sharpest tool in the shed, but then it don't take a genius to pull the trigger on a shotgun."

Butch handed the cell keys to the deputy, who put them in his coat pocket. "Well," said Butch, "He's all yours. Watch yourself, Pooch." Fumbling once or twice for the doorknob, the marshal opened the jail's front door and staggered out into the twilight.

Deputy Pooch was a big man, taller than me, with a barrel chest and a face that was mostly whiskers. He pulled up a chair from the office and sat down facing me, a sawed-off shotgun cradled in his arms.

"You seem like a nice feller—for a murderer," he said, "but I've got a boil on the back of my neck that's hurtin' me somethin' awful, and I don't feel much like talkin'."

"This is your lucky night," I said. "Neither do I."

I lay back on my cot and let my thoughts run. The darkness and the quiet gave me nowhere to go but into myself. Feelings I was able to hold at bay during daylight came to haunt me in the darkness. I looked at my fears and let them take me where they would.

I wondered if Marshal Ridgeway had received my telegram or even the letter I sent him from Red Lodge.

I wondered if Pandora, she of the tawny skin and raven hair, still shed tears for me. I closed my eyes and saw again in memory her dark, deep eyes. I recalled the way her voice sounded when she spoke my name—serious and respectful-like, as if it meant something. I craved Pandora like a drowning man craves dry.

Worse than the loneliness, worse than the fear, was knowing that George Starkweather had outsmarted me, plain and simple. He had slipped my loop and was about to vanish like smoke in a gale. He and Abby— sweet, innocent Abby—would board the train tomorrow and simply disappear. She saw George as her hero and protector, father and family, but she was putting her hopes in a monster.

I lay back on my bunk and stared up into the gloom. Deputy Pooch was mostly quiet, but I could tell he was suffering from his boil. From time to time he'd leave his chair and pace the floor in a kind of restless shuffle. Then he'd sit down again. And all the while I'd hear him grunt from the hurt of it, and now and then he'd whimper sort of quiet-like, just like an old dog.

After an hour or so, he took the lamp into the marshal's office and shut the door behind him, leaving my cell as dark and forlorn as my mood. Even when sleep finally came, it brought little rest. My dreams were a jumble of dark and lonesome places and of people without faces watching me.

The next day, Marshal Butch turned out to be a man of his word—sort of. He made an effort to tidy up my cell, chiefly by putting me to work, in spite of my gunshot wound. I didn't like that very much, but I cleaned out the spider webs and swept and mopped the floor. It hurt my durned side like crazy, but I even scrubbed the walls.

The marshal put on work gloves and snagged that stinking slop bucket out of my cell with a long-handled rake like a man dealing with a sidewinder. He replaced it with a brand new galvanized pail complete with a lid. For the benefit of future prisoners, I suggested he name it the "Merlin Fanshaw Memorial Chamber Pot."

Doc Whittier stopped by again to check on me, and he allowed I was doing well. I thanked him and said I'd been working hard at healing since last he saw me. He said the only long-term effects I was likely to suffer would be a couple of small scars. I thought, *Better a few scars than a permanent resting place.*

Come sundown, Marshal Butch shrugged into his coat and left the office for the evening. Again, Deputy Pooch stayed on to guard me. I stretched out on my bunk, my mind once again on George and Abby.

I thought, *Any moment now, they will arrive at the train station, Abby all excited, looking forward to seeing new places with her father. George will look forward to the trip for reasons of his own, mostly evading the law's long arm. Once again, George will cheat justice, and my failure will be complete.*

I sat up. "Pooch," I said. "What time does the train leave this evenin'?"

"In about ten minutes. What do *you* care? You won't be on it."

"Just curious," I said.

There was no way Pooch could know what was on my mind. I took a deep breath and called his name.

"What?"

"That boil on your neck still botherin' you?"

"Yeah. Hurts so bad I can't hardly think."

I was silent for a moment, then said, "I've had some trainin' as a healer. Mind if I take a look at it?"

The hollow snort of a train whistle sounded clear on the evening air. The northbound was about to pull out, and George and Abby would be on board.

Now it was the deputy who was silent. He closed his eyes, then opened them again. "Don't fool with me," he said.

"I'm not foolin'. Come over here. I can help with the pain."

Come on, come on, I thought. *I'm running out of time.*

The deputy didn't answer. For a long moment, he just sat there, not moving. Slowly, he got to his feet, propped the shotgun against the chair, and shuffled toward me.

I heard the bell on the locomotive ring briskly, the sound clear in the still night air.

Stopping just beyond the bars, Pooch stared at me. His expression was a mix of suspicion and pain. "What are you gonna do?" he asked.

"Come closer," I said.

"This is close enough," he said. "What are you fixin' to do? I'm not lettin' you *cut* me."

I showed him my open hands. "I wouldn't do that,

Pooch. Anyway, I've got nothing to cut you with," I said. "Come closer and turn around."

His pain urged him to trust me, at least a little. Pooch took another step, turned, and pulled his collar down to bare his neck. The boil was angry red and badly swollen. I reached through the bars and gently touched his shoulder. "Easy now," I said.

I grabbed him with my right arm around his throat and pulled him hard against the bars. He struggled, clawing at my arm, but I held on like a bulldog worrying a steer. I brought my left hand up, and in it, the cloth I'd soaked in the chloroform stolen from Doc Whittier's bag. When I covered the deputy's face, he fought like a crazy man, frantic, thrashing about, and then, with a sigh, Deputy Pooch went limp and slumped unconscious to the floor.

The steam whistle came again, a long, mournful wail. The northbound was moving out!

I knelt, again reaching through the bars, and my groping fingers found the keys in Pooch's coat pocket. Seconds later, I was free.

The smell of chloroform was strong in the room. *Well,* I thought as I stepped over him, *I didn't lie to the man. He's not hurting now.*

I found my .44 still in the leather, hanging on a peg in the marshal's office. I buckled the gun on, buttoned up my sheepskin, and stepped outside.

The glittering stars cast their pale glow on the rutted, snow-covered street. Saddle horses lined the hitch rail in front of the Roundup Café, and outside the saloons farther on. Most of the town's business places were closed and dark, but here and there, lamplight glowed in a window or a doorway.

Up the street, at the depot, the train was moving out. I heard the moan of the whistle, heard the labored chuffing of the engine as it began to build up speed.

Too late. It's over. George wins again.

The hell with that! Nothing's over till I quit, and I'm not about to!

I bounded off the snow-slick boardwalk and crossed the street at a run to where a deep-chested Appaloosa stood under saddle with several other geldings at a hitch rack. The animal shied, but a quick glance at the muscles of his forelegs and the stifles in back told me he was built for speed. I loosed his tether and grabbed the saddle horn. "You're elected," I said. "Let's see how fast you can run."

He quick-stepped back into the street, eyes rolling as I swung into the saddle. I leaned low across his withers and slapped him smartly with the reins just to let him know my intentions. Like an arrow shot from a bow, we bolted away toward the train station.

Buildings flashed by in a blur as the Appy dashed toward, and then beyond, the station. In the distance, the train was picking up speed, the glow of the engine's headlamp lighting the way ahead. Wolf City fell away behind us as I drove the gelding at full gallop through the drifted snow beside the tracks.

The wind of our passage roared past my ears and made my eyes water. Beneath me, the gelding's muscles rippled and flexed as he dashed through the drifted snow. I demanded still more of him, and he gave it, surging ahead in a new gait that steadily brought us closer to the speeding train.

Then we were alongside two passenger cars and a mail car sweeping along the rails, their lighted windows glowing in the darkness. I smelled the smoke from the engine, felt a cinder graze my face. Reining the gelding in closer, I leaned out above the flashing wheels and caught an iron upright at the rear of a passenger car with both hands. I felt the wound in my side tear as the speeding train took me out of the saddle. Then my feet found the narrow platform, and I clung to the upright until I caught my breath. I drew my .44, checked its loads, and opened the door to the coach.

A dozen passengers occupied the plush seats along each side of the car. A small potbelly stove put off its dry, steady heat. Oil lamps cast their glow above the carpeted center aisle. The wound in my side throbbed; it was bleeding again.

Tense as a fiddle string, I looked at each passenger in turn. Two men—salesmen, from the look of them— played cards atop a sample case. A middle-aged man sitting beside a lady looked up, startled, as I came in. An old man slept in his seat, his hat pulled down over his face. I scanned the car, but George and Abby were not on it. Dropping my eyes and letting the gun in my right hand hang low at my side, I strode through the car, opened the door, and stepped across the swaying void to enter the second day coach.

It was nearly full. At the far end of the aisle, the conductor passed through, punching tickets. Most of the occupants didn't even look up as I came in, but one or two regarded me with a kind of bored curiosity. Then I saw them, George and Abby.

They sat on my right-hand side about midway down, in a seat facing back my way. George was dressed for travel in a brocade vest, linen shirt, and wool frock coat. His left arm encircled Abby's shoulders. Shadowed by his high-crowned black hat, his face was relaxed as he leaned close to speak to her.

Next to the window, Abby wore the fur-trimmed coat and small hat she had on the day I first saw her. Her auburn curls caught the lamplight and framed her face. She smiled, listening to George.

I came slowly forward, and two seats away, took a stand in the center of the aisle, my left hand grasping a seat back for balance as the car swayed on. I brought my .44 to bear on the center of George's vest. "Hello, George," I said.

Somewhere, a woman screamed. The conductor looked up, his eyes on me. George lifted his face sharply toward the sound of my voice, saw the gun, and froze. His eyes widened, then narrowed in recognition.

"Hello, Bodacious," he said. "I didn't expect to see you here."

"I'll bet you didn't," I said. *"Stand up!"*

George smiled. His arm still around Abby's shoulders, he shrugged. "All right, son," he said. "There's no call for us to be uncivil—" and then he suddenly stood, and the short-barreled revolver he carried the day of Pronto's shooting appeared like magic in his right hand. He leveled it at me and cocked the hammer.

"Now, son," George said, his voice as calm as a pond of water on a still day, "we both know you won't use that smoke wagon. You can't take the chance of killin' one of these innocent bystanders. And you surely won't risk a bullet hittin' Abby."

He laid his left hand gently on Abby's shoulder as if to steady and assure her.

"As for me, I can put you down without the slightest risk to my daughter. Besides, you've come at me with a gun, and I've got every right to defend myself— includin' the use of deadly force. So just drop that .44, or I'll drop you!"

I looked at Abby. I expected to see confusion— terror—on her face, but I didn't. Her expression was calm, marked with the cool intelligence I'd observed before. She seemed mildly curious, as if she was waiting to see what would happen next.

I heard the passengers' exclamations of surprise— fearful, tense, and worried. Down the aisle, near the conductor, a woman tried unsuccessfully to stifle her sobs. George Starkweather wouldn't hesitate for a moment to use his gun. He had me, and he knew it. Slowly, I lowered my revolver and let it drop to the floor.

George's eyes glowed. He smiled as he aimed the short-barreled Colt at my head. "I underestimated you," he said. "Now I'll do what I should've done before—"

What happened next was so sudden, I couldn't follow it. Abby's small hand came out of that muff in a blur, and in it was a nickel-plated revolver that she instantly pressed right up under George's chin!

"Drop it or die," she said. *"Do it now!"*

Astonishment stamped George's face. His mouth agape, the muzzle of Abby's pistol pressed against his throat, as best he could, he cut his eyes down toward her. I had never before beheld a man so surprised and so confused. Whatever he saw in Abby's face shook him to his roots. Slowly, he lowered his gun and let it fall.

"You're under arrest, George Starkweather," Abby said, "for bank robbery, rustling, and murder."

From somewhere—maybe also from her muff—Abby produced a set of hand-cuffs, and in a trice, shoved George back in his seat, and cuffed him. Then she stepped out into the aisle.

"What the bloody hell!" George said, looking up at her.

George had nothing on me on that score; inside, I was asking the same question.

"George Starkweather," she said, "I'm not your daughter. My name is Abigail Bannister. I'm a special agent of the Pinkerton Detective Agency, and you, sir, are my prisoner."

I was too surprised to even pick up my gun from off the floor. I stared at her. *"Pinkerton?"* Flabbergasted as I was, it was the only word I could get out.

"Pinkerton," she said. "And who are you?"

For a split instant, I couldn't even remember my name; then it came to me. "Deputy U.S. Marshal Merlin Fanshaw," I said, "workin' undercover." I was beginning to get my wits about me again. "It appears you've arrested my prisoner."

She smiled. "Actually, I've arrested *my* prisoner," she said.

I knew it was time to back off. "I stand corrected. Thanks for makin' your move when you did; I'm obliged to you."

She laughed a throaty little laugh. "I couldn't let him commit *another* murder, could I?"

I looked up to see the conductor mop his brow with a handkerchief and replace his trainman's cap. "Extraordinary, Miss!" he said. "As cool as ever I seen!"

George was sitting stiff and stone-faced in his seat, staring straight ahead. I guess he was trying to ignore the muzzle of the pistol Abby still held on him.

"I've got some extra shackles in the mail car," the conductor said. "I'll fetch them if you like."

"Thank you," Abby said, "but I think these cuffs will suffice." She looked at me. "The deputy here and I will keep our eyes on him."

"If you say so," the conductor said. "You want to take your prisoner back to Wolf City? I can stop the train and have the engineer back it up to the station."

All this time, the train had been speeding on, the car rocking and the wheels clacking on the rails.

"Yes," she said, "if it wouldn't disrupt your schedule too much."

"Glad to do it," he said, and reached for the emergency cord. "Over the years, this train has been delayed by blizzards, floods, and migratin' buffalo—not to mention hotboxes and derailments. We might as well take a few minutes to deliver a bad man to jail.

CHAPTER 20

Supper with the Boss

The conductor took charge of the situation and applied the air brakes. When they'd squealed the car to a halt, he explained to the still astonished passengers that the train was returning to the station, and went forward to tell the hogger to reverse the engine and take her back to Wolf City.

He also ushered the closest passengers away from our sullen prisoner. They seemed happy to put whatever distance they could between themselves and him.

Handcuffed to his chair, George stared at Abby and me with an expression that could have boiled water. If looks could kill, our funerals would have been held tomorrow morning. A thorough search of his person turned up a second pistol, two knives, and a pair of brass knuckles.

"You surely do go loaded for bear, Cap'n," I said.

Abby and me moved a few seats away where we could talk and still watch George while we waited for the train to get back in motion.

"You forced my hand," she said. "I hadn't planned to arrest him until the train reached Billings."

"Sorry about that. I thought I was rescuin' you."

Abby smiled. "Well, you did provide a timely distraction."

"Why take him back to Wolf City?"

"It's the nearest jail. Also, I'll need to report his capture to the main office in Chicago."

"George broke out of Montana's territorial prison," I said. "He led the robbery on the Cattleman's Bank of Dry Creek and personally murdered a bank teller there. But I reckon you already knew all that. Maybe you don't know that most of the livestock the gang stole came from ranches in Montana. I expect the territory will want first crack at him."

Abby nodded. "Very likely," she said. "Wyoming will want him too, but I imagine they'll grant extradition to Montana."

The steam whistle shrieked three short blasts. Glancing out the window, I couldn't see a thing; it was still dark night, but I felt the change of motion and the rocking of the car as the train backed toward the station.

I wondered what sort of reception I'd face when we arrived. If Marshal Butch and Deputy Pooch didn't shoot me on sight, the owner of the Appaloosa horse I commandeered just might.

At the station, when we were escorting George out the door of the car, the first voice I heard had a blessedly familiar ring.

"Good evenin', Deputy. Nice night for a train ride."

U.S. Marshal Chance Ridgeway stood on the platform, tall and lean in his high-crowned Stetson and long black overcoat. I can't recall ever being so happy to see anyone.

Two hard-looking men, also in full-length overcoats, stood by his side together with town marshal Butch Wilson, who looked confused and unhappy. I think my escape and return with George had plumb ruined his day.

His eyes on George, Ridgeway said, "'God's mill grinds slow, but sure.' Isn't that right, George?"

"It ain't seemly to gloat over dumb luck," George said. "I've been brought in by a couple of damned kids!"

Close by, the engine sat blowing and puffing from its exertions. Over the sound of its breathing, Ridgeway, unruffled and grinning, said, "Those 'kids' would be Merlin Fanshaw, my deputy, and, if I'm not mistaken, Miss Abigail Bannister of the Pinkerton Detective Agency." The Marshal tipped his hat and smiled. "I'm Chance Ridgeway, U.S. marshal from up Montana way. I'm delighted to meet you, Miss Bannister."

Abby offered her hand and Ridgeway took it. "Thank you, Marshal. I've heard a great deal about you."

Ridgeway's smile widened, and, in the lamp glow shining through the passenger car window, his ice-blue eyes twinkled. "My faults are carved in stone and my virtues are written in sand," he said, "but I try to do my best."

Why, the old scamp is actually flirting *with Abby,* I thought.

He turned to the hard-looking men. "Get Mr. Starkweather's baggage off the train, boys, and escort him over to the Wolf City jail," he said. "Lock him up and stay with him."

The men flanked George on both sides and moved him off up the street. Marshal Butch stayed behind with Ridgeway and me. He still looked like he'd been weaned on a pickle.

"Howdy, Butch," I said. "I hope Deputy Pooch is all right. I sure hated to knock him out that way, but I had a train to catch."

"Oh, he's fine," Butch said. "Apparently, that boil on his neck broke open when he slid down the bars, and he woke up feelin' no pain. In Pooch's book, you're one first-class healer."

Turning to Abby, Ridgeway said, "Will you join Merlin and me for a very late supper, Miss Bannister?"

Abby smiled. "Thank you, Marshal, but they're holding the train for me. As soon as I telegraph the home office, I'm headed north to Billings and then back to Chicago."

She looked at me with interest—like she was seeing me for the first time. Her smile was merry, but there was mischief in her eyes. "I really wish I could stay," she said. "The last time Merlin and I dined together was at our own personal Al Fresco Café."

I grinned. "Yes," I said, "where the management keeps the temperature low."

Abby laughed. "Take care," she said. "I expect I'll see you at George's trial." Then she walked away, stepping nimbly through the billowing steam from the engine toward the lights of the telegraph office.

We watched Abby until she went inside the office, and then Ridgeway turned his attention to city marshal Butch Wilson who now fidgeted under Ridgeway's stare. He cleared his throat. "Can I . . . Is it all right if I go now?" Wilson asked.

"My stars," said Ridgeway. "I forgot you were still here! Yes. Run along, why don't you? My men will watch over the prisoner, and your jail."

Butch slunk off like a kicked dog. I couldn't help feeling sorry for the man. I'd been under Ridgeway's cold stare a time or two myself.

Butch's departure left me alone with Ridgeway. The marshal turned to me, smiled, and extended his hand. His grip was firm. "Good to see you, son."

"You, too, Chief," I said. "When did you hit town?"

"Late this afternoon. Came in on the stage with those men, deputies Murph Deakins and Ab Green.

"I'd have been here sooner, but I had to make a stop at Buffalo. The district judge there's an old friend of mine. When I explained the situation, he gave me a court order directing your immediate release. He also sent a telegram to the city attorney here, but when we hit town, his office was closed, so we went to his house. That's where we were when you broke jail and took your train ride. You're full of surprises, son."

"I was a day late and a dollar short," I said. "I caught up with George, but Abby made the arrest."

"We can talk about it over supper," Ridgeway said. "I'm told the food at the Sherman is pretty good."

We entered the hotel dining room by way of the lobby and hung our coats and hats on the hall tree inside the door. The restaurant was quiet at that late hour, with only a few customers on hand. Green-shaded lamps cast circles of light on the tablecloths and brought out the shine of crockery and silverware. Potted palms and ferns decorated the room, and pictures in heavy gilt frames graced the walls.

It was all mighty elegant for a small cow town in Wyoming. I had a pretty good idea how I must look after my two days in the local hoosegow, and for a moment, I felt as out of place as a hog in church. The waiter, however, seemed to take no notice of my appearance. Instead, he smiled and showed us to a table just as if I looked halfway decent.

After he poured us each a cup of coffee and took our orders, he headed back to the kitchen, and Ridgeway and me were left alone.

For a moment, the marshal sipped his coffee and studied me in silence. Like Butch, I found I could not meet his gaze. Instead, I looked down at my folded hands. Still without speaking, Ridgeway took an object from his pocket and slid it across the table to me. I recognized it instantly. It was my deputy U.S. marshal's badge, the one I'd left with Ridgeway back at Dry Creek.

"I thought you might want to wear this again," Ridgeway said.

I looked at it; it was mine, all right; the five-pointed star in a circle I had been so proud of. There was the dent it had acquired the day I rode the gray bronc for Arnie Moss. And there were the tiny scratches made while I lay in the rocks the previous fall hunting antelope. Yes. My badge, all right.

I slid it back to Ridgeway, my vision blurred. "I'm sorry," I said. "I can't wear this. Not any more."

Ridgeway said nothing, but there were questions in his eyes.

"I failed. George Starkweather snookered me, and it took Abby Bannister to bring him down. She's a whole lot better undercover agent than I am. You've got my badge and my regrets, Chief. I quit."

Ridgeway silently fingered the badge, rolling it back and forth on the tablecloth. He sipped his coffee again and set the cup back in its saucer. When he spoke, his words were more an observation than a question. "Your injured pride is beatin' the hell out of you, ain't it, son?" He paused. "Before I accept your resignation," he said, "I'm goin' to need a complete account of your time with the Starkweather gang—clear back from the day you left Dry Creek.

"Some of it I know. Some of it I suspect. I have the letter you mailed from Red Lodge and the telegram you sent from Wolf City. In any case, I need to know what happened, and I need to hear it from you. Just take your time and tell me everything you can remember. You talk; I'll listen."

I don't know what it was about Ridgeway. I'd already confessed my failure. I had told him I was quitting. The old manhunter didn't turn a hair. He simply sat in the chair across from me, sipping his coffee, studying me with those ice-blue eyes.

I had no intention of talking about my failures or recounting the details of my time with the gang. And yet, somehow . . .

All of a sudden, I opened my mouth and words poured out like beer from a broken keg. I told Ridgeway everything I could recall of my time with the outlaws, from the night I left Dry Creek with Rufus Two Hats to the shooting of Pronto Southwell and George's framing me for murder.

The waiter brought our orders and set them before us. It's probably a mark of my sincerity—or maybe my guilt—that I forgot all about eating and continued to talk. And Ridgeway continued to listen. Customers finished their suppers and left the dining room. Our coffee and our meals grew cold. *So much for my not talking about my time with the Starkweather gang,* I thought.

Finally, when all the water had run out of the dam and only the mud remained, I fell silent. Ridgeway pushed his plate aside, cleared his throat, and said, "Thank you, son. That was a good report. Now it's my turn to talk and your turn to listen. Just take a deep seat and set easy while I fill in some gaps."

Before Ridgeway could begin, the waiter came back to our table. His eyes dropped to our plates, then raised again. "Something wrong with your orders, gents?" he asked.

"No," said Ridgeway. "We just got to talkin' and let our vittles get cold. Take them plates back to the kitchen and set 'em in the warmin' oven awhile, will you?

"Certainly, sir," the waiter said, as if customers ignoring their meals were the most natural thing in the world. He refilled our coffee cups and whisked our plates away to the kitchen.

"The day after you 'killed' Glenn Murdoch and broke Rufus Two Hats out of the Dry Creek jail," Ridgeway said, "you were the talk of the town. Glenn put on false whiskers and a derby hat and caught the stage to Silver City. From there, he took the train to his sister's place in Nebraska where he helped paint her front porch and got caught up on the family gossip.

"Meanwhile, back in Dry Creek, we gave Glenn a hero's funeral. Filled a casket with two hundred pounds of rock and planted it up on boot hill. I made a speech, the McNabb girl sang 'The Unclouded Day,' and everyone had a fine time saying good things about Glenn. Too bad he couldn't have been there; he'd have been plumb tickled to hear how well thought of he was."

Ridgeway paused and took a sip of coffee. Then he continued. "Of course, the whole town was pretty upset with you. There was some talk of forming a posse and setting out in pursuit of you and Rufus, but nobody really wanted to leave town. No beer out there on the prairie, you know.

"We sent out telegrams to all the peace officers around and printed up some posters describing you and your dastardly deed. You can imagine how surprised I was when I got a telegram back from Horace Wisdom over in Columbus, sayin' he'd took you down with a shotgun! I caught the next train to that city and was some relieved to find the deceased was not you. I informed Horace of that fact and shipped your little gray horse back to Dry Creek.

"After that, there was nothin' to do but wait. I am a patient man, as you know, but it was some time before your letter from Red Lodge arrived at my office. I have to admit I was growin' a mite restless.

"Your letter was thorough and complete. I found the news about George's 'daughter' to be particularly interesting. Likewise, your account of the bank robbery at Blue Rock. I sent some men down to the rustler camp on the Yellowstone, and they arrested Shorty Benson and a couple of other long rope artists.

"The map you drew of Arrowhead ranch was helpful. I sent some men out, but by the time they got there, George had already vacated the premises. The new owner had a line rider on the place when my war party showed up, but he had no idea where George had gone. I called my deputies in and continued the investigation while I waited for further word from you.

"That word came three days ago with your telegram.

When I saw the name 'George Shannon' in the message I knew we were closing in on Original George at last."

I had sat and listened to all this with mixed feelings; warmed to know Ridgeway had made that trip down to Columbus to get my body, but chilled at remembering some of the things I'd been through.

"Yeah," I said. "Trouble is, the kid at the telegraph office was on George's payroll. He told Slippery Mayfair, and Slippery told George. From that point on, my secret was out. When I had to face down Pronto Southwell, George used the shootin' to get me locked up. I was in some danger of bein' hanged for murder."

"I'm glad that didn't happen," Ridgeway said dryly. "Stretchin' hemp is beyond the call of duty for an undercover man."

I chuckled. "I'd say so. I got strung up once back in eighty-four. Didn't care for it much."

The waiter came back to our table and warmed our coffee again. "Much obliged," Ridgeway said. "I believe we could eat those orders now, if they're still warmin'."

"You bet," said the waiter, and turned away toward the kitchen.

"Speakin' of undercover men," I said. "Is that dude in the derby hat—the 'hat salesman'—one of your men?"

Ridgeway's smile widened. "He is," he said. "He's a special agent dealing with banking and financial matters. Soon as I got your telegram, I sent him on ahead.

He's helping implement a court order seizing George Starkweather's assets. We may not get all the stolen money back, but it looks like we'll recover a substantial portion of it."

"What about Slippery Mayfair? It's his bank."

Ridgeway looked thoughtful. "Yes," he said. "Well, it appears the dishonorable Mr. Mayfair is as slippery as ever. Even with your testimony, I don't believe we have enough to convict him in a court of law."

Still, I was beginning to feel better. "Well, at least you'll put a dent in his capital reserves. Knowing Slippery, that'll hurt him more than prison."

"His time will come," Ridgeway said calmly. It was both prophecy and promise.

The waiter returned with our plates and set them before us. I had ordered beef stew, and Ridgeway had asked for fried chicken. Neither order seemed any the worse for having been sent to the warming oven, and we both fell to eating with a will.

When we finished, Ridgeway leaned back in his chair and sighed. "Those vittles were larrupin' good," he said. "I expect we'll sleep well tonight."

"I don't know how you can be so durned cheerful," I said. "No matter how you look at it, it was Abby who caught George Starkweather."

"With your help. If you hadn't broke jail and caught the train, things might have turned out different."

"Maybe. I sure was surprised to learn Abby's a Pink. How'd she get on George's trail?"

"There's quite a story about that," Ridgeway said.

"Seems like when George was still in the pen, he got to feelin' sentimental and asked Slippery Mayfair to try to find his old ladylove, Sally Weems. Slippery hired an investigator in Kansas City and put him on the case. He told the detective that his client's name—when Sally knew him—was George Starkweather, but that he had since changed his name to George Shannon.

"Well, one day this peeper's talkin' to a lady friend in a downtown restaurant, and he mentions this case he's workin' on. He also drops the name George Stark-weather, and that rings a bell. His friend just happens to be a Pinkerton agent name of Abigail Bannister and she's heard of George Starkweather.

"Abigail goes back to the office and looks up George's record. She finds George has been doing life without parole at the territorial pen in Deer Lodge, but he has recently took himself an unauthorized vacation. He's wanted by the law, and he's worth a thousand dollars, pig or pork.

"The detective tells Abigail he's hit a dead end in the case. She asks him if she can work on it herself, and he says sure, go ahead.

"Abigail sends Slippery a letter, saying her mother is the Sally Weems in question, but that her mama passed away some time ago. She also says George Shannon is her daddy and that she sure hopes she can meet him some day.

"Slippery passes the letter on to George, who swallows the hook like a trout hitting a mayfly. He invites Abigail out to his ranch, and the stage is set."

I hesitated to ask my next question. "Did Abby know I was a lawman?"

"Nobody did. Far as she was concerned, you were just another outlaw."

I recalled how helpless Abby looked the day we found her in the wrecked coach beside the road to Blue Rock. I had worried about her innocence in George Starkweather's violent world, but my concerns had been needless. Clearly, Abby had proved herself more than a match for the bandit chief. I both envied and admired her for that.

"If you still want to quit," Ridgeway said, "I'll accept your resignation. But I figured I owed it to you to tell you the truth. You accomplished your assignment; you didn't fail."

Ridgeway ticked off the points on his fingers. "George Starkweather, ex-convict, murderer, thief, and world champion evildoer: arrested and returned to prison. Every known member of his gang of cutthroats: dead or in custody. Stolen money from bank robberies in Montana and Wyoming: mostly recovered.

"And last but not least," he said, "you spent a season with those murderous malefactors and did *not* get yourself killed! I call *that* a success."

I grinned. "So do I," I said. Then I felt a little sheepish as I added, "If it's all the same to you, I think I'll pin that deputy's star back on now."

Ridgeway slid the badge across the table to me. "It's all the same to me," he said.

Center Point Publishing
600 Brooks Road ● PO Box 1
Thorndike ME 04986-0001 USA

(207) 568-3717

US & Canada:
1 800 929-9108
www.centerpointlargeprint.com